ASSIGNMENT
in SAIGON

- - - -

COLD WAR SPY THRILLER, #6

BY BILL RAPP

coffeetownpress

Kenmore, WA

coffeetownpress

A Coffeetown Press book published by Epicenter Press

Epicenter Press
6524 NE 181st St. Suite 2
Kenmore, WA 98028.
www.Epicenterpress.com
www.Coffeetownpress.com
www.Camelpress.com

For more information go to: www.coffeetownpress.com

www.billrappsbooks.com

Assignment in Saigon
Copyright © 2024 by Bill Rapp

ISBN: 9781684922246 (trade paper)
ISBN: 9781684922253 (ebook)

LCCN 2024940168

Printed in the United States of America

DEDICATION

For my wife Didi, whose support throughout my writing career has been invaluable.

ACKNOWLEDGMENTS

As so many of my generation, I had already read several histories and assessments of the US involvement in the long-running wars for Vietnamese independence. These include Stanley Karnow's encyclopedic "Vietnam: A History", General Bruce Palmer's "The 25-Year War," Lt. General (Ret.) Harold Moore's and Joseph Galloway's "We Were Soldiers Once and Young," Neil Sheehan's "A Bright and Shining Lie," and Philip Caputo's memoir "A Rumor of War." For this book I decided to examine a number of more recent studies of the American decision to become directly engaged in the Vietnamese war for independence and its immediate aftermath. I found Fredrik Logevall's outstanding two volumes, "Embers of War" and "Choosing War," which cover in great detail the evolution of US policy from 1954 to 1965, to be especially useful. Max Boot's study of the career of Edward Lansdale provided helpful insights from a slightly different angle, and James Warren's "The Year of the Hawk" followed along similar lines. Richard Shultz also provided helpful material in "The Secret War Against Hanoi." Mark Moyer takes a more sympathetic view of American efforts and deliberations during this period in "Triumph Forsaken," while Colonels (Ret) William Haponski and Jerry Burcham put a much more negative imprint on our efforts and strategy in "Autopsy of an Unwinnable War: Vietnam."

The overwhelming number of fictional treatments focus on our military engagement after the time covered in my book. One exception I found and can heartily recommend is Ward Just's "A Dangerous Friend." I will reserve comment on Graham Greene's flawed "The Quiet American."

VI • BILL RAPP

Numerous individuals contributed to my own efforts to capture something of those eventful days in our country's history, including Tom Gruszauskas, a high school classmate who served in that war and was generous enough to read through the manuscript and provide comments on the setting and tone. I am also grateful to Jennifer McCord, the senior editor at Coffeetown Press, who once more held me to her and my publisher's high standards in terms of the narrative and character development, which made for a better story and a much better book.

Despite all this assistance, if there are errors in fact or shortcomings in storytelling I will occasionally plead poetic license but always accept full responsibility.

PROLOGUE

This was not over—not by a long shot. Despite the armistice and division of Vietnam into opposing statelets, Henri de Couget knew that this entire mess was not finished yet. No matter how much he hoped, no matter how hard he would work to start a new life in the southern half, now an independent state in its own right, this war would continue until one side or the other was thoroughly beaten. The Communist leadership in the northern half would not give up their dream of an independent and unified country. That meant that the battles, the suffering, the discomfort, the dislocation, and the challenges of finding his place in the new world that surrounded him would continue.

He studied the path ahead: just more of that damn jungle, and once again, it threatened to swallow him. It wasn't just the overgrown vegetation that seemed to surround him everywhere he went, that held only dangers and death, the torment that had plagued so much of his past in this country—snakes and insects, the heat and the humidity…and the Viet Minh, those communist bastards. As he made his way south through the thick, lush vegetation that gripped his legs and grabbed for his arms, he remembered that there had been a fleeting relief of sorts from those things, even if temporary. No, those few good moments seemed to disappear like a wish. Every day seemed to bring new threats, new danger, and new discomfort. Yet, he had some hope. Now.

That is, if they ever got through this goddamn monsoon that always seemed on the verge of washing him and the world around him into some kind of global sink hole. It was one of the worst things about Indochina. There seemed to be no end to the downpours that lasted from May through September. Every bit of clothing was soaked, every habitable space was flooded. Everything, and he meant everything, became drenched to its core. No light, no air; the sky was nothing more than water. He had almost wished for an ark at times to carry him away.

That goddamn rain had been the worst part of the days and nights, all forty-five of them, at Dien Bien Phu. The never-ending flow had turned their trenches into small rivers of sewage running up to and often over your knees, your feet nothing more than sodden clumps of cotton and leather. The rain was even worse than the constant bombardments and sniping from those damn communist guerrillas in the hills surrounding the French base. At least you could shoot back at them. You didn't dare go out to pick up the airdropped supplies that our pilots and the Americans tried to bring for relief. Much of that stuff, at least half, had been lost to the Viet Minh.

How the hell had those scrawny bands of jungle fighters been able to bring so many troops and so much artillery to the valley? And then set it all up on the hillsides facing our camps? They were little more than medieval peasants. But they were tough little bastards. He'd give them that much. They were well-led, too and right at home in that godforsaken jungle. He still couldn't understand how the French gunners and fighter pilots had been unable to destroy them. Hell, we couldn't even suppress the anti-aircraft fire that kept most of our planes too high to find the drop zones.

Well, damn it all and screw them. He at least, Captain Henri de Couget, had made his escape. Theirs had been the only breakout attempted, isolated as they were at the Isabelle outpost to the south when the final surrender came on May 7, 1954, and even that had been a miserable failure for the most part. He had been lucky, though. Hidden in the midst of a group of Tai tribal fighters who had been serving with the Foreign Legion, he had escaped those Viet Minh bastards—tough and capable, no doubt about that—but bastards all the same.

Lord knows how long he would have lasted if he hadn't made it out, first on the long march to captivity and then in the camps. So many comrades had been left to die along the way, no surprise that. Many were pretty far along in the first place. The meager rations and the work regimen in the camps knocked off a whole lot more. He had heard that as many as sixty percent of those poor sods who surrendered never got to see home again.

Yes, he had been one of the lucky ones, arguably the luckiest. Two other Legionnaires who had escaped with him had not made it, at least not this far. One had passed along the way from a combination of dysentery and malaria, his body left to rot in the jungle. The Tais would not even let him stop to bury his comrade. The other had passed shortly after they arrived at the Tais' home village in the mountains of central Laos.

They were good people, the Tais, and they hated the Viet Minh even more than the French did. These villagers had tried to save his friend, but the infections had gotten worse and gangrene had done the rest. It was all too late by the time they made it to the village hamlet.

Now that that miserable rain had finally stopped—and he was healthy enough to march—he could make his way south to Cochin China, the southern portion of Vietnam around Saigon and the Mekong Delta. There the French presence had been solidified and Ho Chi Minh and his damn Viet Minh would be kept at bay. His own government in Paris and the Foreign Legion fighters had done much better in the south holding on to their patch of ground, better than those fighting in the north, in Tonkin and the northern stretches of Amman down near the center of the country.

But for how long now? Who could tell? No one had expected the Viet Minh to achieve this much. Word had even made it to the Tai village in Laos that Ho Chi Minh and the Viet Minh had held a big parade in Hanoi to celebrate their victory over us on October 9. Four days ago. Hard to believe it was already 1955.

"Do you think we will be safe down there?" she had asked.

He shrugged but did not stop moving. He was afraid that if he did, he and his group would not be able to get started again.

He simply refused to trust the jungle. He knew that this horrible, malevolent world around them would not let him finish his escape. Not if it could stop him. He glanced at the sky and smiled, happy to see the clouds drifting away to the east and the ocean. Any sign of dryness would help.

"That is hard to say," he replied. He looked at the woman, his savior and now his wife—in a way—a tribal, jungle way.

She was right to ask, though. What does happen now? No one expected the Viet Minh to honor the terms of the Geneva peace accords negotiated last year. He doubted either side would, actually, and especially not with the Americans involved as well. True, their presence and role had been growing for years. Now, though, it was their show. We'd see how much they could do with all their money and military power. They had certainly criticized us for being too weak and not aggressive enough. Let's see if they learned anything and can do any better. He did wonder what that would all mean for him, though.

But for now, that was not his problem. Nope. He had other, more immediate worries, like how he would make a living in what was left of Vietnam, or the Vietnam that he and his countrymen had known. His common law wife from the Tai village and the small group of her relatives would escort them to Saigon, the new capital in the south, where they would start over. She had been his greatest surprise and true reward. The funny thing was, he couldn't tell you why he deserved a reward like her, a woman who had nursed him to health and stayed by his side every night since he first arrived in her village, a man who felt more dead than alive. That part, at least, was over now.

Maybe he and his wife could build a build a prosperous new life together. A return to France was out of the question, at least for now. There was nothing for him back there. True, he came from a long line of French military men, all of whom had served with distinction for centuries. One had even stood by the Emperor at the battle of Jena and survived the retreat from Moscow, only to fall at Waterloo. Perhaps he should have fallen, too, here in the jungles of Indochina. But in the end he realized he had no desire to die a hero's death in this godforsaken patch of hell with its rats and leeches and ants and snakes, all of them hidden deep in the countryside. Saigon offered more, especially now that the Communists were stuck up north...at least most of them. Hopefully, the Americans would keep it that way. Theirs was the new empire in Asia.

"Will it depend on the Americans? Do you expect much from them?" she persisted.

"Perhaps," he answered. "Then again, I don't really know what to expect."

Then he mumbled some words that were directed more at the jungle than anything else. "And neither do they."

CHAPTER ONE

The Paris of the Orient, or so it was said. As Baier surveyed the heart of the city, though, he was stunned by the contrast with his first view of the South Vietnamese capital from a height of several thousand feet in an airliner circling the sprawling metropolis Saigon had become. The population was nearing two million—if it hadn't already left that number behind. The approach swept over neighborhoods of ramshackle housing, more huts than homes, piles of garbage, and mobs of cars, bicycles, rickshaws, and people. A sea of human and vehicular traffic flowed over a fetid landscape swarming with a combustible cocktail of disease that included malaria, typhoid, dysentery, and just about anything that could kill you, or so he had read in his briefing notes.

In the city center, however, Karl Biaer felt as though he entered an alien planet. Here, he could see what they—whoever they were—had meant by the comparison with Paris. Of course, the real thing was so much more splendid and more beautiful. But Saigon definitely had some attractions. The major boulevards were open and lined with cafes, shops and restaurants, much like the real Paris. Even many of the people gave off an air of western ambience, especially the thousands of French *colons*—or former *colons,* the French administrators, rubber barons, and entrepreneurs who had previously ruled this French colony. But they still lived and appeared in many cases to thrive here, despite their recent history and lost war. That, however, as he was soon to learn, was the most appealing public face to the city. And looks could be so deceiving.

But there was still the damn weather, which seemed to hang over this second Paris like a damp cloth. Jesus, but it was humid, as well as stinking hot. Baier guessed that was something you had to expect when you lived in the tropics—no matter for how long, or how short. His recent assignment to Saigon was open-ended... sort of. It was already New Year's Eve, 1963, just shy of two months after the coup and assassination of South Viet Nam's erstwhile and erratic president, Ngo Dinh Diem, that had occurred earlier that year on November 1. More like a dictator and mafia don, if you asked just about anyone in Saigon, outside the American military. And it was his, Karl Baier's, government that had made that coup happen, or at least had blessed it and allowed it to happen. This after years of worshipful praise and billions of dollars of support for the Diem government.

Just what the hell had happened, Baier wondered. How could all those highly-placed advisors in Washington, influential congressmen and Senators like Mike Mansfield—reputedly an expert on Southeast Asia because he had taught university courses in the history of the region—gotten it so wrong? Even John Kennedy, the President who many believed ordered the coup, had sung the man's praises just a few years ago. Now, we were in a real mess. By 'we,' Baier meant his country and his organization, the Central Intelligence Agency. The South Vietnamese were not much better off. Most were searching for a way forward, or out.

"I need you to go out there for a while to help our station sort through all the chaos and confusion that seems to reign," the Director, John McCone, had said. "Help our Chief of Station. I don't mean to suggest that he isn't up to the task at hand," McCone had added. "Quite the contrary. But Lord knows that anybody could use some help in a place where there are so many actors in a cast that's constantly changing, and where it's never entirely clear who our friends and enemies are."

The Director sighed, then continued. "And that's only a little more confused than things here in Washington these days. I'm pretty sure our COS could use some help in sorting all this out from someone who knows Washington's perspectives and needs. You know, he probably still feels brand new out there."

"How long has it been?" Baier asked.

McCone thought for a moment. "Let me see. He replaced his predecessor last summer, after some jerk blew his cover. So, he may still be getting his proverbial feet on the ground. And that can be pretty slippery, given all that's going on."

"But what you're asking for sounds more like an Aardwolf, and those are written by the Chief of Station, Sir."

"You mean those think pieces sent in from the field?"

Baier nodded.

"Those are all well and good. And usually pretty useful. But as I said, our man out there now is just too new to the place. And besides, he has a damn big station to run." The Director shook his head. "No, I think that would put too much on his plate right now."

Baier took a moment to marshal his thoughts, staring out the broad windows that lined the wall of the Director's office on the seventh floor of the new Headquarters building in Langley, Virginia. Bare trees spread across a short range of hills that swept around mansions and down along rocky hillsides, all the way to the rapids of the Potomac River before it flattened out into the broad swath of still water that slid into the Chesapeake Bay and then the Atlantic Ocean. When he looked back at his boss, Baier focused on the knot in the director's navy-blue tie that looked as though he had fastened it to his neck that morning, but without any visible physical discomfort. Baier finally protested that he knew next to nothing—actually, exactly nothing—about the region and the country in question. He was a Europeanist at heart and by experience and background.

"Heck. Sir, I feel slippery, and I haven't even gotten there yet. It's all new territory to me."

"That's okay," McCone assured him. "You can bring a fresh perspective, that of an outsider without a lot of baggage. Besides, I trust your judgment of people. Look what you were able to sort out in Turkey last year..."

"On issues that were much closer to home for me."

McCone waved his words away. "No matter. You're also a quick learner, and there will be no shortage of teachers. In fact, that could be your biggest challenge, deciding whom to listen to among all the self-anointed experts out there, all of whom appear to approach the issue of Vietnam with a different view and background. Your problem will be not allowing your experiences in Europe to dominate your thoughts and interpretations of what's going on out there and where it's heading."

"Like the French did?" Baier asked. The question was only partly rhetorical.

Baier smiled and waited a few seconds, making sure he phrased his next question carefully. "Are you sure I'd be able to add anything to the report you just turned in? The one from your own trip to the region earlier this month with Secretary MacNamara."

"Yes. In fact, I wish you hadn't read that. I don't want you to be influenced by my own thoughts and conclusions." He smiled. "I'm no expert on the region either."

The Director rose from his chair. "But back to the French. They had their own ambitions and perspectives as well. Some more global, given their recent history."

"You mean getting their butts kicked by the Germans and losing their colonial empire?"

"Yes. And none of that helped the French get a realistic view of their future in the country, or in Indochina more broadly." He slid his arm around Baier's shoulder as he led his Special Advisor for Strategic Affairs to the door. "I'm sure you'll be able to avoid that. That's the main reason I'd like to have you out there."

McCone sighed, then turned to the window and the expensive real estate in the forest and hills just beyond the gate. When he spoke, it was as though he was addressing the neighborhood instead of his assistant. "I take the work of our analysts downtown, and I'm happy to do so. I think they've been right about the difficulties we face there all along. For years now. But I also think a fresh and timely field assessment of some sort would help inform the policymakers who are charging ahead and all too often with what appear to be blinders on. I know it will help me help them sort things out."

Baier paused and studied the Director, his face wrinkled with thought and worry despite a smile the man had tied in place to hide the doubts and anxiety that must have filled his head whenever he thought about the looming quagmire of Southeast Asia.

"Wouldn't it be better to send Landsdale back out there? He's the one with the experience and background in the region. He also knows the people who matter better than I ever will."

McCone shook his head. The smile did not move. "The poor man's got too much baggage. No one wants to listen to him anymore."

"But how's that? He did a great job in the Philippines. And he spent some valuable time with President Diem and his crew a few years back." Baier paused. "Excuse me, former President Diem. But Lansdale still knows what's going on out there."

"That's a big part of his problem. He's too close and his mind is already set. Plus, he keeps telling people back here how mistaken they are and how little they know."

"Maybe he's right."

"Maybe he is. But I need you to go out and bring back a new unvarnished truth, as it were. I need a fresh perspective to help me make our Agency's case here in town."

"Whatever that may be."

The Director's smile shifted and broadened, as though a small sliver of relief had found a home. "That's right. Whatever that may be. It, like everything else on this issue, is evolving day-by-day. But I want our role to be clear and objective. That is our mission, after all. And I want it written by someone who was there explicitly to write just such a report." The Director paused. An index finger rose. "One word of warning, though."

"And that would be?"

"Don't let yourself get wrapped up in some new operation." The finger waved as Baier started to interrupt, "Now, now, I know how you operations people think. You can't resist stepping into some new adventure. And the COS will probably be happy to have you do so, especially if it promises to provide some valuable new intelligence."

"Please, Sir, I…"

"Just remember what your real mission is. See if you can become an analyst for a brief time."

"That's a tall order for someone like me, Sir. I've never done anything like that before."

"I know. But do it now anyway."

• • •

In the end Baier had agreed to go. Of course, he had. You don't blow off the CIA Director, not if you want to maintain a career that had had its share of the proverbial ups and downs. Everybody had those, of course, or at least most people did. But his treatment after returning from Turkey had definitely been one of those 'ups.' He had exposed not only a Soviet operation behind the murder of three CIA assets in Turkey, one that had threatened to jeopardize the Agency's and the U.S. position in the region and beyond, but also the treasonous behavior of one of the CIA's own who had—perhaps unwittingly—assisted the Soviets in their efforts, and this as the Cuban missile crisis was coming to a head. Baier had been given the enviable position of Special Advisor to the Director on Strategic Issues as a reward: a seventh-floor job with a spacious office just down the hall from the Director's room, and all the perks and influence that went with it. And at this point in time, there was hardly a more strategic issue for the United States than Viet Nam. So, how could he say no?

"This is going to be a tough one for you, my friend," Ralph Delgrecchio said. Delgrecchio had been at Baier's side for nearly every adventure—and misadventure—throughout his career, a wing man whom Baier had come to know and trust. Unquestionably so.

"Yeah, no shit. Tell me something I don't know already, Ralph."

"Okay, but for you it's going to be tougher than most."

"How so?"

"It's because you're so tied to Europe." Delgrecchio held up his hand to block Baier's interruption. "That has served you well, if only because of your personal background and the fact that Europe—and Germany in particular—has been the front line in the Cold War. But for a place like Indochina that can warp your perspective and your outlook."

"Again, how so?."

"Because there's a whole new set of factors at play. It's almost like the place is virgin soil. No history of civil society or democratic political aspirations. Just foreign occupation and colonial oppression. And that goes way back to ancient times with the Chinese in there."

"Shouldn't that make them more open to us and what we're trying to do there?"

"Not necessarily. Our western perceptions and intentions keep running up against a whole brew of anti-colonial aspirations, communist idealism, and a willingness to endure hardships and oppression as the natural order of things. Something we shed centuries ago."

"You make it sound pretty hopeless, Ralph."

Delgrecchio shrugged. "Not really. I can't pretend to know how this is going to turn out. But most of the people making the decisions back here haven't a clue right now. They're looking at this from a broader strategic angle that is meaningless to the people who actually live out there. And who are doing the fighting and dying. You're going to have to figure things out all by yourself and bring whatever bad—or good—news you've got back to a Director and an Agency committed to the truth. And committed to delivering that truth to those in power. Whatever that may look like, or however uncomfortable that may be."

"Well, of course. That's what it's all about. And our reporting and analysis hasn't shied away from that so far."

"And the pressure will keep going up as you arrive out there, my friend."

"I hate to sound like s broken record, but again, how so?"

"We've already invested a lot. We've got what, 15,000 military advisors working with the South Vietnamese army already, and it looks increasingly likely that that number will jump several thousand more in the near future, maybe even the next few months. President Johnson has already made it clear that he will not reverse or even alter Kennedy's policy, which means continued engagement. If not more."

"Ralph, you're telling me my assignment is useless?"

Delgrecchio shook his head. "Not entirely. Just that you can guess what the policymakers back here want to hear."

"And McCone's purpose in sending me there?"

"I can't pretend to read the old man's mind. But my guess is that he wants to go downtown with a balanced view, to put some realism in the discussion and what the big boys can expect when they decide on their way forward." Delgrecchio paused to study his friend. "And Karl, this assignment will be different, very unlike the others you've had."

"Why is that?"

"It will be tied to you personally. More than any operation. In a way, you're predicting the future, my friend. Almost like a real analyst." Delgrecchio took Baier's hand. "And good luck with all that."

• • •

Before he gave the Director his final answer, though, Baier needed to speak with his wife, Sabine. They had been separated before. Once, in fact—during and just after his sojourn in Turkey, and that had introduced an unsuspected strain in their marriage. Of course, that had been because of Baier's infatuation with a Turkish woman of Greek heritage, an affair that had, thankfully, not been a full-blown thing. Never even consummated, in fact. But it had still been a proverbial matter of the heart, one that had grown, Baier suspected, as much from the dangers and sense of mission they had shared, as from the woman's deep, dark beauty. Neither had been prepared to make a full romantic commitment, but Baier had nonetheless not been able to hide his foreign attraction from Sabine. She was far too smart for that to happen.

Their brief separation—six months—had allowed them both to see how much they meant to each other and how little they looked forward to a life apart. Especially after what they had been through together, from those heady days in war-torn Berlin, through captivity in East European prisons, and escapes through a newly-minted Berlin Wall. Now, Baier was supposed to go away once again. And this one could stretch on indefinitely. One could just never tell with a war zone assignment, especially one with such a vague purpose and deadline. Moreover, it was a war zone, and Sabine would not be able to accompany him, as she had on other assignments. Until Turkey, that is.

"I'm sorry, Karl, but this sounds a bit like a wild goose chase. The timing could also be better, For us, I mean."

They sat side by side on the sofa of their home in Vienna, Virginia, a small town about fifteen miles from the District of Columbia, or 'the District,' as most in the area referred to Washington. Ever since the completion of the new Headquarters building down the road, though, that small town had grown, in part, into a suburb of the CIA Headquarters. Thankfully, Baier and Sabine were holding hands. That, Baier hoped, would make this conversation a little easier.

"I really don't see how I can refuse," he said. "I mean, the Director himself requested it. And you can see how this whole mess in Vietnam is coming to absorb more and more of the Administration's attention. If my country needs me, I can't very well refuse to serve."

Sabine squeezed his hand hard enough to push Baier's knuckles together like a vise. "But do they really need you? It's not like you have a lot of experience in that part of the world. In fact, you don't have any at all."

"Yeah, I know that and said as much. But there aren't many in our government who do. McCarthy and his Republican lickspittles saw to that when they launched their campaign about the Democrats 'losing' China."

"That was despicable. Anyone with a brain could see that Chang Kai Check 'lost' China all by himself. Himself and the rest of that incompetent and corrupt gang around him. Besides, it was never ours to keep or give in the first place."

"Oh, I agree. Then they went on to purge most of the regional experts at State and elsewhere for complicity in what they claimed was a Communist plot."

"Are you telling me there's nobody left?"

"Not exactly. But those few dissenting voices aren't listened to anymore. Now we're stuck with people like me, who have to try bring some balance to the discussion."

"Balance?"

Baier nodded. "That's right. The discussions at State are dominated by Europeanists…"

"Like you."

"Yeah, like me. But many of the decisions about our presence and policy in the previous decade especially were taken with an eye to their impact, in large part, on the future of Europe, not Southeast Asia. There are some who think that has put us on the wrong path."

"You sound like you've already made up your mind."

"No, I haven't. But I think the Director wants to make sure he's getting a full account of what's going on there from someone who has a better sense of the policy debates and dynamics in this town. And, I suspect, someone who can get closer to the truth down on the street and in the hamlets than some high-level member of the Cabinet."

Sabine sat back against the sofa's cushions, studying her husband as though she had just discovered a fatal flaw in his argument. "Don't you people have the analysts for that?'

"Yes, of course. And they were the ones—or at least among the first—to express skepticism about this Diem guy and his corrupt family and friends. And how poorly he and his gang had fared in building any kind of popular support and legitimacy. They were also the ones who gave the French little chance of holding on at Dien Bien Phu, which Eisenhower and Dulles—the Secretary of State—just blew off. 'Oh, they've got air superiority and plenty of napalm,' they said. Or something like that. In fact any skepticism I have comes from talking to those guys."

Sabine sat forward and brought Baier's hands to her chest. After a moment she dropped them and smoothed the plaid woolen skirt over her thighs and down past her knees. When she looked up, Baier noticed that there were tears in her eyes. "Karl, I know you have to do this. But I will still miss you. And I know I can trust you. But there is still some doubt that nags at me."

Baier's heart melted. He grabbed her wrists and passed his hands back up over her palms and held on tight to her fingers. "You could trust me before. And believe me, I am not going to do anything to jeopardize our marriage. I doubt the environment there is very conducive to that kind of thing, in any case."

"And how long will it be?"

"I can't say for sure. The Director said something about six weeks. I can't see it stretching much beyond that. But you never really know in this business. I guess it depends on how things unfold there. With the way things are going since the coup against President Diem and his assassination, it looks like we're going to slip further and further down a rabbit hole."

"I guess I should be happy that we got to spend Christmas together."

"Yeah, well, there is that. And I'm glad, too. Very glad that I had you back for that at least." He paused and brought Sabine's hands together. "And I'm sure I'll be able to get back for the occasional R & R visit if this assignment drags on."

Sabine pulled her hands free and stood, smoothing her skirt over her legs again. "Well, I know that you will do your best. You always do. And you know that I'll be waiting. Just make sure you come back in one piece when you do."

Baier stood and pulled his wife close to his chest. He felt the warmth of her breasts and heartbeat. "No need to worry about that. I have no plans to play the hero."

• • •

Nhu Van Kim was late for work once again. He rushed to his car and threw himself into his seat, settling his slim body behind the driving wheel. These American cars now came almost regularly with seat belts, but he decided to skip buckling the damn thing because he was already behind schedule.

The knock on the window sounded light but firm. A stranger stood there, bent slightly at the waste, as though the stranger wanted to avoid alerting anyone else. The man outside glanced through the rear window. To see if Kim was alone? The stranger needn't worry about that. Especially at this early hour, when most people—like him—were leaving for work. But he could tell this man standing by his car definitely wanted his attention.

He studied the thick short fingers of this stranger for a moment before rolling down the window. The stranger wore no rings, although it was clearly his left hand that leaned on the door. Not married, he guessed. He glanced up and recognized a vaguely familiar face. He could still not place the fellow, though. From work perhaps, he wondered. The man also appeared to be alone. Well, he would have to tell this guy that he needed to leave. It was not a good time for a conversation. He had to get to work, and quickly. His colleagues at the National Police would notice if he was late again. Besides, he had a meeting later that day with the Americans.

"What is it? Are you having car trouble?" he asked.

Odd, but he did not remember ever having seen this man in the parking lot of his apartment complex before, and certainly not in the building itself. He wondered if the stranger even lived in this area of Saigon. Then again, most people from the National Police and other security services did. The man must have come from somewhere else.

"Mister Kim?" the stranger asked.

"Yes. How can I help you?"

Then, it all happened in a flash. The revolver rose from behind the stranger's back, in his right hand. The gun stopped just short of Kim's temple. He never had time to object or protest. The blinding light and the loud crack, almost like a sharp peel of thunder, was the last thing he saw and heard as he left this world behind.

CHAPTER TWO

"Happy New Year, Karl. How did you spend the holiday?"
"Trying to get over the jet lag and get my body accustomed to the new time zone. So, mostly I slept a lot. On and off, of course."

"Yeah, I figured as much. There probably wasn't much else to do since you couldn't watch any bowl games. Especially not since your alma mater, Notre Dame, doesn't play in any. Some people gather in the wee hours here to watch those things together, but I was pretty damn sure you would not be up for that, literally or figuratively."

"Thanks, Frank. You guessed right on that one."

"So, tell me. What's the scuttlebutt from the seventh floor these days?"

Frank Crockett, the Chief of Station in Saigon for the last six months, sounded eager for any intelligence Baier could provide from Headquarters. Baier had learned years ago not to call the man "Davey," a reference, of course, to his family name and the fact that he grew up in eastern Tennessee. His family had no ties to the famous frontiersman, especially considering that this Crockett family originated in Pennsylvania and only moved to Oak Ridge when his father got a job as a nuclear engineer at the laboratory there. Some fellow officers in Crockett's incoming class had tried to stick the nickname on Crockett shortly after he arrived at Langley, but a few shoving contests and even a couple fistfights after work when one or both sides had downed a few too many beers settled that issue once and for all.

Like so many officers in the field, Crockett was happy to be abroad and away from what was proverbially known as

'Hindquarters.' But he did miss the information and insights from Washington, and any news from the Agency leadership in particular. In most cases it was little more than corridor gossip, or 'rumint,' as it was known in the building since it was basically rumors. Crockett had been able to spend the bulk of his career overseas and away from Washington with several very successful tours in Korea, Bangkok, Taipai, and Indonesia, all of them demanding postings in a changing Asian landscape. Not only had he gotten to see some of the old colonies battling for their freedom after the Second World War, demanding that the West live up to the principles it espoused to fight Nazism and Japanese imperialism. He had also seen the kind of role—and appeal—Communism held for those chasing after ideals like freedom and self-rule.

Now, he had a new challenge to add to those, one that stemmed from the politics back home. In Crockett's elevated position as the chief of what was coming to be the Agency's largest deployment ever, the desire in the field for current information on the ins and outs of internal Agency politics was especially strong. He had probably spent the entire week since the cable on Baier's assignment had arrived trying to read between those bureaucratic lines.

"Are you interested in gossip, of which I have little in any case, or are you trying to discern my real reason for coming out here?" Baier asked.

"Well, both, actually." Crockett leaned back against his chair and rolled the coasters about a foot from the desk. There were still several feet to go before his back met the wall and window, given the spacious quarters in his office. That still didn't feel like it helped the air circulate. Baier grew hotter and more uncomfortable by the moment as he sat there in his cotton, navy blue suit and tie while the station chief sat nestled in his chair with short sleeves and an open collar. "First, though, I'd love to know what sort of reception McCone and our reporting are getting downtown."

Baier pulled his jacket off and folded it over the corner of the sofa set against the wall. He took his seat next to the jacket. "Hard to say, Frank. I mean the old man is invited to all the big powwows at the White House, and he takes along our stuff. But I get the sense that even if LBJ's attention is focused mainly on the election later this year along with his dreams of building the 'Great Society,' his advisors have their minds made up already. I mean, it's basically the same crew that Kennedy brought to town, and those guys all think they're smarter than everyone else anyway. So why bother to pay attention to our or anyone else's reporting and analysis? Especially the stuff where our analysts are basically telling that team that they're chasing a fool's errand."

Crockett's smile widened almost enough to fill the room. "Don't tell me they actually said as much."

"Well, not in so many words. But our people have pretty consistently pointed out that the heart of the guerrilla insurgency here lies in the south and that the Viet Cong do not rely solely on weapons and men from the North. It's more than a war of aggression from the north, which is how the people around LBJ see it. To be sure, Hanoi provides the broad strategic direction and some supplies, and Ho remains the most popular guy in the entire country—North and South. But an expanded bombing campaign is not going to force those guys to give up, nor will it have any appreciable impact on the supply chains for the VC, regardless of where that stuff's coming from." Baier paused to study Crockett's face, which stayed open and happy. "At least that what our analysts are saying."

"Good. That's corresponds to what we've been reporting as well. I'm glad we're all in sync on that. What about our reporting on the inability of these governments in Saigon to build any kind of popularity or legitimacy?"

"Oh, the consumers downtown are getting all that. But the general sentiment appears to be that that sort of thing—you know, the reforms and popularity--will come later. Let's stabilize the political and military situation here first, then we can get on with the institution-building, democratic governance, and all that other stuff afterwards." Baier paused to catch his breath and let out a grin. "At least, that's what I've picked up back in the halls at Langley. I do not go downtown with the Director, you know."

"Yeah, I can understand that. You know, though, that gives me an idea on something you might be able to look into at the start here. But, as you've probably guessed, I'd really like to know the real reason you're here. McCone was pretty insistent in the cable you that come out here. It wasn't like I had much of a choice."

Baier's grin grew into a smile. But his was not nearly as wide as Crockett's had been. "Oh, hell, Frank, I understand. I knew it was only a matter of time before we got around to that." Baier leaned forward and loosened his tie. He thought for a moment about pulling it off. He could feel the dampness spreading around his shirt collar already, and it was only the middle of the morning. "Please believe me that there is no hidden agenda or ulterior plans hidden in my being here."

"Then just what does McCone expect a Europeanist and German and Soviet expert to accomplish here?"

"That was my question to the Director as well. In fact, I told him I had less than a little experience in or knowledge of the region. And the word 'little' exaggerated both."

"And his response?"

Baier shrugged and sat back. "He said he didn't care. For some reason he valued my judgement and thought that another pair of eyes and over fifteen years of experience would help us work our way through the mess out here. And hopefully, back in Washington. I get the feeling sometimes that he feels a little beleaguered downtown when he has to join a table with the likes of McNamara, Rusk, and Bundy. And I really want to add that he does not think that you've been doing a poor job or have been slacking in any way."

"Well, that's certainly good to hear."

"I mean it, Frank. It's just that this is such a new and unique situation for us. Hell, not just for the Agency, but for our country as well. Anyone working out here could use all the help Langley can provide, including help at figuring out what Washington is up to and what it needs—not just what it wants. In that sense, I really am at your disposal. Understanding, of course, that I've got to put together that report the Director wants. It's my primary objective."

Crockett rolled his chair forward and leaned his elbows on his desk. "Okay, I got it, Karl. And thanks, I appreciate your openness on this. Then let me run some things by you."

Baier leaned forward, opened his hands and rested his wrists on both knees. "Please."

"We've begun running a pretty active paramilitary campaign, working with some of the Hmong tribes in Laos."

"Laos? I've heard a little bit about that program, but I can't help but ask myself if there isn't enough to do in Vietnam."

"I think you'll find out soon enough that the countries in this region are all interconnected in some way. The entire region was a French colony, you know, not just Vietnam..."

"Yeah, I've picked up that much."

"...And Laos, which was experiencing its own very active Communist insurgency until the ceasefire and peace talks put that war on hold back in '62, provides a very valuable location to keep tabs on what is going on the Vietnam. And that includes the roll the North Vietnamese have been playing in that country and are likely to play in the future." Crockett sighed. "I realize we're not supposed to be there, given the terms of the ceasefire in Laos, but Ho Chi Minh and his boys haven't exactly shied away from using Laos either. I'm not sure who went in there first, but we're both there now. And believe me, Ho and his boys are very active these days. There is plenty for us to do."

"How so?"

"Well, those tribes are no friends of the Vietnamese in general, and the Commies up north in particular. They tended to work pretty closely with the French. And their territory sits astride the main route Ho's and Giap's boys use to bring what they do supply down south. Not to mention the occasional troop deployment and advisors."

"Okay, I got it."

"Good, because if we do need to become more active along that trail—some wise guys labelled it the Ho Chi Minh Trail a while back—a lot of that is likely to happen in conjunction with our Hmong allies. Some Tais, too. They're another cooperative tribe in that region. But it also gives us an excellent vantage point to keep track of what is moving south."

"You know, the White House and Pentagon seem to think that

airpower will solve all our problems. Maybe they'll just bomb the shit out of that place."

"Good luck with that, is all I can say. It's the thickest fucking jungle you can imagine, Karl. I mean it. And as the French learned, that's the environment the Viet Minh—and now their successors, the Viet Cong—work best in. Plus, I'm sure the regular North Vietnamese battalions are just as adept at the style of jungle warfare we're up against here with the Viet Cong. I just hope it doesn't take us as long to learn our lesson."

"Okay, good," Baier responded. He started to stand. "That would also fit in well with what the Director wants me to do. That sounds like an important element in the story here. I'll make arrangements for a visit up there *toute suit*, as the French say."

"Yeah, a fat lot of good it did them." Crockett held up his right arm. "Just a minute, though. Don't run off just yet. There's a more immediate issue that you might be able to help us on more quickly." The smile returned. "And it should help with your report." Crockett held up two fingers. "A true two-for-one assignment."

Baier sat back down. This time he gave up and finally pulled his tie off completely. "Whatever you need. What is it?" He held up his hand with an open palm. "Although I should warn you that the Director told me to stay away from getting involved in any operational matters."

"Told? Was that an order?"

Baier shrugged and smiled. "I took it more as advice. That is, as long as I get the real work done."

"Well, then as you may already know, one of the main reasons we supported the coup that installed this General Minh was his promise to pursue the war here in the South more aggressively and to focus greater efforts on building a capable South Vietnamese army."

"Sure. You mean the ARVN, as it's now called. The Army of the Republic of Vietnam."

"That's right. Well, there are rumors floating around that Minh's aggressiveness is waning. In fact, he's allegedly been reaching out to Hanoi about starting peace talks to create a reunified Vietnam, and one that is neutral."

"And the logic behind that?"

Crockett sighed and shook his head. "Once you've been in this country a few more weeks you'll understand the logic. It's pretty obvious, actually. If any government in Saigon wants to establish some popular support it will need to find a way to end the fighting. The people are sick and tired of war. It's been going on since 1946 just after Ho Chi Minh declared Vietnam's independence from the French. And the locals don't really care what form of government they have. Just so long as it isn't one imposed by the French, or by us now that we've replaced the French in the eyes of most locals. It has to be Vietnamese."

"And that explains Ho's popularity?"

"Pretty much, yeah." Crockett's head was shaking up and down as though he was listening to music. "They don't really give a shit if it's Communist or not. They may regret it later, but for now they just want it to be Vietnamese and at peace."

"But isn't that similar to what we want? Except for the Communism."

"True enough. But it looks like there's a long way to go before we get that far. If we ever do with the clowns that are running this place."

"And you'd like me to see what I can find out? About Minh's reputed outreach, I mean."

"Yep. You can imagine how that kind of reporting would be appreciated back home. We're looking, of course, but another pair of eyes couldn't hurt. Just what are Minh's plans and how much outreach has he really done?" Crockett glanced out the window and back before continuing. "It would also be nice, of course, to get the North's read on this. But then, we don't have the sources for that kind of reporting."

Baier stood again, grabbed his jacket this time, and started for the door. But once again, Crockett called out and stopped Baier before he could get out of the office.

"There's one other thing you should know."

"And that would be?" Baier asked.

"I know you've only been here for two days—if that. But you have no doubt noticed that Saigon does not suffer from a lack of foreigners. Westerners especially."

Baier turned and leaned against the door frame. "Yeah. And?"

"One of the loudest is an American. Some old codger from the OSS who spent the last days of the war in Vietnam. Mostly to keep watch on the Japanese and make sure any American pilots who crashed or landed here got back to our side."

"Okay. Am I supposed to avoid this guy? Or can we make him more useful?"

"That would be hard to impossible. Either way. I'm sure he'll find you out at some point to bend your ear on how screwed up the French were and how we are following in their misguided footsteps."

"And why does he care?"

"Claims he got to know Ho Chi Minh pretty well. Was even present in '45 when Ho declared Vietnam's independence. Got him to plug in some wording from our Declaration of Independence and even help him write some letters to Truman."

"That sounds pretty interesting, if futile."

"Yeah, apparently Ho and his minions never heard a word in reply. Completely ignored."

"Well, he's not being ignored anymore."

"Nope. But don't let this guy monopolize your time here. He'll keep you from getting any real work done."

"Okay. And his name?"

Crockett shrugged. "Something Irish, I think. I can't remember it exactly, but I always think of pickles when I see him. Something similar to that."

"Thanks, Frank. That's not much help, but I'll keep it in mind."

CHAPTER THREE

O ne thing Baier had no trouble acclimating to was the food. It was simply delicious. The wide variety of noodle dishes, the fragrant chicken and pork concoctions—some of them pretty damn hot—would make for a pretty enjoyable tour here. That is, if there wasn't a war going on and threatening to get bigger and deadlier.

There was clearly a heavy French influence, which he was enjoying at that particular moment during his breakfast at the Continental Hotel. The rich and strong coffee beat the hell out of the Maxwell House he normally drank at home, and it reminded him of the strong German coffee that had spoiled him every morning during his assignments there and travels to visit his relatives in Baden. The *pain du chocolat* were not bad either. In fact, two were resting on his plate just waiting for Baier to finish his soft boiled egg.

"Mr. Baier. Sir."

Baier glanced up from his cup to see a young American civilian hovering at his table, dressed appropriately enough in khaki slacks and a plain white, linen, short-sleeved shirt. Baier was going to have to pick up a couple of those. For today, he had put on a pair of gray slacks, one half of a suit he had brought from Washington. He left the tie and jacket in his room. Baier may have been a special advisor on the seventh floor, but he wasn't stupid.

The young man held out his hand, which Baier took as he stood.

"Crockett said I should stop by to help get you started. I gather you're new to this country, and the entire region." He surveyed the dining room. "Accommodations okay? We hope to get you into some permanent housing as soon as we can, but, as you can no doubt imagine, coming here midway during the normal rotations has made that pretty difficult. Especially gearing up as we are."

Baier nodded as he sat back down. "Oh, this place is fine. Quite nice, actually. It will certainly do for my time here, which I doubt will be that long anyway. And, yes, you have gathered correctly. This is all new territory for me. I certainly appreciate the help."

"Great. Frank thought you'd like the hotel. A lot of history both here and in the neighborhood."

"Really? Like what?"

"Well, most of the main buildings were put up at the end of the last century. I guess the French wanted to leave their mark, so to speak. The Cathedral, Notre Dame—no relation to your college, of course…"

"Of course."

"…was built then, along with the Opera House and the Post and Telegraph Office. The Hotel de Ville as well. The street used to be called the Rue Catinat but was renamed To Do Street in '55, shortly after the peace agreement in '54, which ended the French attempt to reimpose its colonial rule. The square got a new moniker as well. From Place Garnier to Lam Son Square."

"Okay, thanks for the history lesson. I'll have to check those places out. But let's get back to the business at hand. How about starting with your name and a little bit about yourself."

The American sat and looked over the spread on the table before taking in the senior Agency officer. Then he shook his head and smiled. "Oh, sure. I wasn't sure how much you knew about the Station. My name is Fred Harnett. I think you met my brother in Berlin. It was on that exfiltration of the KGB guy you knew."

Baier almost laughed. "Oh, hell, that's right. He was terrified when I first spoke with him. I think he was afraid I was going to shoot him, or worse, ruin his career. He had lost the Russian when he dropped him off short of the safehouse, and the Russian promptly caught a subway to the *Bahnhof* at the Zoo for a quick train trip to Paris."

"That's right. He was afraid he had lost a very valuable asset through his carelessness or inexperience. Or both. He was really relieved when you let it ride. I guess you had an inkling as to what the guy was up to anyway."

"Yes, I did. And it all turned out just fine in the end. Although it was quite an adventure getting there." Baier lifted the carafe. "Can I get you some coffee? I'm afraid I've pretty much finished this one."

Hartnett thought for a few seconds, then nodded. "Thanks. I think we can talk openly enough here." He glanced around the hotel restaurant. "We do have an office set up for you..."

"Yes, I saw it the other day when I checked in with Frank."

"Good. But it's still more comfortable here." Hartnett glanced at his watch. "And it's pretty deserted by now."

Baier motioned for the waiter to bring another serving of coffee. "Yes, that tends to happen when you sleep in as late as I have the last few days. But I think I'm getting my body adjusted to the new time clock here in Asia. It's certainly been more of a challenge than when I go to Europe."

"Good enough. So where would you like to start? Frank gave me some ideas, things he had run by you earlier, he said."

Baier held up a finger. "First, though, I'd like to know more about you. It always helps to get a feel for where your colleagues are coming from, what sorts of things make him or her tick."

"Well, I joined our company in 1956, three years before my brother. We grew up in Chicago, as you may already know. But unlike my brother, who stuck around to attend Loyola University in our home town, I wanted to skip the winters and get some more sun in my life. So, I headed out to southern California, where I enrolled at the University of San Diego."

"Did it work? Did you get the extra sun? I hear that place has an almost ideal location in San Diego, practically sitting right on the beach." Baier took a sip of coffee. "It would be hard to study there, though. Or so I would imagine. Not like Notre Dame, where I went to school. Once the football season is over you're pretty much locked in for the winter with little else to do but study."

Hartnett smiled, while his eyes took on a far-away look. "You make Notre Dame sound like a monastery. It can't be that bad. But yeah, it was pretty nice in San Diego. The sun, the girls, and even the studies all worked out very well for me. Shortly after graduation I applied to our organization, and about a year later I was in and moving to Asia. This is my third tour, after initial runs in the Philippines and Malaysia."

"Okay, good. So, the two things that intrigued me and where I think I can help while still following my orders from the Director are learning more about the work we're doing with the Hmong, which I gather is in Laos primarily..."

"Yep. I can help set up a visit out there."

"And the more immediate issue of where the Minh government might be going with some sort of outreach to Hanoi."

Hartnett sat back as the waiter brought a cup and saucer for him, then placed a fresh carafe of coffee on the table. Hartnett watched him return to the kitchen. He sighed. "That's a tough one right now."

"How so?"

"Well, you know we—I mean our government—supported Minh's elevation in part because he promised to pursue the war effort more aggressively. And our military, or the MACV, in particular, is really committed to making sure that happens. They do not like anyone throwing cold water on their own efforts to get the Vietnamese to improve their military and its effectiveness, as well as their political or philosophical commitment to fighting the Communists."

"We're not about to run around here with our heads in the sand, are we?"

"Oh, I agree," Hartnett continued. "But we'll have to be sure to avoid the folks at MACV."

"You mean the Military Assistance Command Vietnam?"

Hartnett nodded vigorously. "That's right. The command center, as it were."

"Well, that works for me. I want to talk to some Vietnamese about this. What's our liaison relationship like?"

"We have a pretty good one with the National Police. That's where I'd recommend we begin. There are some Vietnamese there who were transferred in from the old Sûreté. That's the security service the French built up when they were still running the show here." He saw Baier's puzzled look. "Those locals got folded into the NP by Diem a few years back when the French left—for the most part--and there are many who still resent the way they were treated."

"Over what? What was wrong?"

"Well, many thought they were underappreciated and then bypassed by friends and allies of the Diem family. And there are those who feel the same way about how Minh and his cohort are running things now. It's just one of the minefields. So, we need to tread carefully, as it were."

"But that should give us some openings among the discontented, as it were."

"Oh, for sure. Then there's also the Nhu factor. I'm sure you heard about him, Diem's brother-in-law."

"I recall him being a major power behind the throne, as it were, as well a major reason for Diem's overthrow. He got shot, too."

Hartnett poured himself some coffee and took a sip. He had his eye on the last *pain du chocolat*, so Baier passed him the plate.

"Thanks." He immediately stuffed about a third of the pastry between his teeth. When he finished chewing, Hartnett said, "That's close. He was hung. But interestingly, he had also begun to reach out to Hanoi."

"Go on. I recall some reporting along those lines," Baier said.

"He—and others in the regime—had a sense that we were growing more and more disenchanted with the corruption, authoritarianism, and general lack of effectiveness in the government, so he started to look for other allies. I doubt Ho and his group would have given that bunch much more than the time of day, but you have to be aware of the underlying anti-Americanism among many of the Vietnamese."

"Because they see us as simply replacing the French as the new colonial power?"

"That's right. Plus, the fact that we're basically taking over the war effort. It probably won't be long before we're running this whole place. So, we have to maneuver around that. But there's so much internal plotting and corruption and backstabbing that we're generally able to find someone willing to talk to and work with us. Maybe not forever, but at least for a little while."

"But how does that relate to getting pissed off about being folded into the National Police?"

Hartnett swallowed some more of his pastry. "Well, the guys who worked in the old Sûreté had developed a pretty strong sense of autonomy. Superiority as well. And they weren't too happy about losing that."

"Which brings us back to the ex-Sûreté people as the most likely ones to be open to our approach?"

Hartnett set his cup down and finished the roll. "Exactly. Let me see what I can set up today and maybe we can meet up with somebody or somebodies tomorrow or the day after. In any case, I'll put something together."

"Great. Thanks, Fred."

Harnett brushed his fingers clean after the *pain au chocolat* disappeared. "I'd better get into the office. Will I see you there?"

Baier nodded as he stood. "Definitely. I need to do a lot of background reading to see what else you all have been up to. And this is a busy place, so it's probably going to take me a while."

Hartnett rolled his eyes and pointed toward the ceiling. "Damn, I almost forgot. Frank has set up an appointment for you to talk with the Ambassador and the Deputy Chief of Mission tomorrow. I'd recommend talking with them separately, though."

"Why is that?"

"Well, the Ambo is pretty gung ho about our programs and effort here, while the DCM is a bit more skeptical. I think you'd get a more honest opinion from both men if you spoke with them apart."

Baier paused as he studied the remnants of coffee in his cup. He topped that off then looked over at Hartnett, who was pushing his chair back. "Okay, good idea."

"There is one other thing," Baier said.

"Yes?"

"Frank also mentioned some old OSS guy who was stationed here near the end of the war. I gather he got to know Ho Chi Minh pretty well and was even at his side when the old man declared Vietnam's independence at the end of the war."

"Oh, yeah. He probably meant this guy Pyle. What about him?"

"Well, I'd like to meet him. I came from the OSS as well, you know. It's always nice to meet up with some old colleagues."

"Did you know him?"

"Not really. I spent all my time in Europe defeating the Nazis."

"Lucky you."

"But he does sound like an interesting character to talk with. Any idea where I might find him?"

Hartnett smiled and shook his head. "No. The guy moves around a lot. Kind of a gadfly. He's hard to pin down. I guess he has all kinds of contacts from his time here. Pretty much a permanent resident of the city nowadays."

"Does he have an address or a particular hangout?"

"Not that I'm aware of. But don't worry. I'm sure he'll find you."

• • •

Baier was right already about one thing. There were a helluva lot of files to read through if he was going to catch up on the operations, targets, and requirements for Saigon Station as the American involvement in Vietnam expanded. For now, though, he decided to concentrate on any reporting or insight his colleagues had collected on just where the Minh Government was heading—in terms of its relations with Hanoi, that is. He did not recall seeing much along those lines back at Headquarters, not that he had much time to focus on developments in Vietnam specifically, not with the ongoing crises around Berlin, programs to support the Non-Proliferation Treaty Kennedy had negotiated with the Soviets, colonial revolts against the French and British in places like Algeria and Malaysia, and the opportunities they were giving the Soviets and Chinese to meddle in African and Middle Eastern affairs. And the Middle East itself looked as though it would keep Washington occupied for years to come.

But the other reason he had not seen much was that there was so little there. The file was pretty damn thin. On this issue, in any case. Which made some sense, because the Embassy was probably prepared to rely on its own relations with the Minh Government and figure that they—the Embassy, that is-- would be able to learn whatever Washington needed to know. In their minds, all we had to do was just ask the buggers. After all, we were practically financing the damn country. Yeah, right. If only it was always that easy.

Baier sat back in the small, but comfortable office the Station had provided just down the hall from the Chief's. The window looked out over Ham Nghi Boulevard, the main drag that ran in front of and around the half-moon shape that contained the five-story building housing the American Embassy. From the outside, the place looked so colonial, almost like a picture from a Joseph Conrad novel: white brick and plaster, lots of windows for the air to circulate around and shades to hold off the afternoon sun. Not that those provided a whole lot of relief. Thank God for air conditioning. Although that seemed to work only enough to make the environment almost habitable. But Baier guessed you had to expect as much, working in a tropical climate like Vietnam's. He'd survive.

The one thing, though, that really bothered Baier was the proximity to the street below. There was, after all, a war going on. The small concrete pillars looked as though they might hold off a bus or something large and slow. But a smaller vehicle or scooter would make its way though, and pretty easily. And they wouldn't need to go very far, since the barriers—if you could call them that—were only a few yards away from the building. Not much more than what you'd need for a first-down; and with all this glass to act as shrapnel, a bomb could do a lot of damage. Baier stood and shoved his desk toward the corner to get it as far as possible from the center of the room and a possible blast route.

Then it was back to the files. Baier selected the one on his desk that covered the special operation in Laos with the Hmong tribes there. Now this one had more material and made for more interesting reading.

CHAPTER FOUR

Hartnett was true to his word, if a little delayed. It took him two days to set something up with the deputy chief of the National Police's Counterinsurgency squad, the group that functioned as the Station's main interlocutor. That office also functioned as the principal Counterterrorism unit, which made sense, from what Baier could see, since the terrorism in country stemmed pretty directly from the communist insurgency.

That this group would serve as the Station's most important point of contact within the local service also made a lot of sense, of course. Those were the guys within the security services most directly involved in countering the Viet Cong, especially in the larger cities like Saigon, Hue and DaNang. From what he had read and heard, Baier suspected that the close working relationship the Station enjoyed with that service also stemmed, in part, and benefited from the service's ability to operate in that urban environment. Those were the prosperous cities with an active and outward looking entrepreneurial and western-educated population. But he was glad to see that this had not prevented Agency officers from working the rural areas as well.

Nguyen Van Trongh was one of the many Catholics who had fled the North after the Geneva conference split the nation in two at the 17th Parallel back in 1954. He was not directly related to the Diem clan or even close to the family socially, which made him a bit of a rarity among high-level officials in the Saigon government. It was also speculated by Hartnett and others in the office that Nguyen Van Trongh had not been entirely corrupted by that regime and its extensive patronage network. He had clearly impressed somebody in the Diem family during the flight south, or at least that was the word that Hartnett had picked up around the Station and at the National Police Headquarters. It must have been close to the truth if the leadership analysts at Headquarters had seen fit to include it in the man's biography. That he had been retained after the coup against Diem also spoke to his professionalism and capabilities.

"He's one of those officers left over from the coup who is less anti-American," Hartnett explained. "That should help us get a better reception. At least I hope so."

"Don't tell me there's an undercurrent of that kind of thing in the National Police. That's not going to make any of our jobs easier over here," Baier exclaimed.

Hartnett's face took on what Baier thought looked almost like that of a sad, disappointed clown who had tried so hard to please a skeptical crowd. "I think we're beginning to see some resentment now."

"Resentment? Over what?"

"Over the fact that we're moving into a role that does a helluva lot more than merely advise the government here." Hartnett waved his hands, then paused to shrug. "But it's not that bad. At least not in the NP. Not yet, anyway. Or let's say it's not that pronounced. But you've got to expect it to be there for some people. I get the sense—shared by the colleagues in the Station I've spoken with—that most in the local service have come to terms with the change. It's not like they're going to solve this insurgency on their own. They really need us to succeed," Hartnett said. He paused and studied the crowd in the street below as the locals went about their shopping or made for one of the many cafes along Ham Nghi Boulevard for their lunch of noodles and fish. "They also need us to survive," he added.

"What about this Van Trangh character. You said he's not one of the anti-American officers at the NP. I'm getting the feeling that he may even be an outlier. Why is that?"

Hartnett pursed his lips before speaking. "Well, as I said, the guy is considered one of the less corrupt officials in the NP, and the word is that he was not one of those who enriched himself during the Diem regime. At least not that much, not enough to show."

"Yeah, that came across in his leadership profile from the analysts. Is he an asset of ours?"

Hartnett shook his head. "No way. We haven't even tried to recruit the guy, from what I've heard. He reportedly told us on our very first visit to the NP after the coup that we shouldn't even try. He would tell us whatever we wanted to know if we just dealt with him openly and on an equal basis. There were limits, of course. Or so he claimed. But I haven't seen any yet."

"Is his Catholicism an issue over there or in his work?"

Hartnett shook his head again. "That depends. Not for his work in the NP. It's easy to exaggerate the Catholic influence here, especially since the Catholics are only about 10 or 15 percent of the population."

"Then what's the problem?"

"It's more a matter of placement. Most of the higher and middle level civil service jobs and the same military ranks are dominated by Catholics. Where the problems come in is that the worker bees and certainly the peasants in the countryside are either Buddhists or followers of Confucius. So, you can imagine how that might limit their effectiveness. Remember those monks setting themselves on fire to protest the Diem regime?"

Baier sat back and ran his hand through his hair before wiping the sweat off his brow with his handkerchief. "Oh, God, yes. The American public had a hard time understanding that. So did I, to be honest."

"I'm no expert on this country, but it points, in my mind, to the depth of religious feeling and commitment among so many of the locals. It's just one more hurdle for this regime. It was especially the case for the Diem crowd, but it's still out there."

"And then I understand there are also various sects that are not really friends to either the government in the south or the one up north. Like the Bo Cai and the Hao Hao."

Hartnett walked to the window in Baier's office to study the crowds once more. "Yeah, although the Diem regime pretty much crushed those guys here in the south—in the Mekong Delta in particular where they were so strong—when he turned the Army loose on the organized crime gangs that ran Saigon."

"So, where do the Catholics fit in?"

"Right on top. Which is a problem in itself, but the Catholics among the ruling clique have got other issues as well."

"Like what?"

"For one thing, they're associated with the French and the colonial period. That religion, our religion as it were, was brought here by French missionaries in the last century. And the converts, of which there are a lot, were educated and lived in a French system. They all—or many of them, maybe even a majority— speak pretty good, and even some fluent French, went to French schools, and travel to Paris and the Riviera whenever they can. The last Vietnamese emperor, Bo Dai, spent most of his time in his French villa, not in the country he was supposed to govern. It's like they're a constant reminder of France's colonial legacy here."

"Well," Baier concluded as he stood, "let's go see what we can find out on our own."

• • •

The drive to the National Police headquarters took almost an hour, largely because of the hordes of civilians in the streets that overflowed from the rickety shop fronts along so many of the main roads. It wasn't the traffic. There were plenty of vehicles; the density easily matched New York and certainly Washington. It was all the bicycles and carts mixed in with the pedestrians that created the spontaneous and surging traffic jams and blockades. And if that wasn't bad enough there was also the heat, plus the humidity. Both those things settled on the open Jeep like it was not moving at all. Which it hardly was in these crowded streets.

It was still early January, and Baier was already dreading the coming of spring and summer. He had heard about the monsoon rains, which made him hope that his assignment would be over by then. Here's hoping, Baier reminded himself almost daily. He still had plenty of time, though.

"Van Trongh's assistant told me that if we wanted to see his boss, we'd have to drive out here. He's spending the day with several classes of new cadets before they receive their onward assignments. Some kind of graduation, I gather."

Hartnett pulled their jeep into a long gravel parking lot in front of a two-story stretch of white plaster that ran the length of two to three city blocks. Rows of small pillars and open windows gave the whole building the look of a cross between a colonial administration building and a primitive industrial plant or warehouse. He was also surprised by Hartnett's energy when he jumped from the driver's seat and trotted up the front stairs. Baier wondered how long it would take him to get used to the climate in this part of the world.

Once Baier caught up to his colleague at the front door, the two Americans breezed past the front desk like they were not only expected but welcomed as sponsors. Baier slipped out of his jacket and draped it over his arm as he followed Hartnett up a set of stairs at the end of the foyer to the second floor. Another twenty to thirty yards, and the Americans sauntered through an office door that had a Vietnamese title painted across a glass front. Baier had no idea what it said, but he figured it must have been an office that their host occupied whenever he was here. Without saying a word—merely nodding in the direction of a young Vietnamese woman seated at a desk just inside the door—they dropped into a pair of wooden chairs across from the receptionist. If that's what she was. Baier had no idea what her job might be, but she seemed busy. She immediately resumed her typing as soon as they sat down.

After about fifteen minutes of sweating and fidgeting—mostly on Baier's part—a middle-aged Vietnamese man approached them from an inner office with his right hand outstretched in greeting. He approached Baier first, clearly forewarned that he was the senior officer.

"Ah, Mister Baier," he said. "Welcome to Vietnam. Have you gotten used to our weather and your new body clock?" he asked.

Without waiting for a reply or missing a beat he continued. "I am Nguyen Van Trongh, Deputy Commissioner for Intelligence within the Special Police Branch. I am so pleased to meet you."

"Thank you," Baier replied. "And thank you for asking. I believe my body clock has adjusted, but it will probably take a little more time for the weather." Baier stood to shake the man's hand. "But I understood that your writ covers terrorism and counterinsurgency."

The Vietnamese officer smiled. "Yes, that is true. It is my main responsibility. But whatever the title, there will be plenty of work for us all, I am sure." Nguyen Van Trongh motioned toward a door on the right. "Please, let's retire to my office, where we can discuss the purpose of your visit today."

Their host led the Americans into an office that looked out over the front parking lot through a wide window open to the morning air. He was dressed in the ubiquitous light-colored, short-sleeved shirt. Baier decided then and there that he would forego suits in this country from now on, except maybe when he had to call on the Ambassador, or some other big shot. Hartnett had clearly made the conversion already.

Two large fans in either front corner pushed as much circulation as possible throughout the room without disturbing any of the papers on their host's desk. He offered both men the sofa opposite the window, while he took his seat in an armchair closer to the door. Baier found himself on the edge of an air stream from the fans, a courtesy he appreciated.

"Would you like some tea, or perhaps a soft drink? We just received a shipment of Orange Crush, my favorite, I have to admit. There is also some Coca-Cola, if you'd prefer that."

Hartnett opted for some tea. "I think I'll try one of your Orange Crushes," Baier said.

Nguyen Van Trongh rose and spoke a few words to the receptionist outside his office. Then he returned to his seat.

"I am sorry you had to wait, gentlemen, but we recently lost an officer, and we have been very busy hunting down his killers. Nhu Van Kim was one of our more promising junior officers, I am afraid."

"We are very sorry to hear that. How did he die?"

"An assassination. One of many by these damn Viet Cong." Nguyen Van Trongh shook his head. "This one is a puzzle, though. He was shot in his car in the parking lot of his housing compound. The VC rarely get that close or are that daring in Saigon. The countryside is another case. We have lost many officials to assassination squads out there."

"Well," Baier added, "I certainly hope you find those responsible. If there is anything we can do, please let us know." He nodded in Hartnett's direction. "My colleague would be a good point of contact."

Nguyen Van Trongh nodded. "Thank you. I appreciate your offer. Now, what can I do for you?"

Baier looked over at Hartnett again, who nodded in his direction. Baier took the lead.

"First of all, thank you for making time in what I am sure is a very busy schedule," Baier said. "I understand there are a few graduations today."

Nguyen smiled and nodded. "Only one, actually." The man's English was outstanding. Baier remembered that his resume had included a stint at the national police academy in Washington. He wondered if there were other connections to the States. "But it is a very good class. Their quality speaks well for the future of my country. I am certain."

"That's wonderful to hear," Baier continued. "But as you no doubt have guessed already, there are other matters we would like to discuss."

"Of course."

"We have been hearing rumors that your current government under General Minh has been reaching out to Hanoi about possible peace talks and a reunification of Vietnam. Could you comment on those rumors?"

"What would you like to know?"

"Well, for starters, are they true?"

Nguyen Van Trongh stared out the window for what seemed like a full minute. He pursed his lips, then leaned forward. Baier assumed that the rumors were more than that, that there was real substance to them, and that Nguyen was considering how much to reveal. When he spoke, the words came out slowly, almost as though they were slipping through a filter.

"There have been some feelers, as you say, to the North. How serious they are and how widely supported is unclear at this point. At least to me."

"Can you give us some specifics on who may be behind this move, as well as an estimate on the strength of the support for this policy?"

"And just what the goal might be," Hartnett added. "Any specifics you might have would be deeply appreciated.

Nguyen Van Trongh paused again. It was clear that he was weighing each response, each word, as to the cost of betraying his government and disappointing his benefactors. "I cannot do that I am sorry."

Baier leaned forward. "Is that because you really do not know? Or is it because you are afraid of those involved? If so, you know we can protect you."

At this Nguyen's eyes widened and his brow rose. "Like you protected President Diem. You know his brother-in-law Nhu also had begun to reach out to Hanoi. Many suspect that that made it much easier to overthrow him."

Baier was checked. This was almost an insult, an accusation and demonstration that memories of the recent coup last year on November 1 and the executions the day after, remained a sore spot. That in itself was hardly surprising. But for a Vietnamese official who would have to work closely with the Americans to throw this in his face, was stunning. Baier realized he would have to move more cautiously.

"Are you suggesting that the outreach to Hanoi is the result of the distrust that the coup and our role in it has generated?"

Nguyen Van Trongh smiled and shook his head. "No, I am sorry if I spoke too quickly and too harshly. But I wanted you to know how much uncertainty there is among us now. That is the real problem for me today." He paused before continuing. "You

Americans have certainly noticed how uncertain and ambivalent the Minh Government is. It is very difficult for me to follow the ins and outs of policy deliberations in my own government these days."

"Yes, I see. But could you give us some kind of estimate, even a wild guess, as to how far along these talks might be? Or have you heard anything about a response from Hanoi?"

Nguyen shook his head. "Mister Baier, I am only a deputy commissioner. You would need to speak with the Director General, or someone in his office. Perhaps Ambassador Lodge should call on him."

"I see," Baier said." He glanced over at Hartnett. "Perhaps we should direct our efforts elsewhere." He turned back to his host. "Thank you for your time."

All three men rose from their places, and the two Americans turned and started for the door. Nguyen Van Trongh remained standing, as though rooted to the spot.

"Perhaps there is one more thing you Americans may find interesting."

Baier stopped and turned. "Yes? What is it?"

"There is another area where your country—and your organization, Mister Baier—would do well to focus on."

"I see. And what could that be? It's hard for me to imagine something more important than a premature peace deal with the Communists in the north."

"Perhaps. But I seriously doubt it will come to that. You see, there is already plotting under way to replace General Minh."

This was the second time that morning that Baier had been stopped nearly dead in his proverbial tracks. By now he felt as though he was losing all trace of any trail, any sense of direction he had possessed when he first rode out to this building. His conversation had moved almost effortlessly from one weighty subject to the next, each with significant and even threatening overtones for the United States. This was turning out to be one hell of an introduction to Vietnam.

"Excuse me? Again? Another coup? Why? And who would lead this one?"

"I am not at liberty to name names. Not yet. You will probably learn of that soon enough. I am aware that you have other sources of information."

"Okay, but why? This bunch hasn't even been in charge for three months. Hell, it's just been two months and some change."

"I mentioned earlier that this government is so uncertain and ambivalent about its future direction. There are members of our military leadership who are very upset with this. They agree that the war must be pursued with greater aggression and a more offensive strategy. They are maneuvering to replace General Minh with one of their own."

Jesus Christ, Baier thought. What a fucking mess. But the Ambassador and MACV would probably be more than happy. At least Baier's conversation with Ambassador Lodge the day before suggested as much. If it really was because of a lack of purpose and focus and the desire for a more offensive approach to the war, then those guys would more than welcome another change in government. They will be more than happy to get this tidbit of intelligence, no matter how uncertain the sourcing. A more aggressive approach by the ARVN would certainly be appreciated. Anything to get those guys off their butts and chasing the Viet Cong would be a good sign of things to come. But what the hell did that say about the need to create a government in the south that could generate the political stability this place needed, not to mention the kind of popularity and loyalty that the Commies in the north appeared to enjoy?

These thoughts swirled around Baier's head like the insects that filled the air above their heads as he and Hartnett descended the steps to their jeep. Then he remembered. He never did get that Orange Crush. It would have tasted really good about now. Then again, he admitted to himself, if I took the time to take a drink, I might miss something.

• • •

During the drive back to the Embassy, Hartnett was unusually quiet, He rarely looked over at Baier, his attention focused instead on the pedestrian sea that surrounded their jeep.

"Checking for possible assassins?" Baier asked. It was only half in jest.

Hartnett's head whipped around as though a sharp wind had snapped his neck. "Excuse me?" he waved his hand at nothing in particular. "Oh, no. Sorry. It's just the killing of that Vietnamese officer. The Kim guy. I think that could be a real loss for us."

"How is that?"

"I hadn't worked with him that much. But I can still say that he was pretty impressive. Very sharp and very pro-American."

"In what way," Baier pressed.

"He clearly liked us. The Station, I mean. And he spoke very fondly of his trips to the States. Family in California, I believe."

"More pro-American than others? More open with us?"

Hartnett paused to think. "Yeah, I'd say so. Definitely more than most."

"But not a recruited asset?"

Hartnett let a light laugh escape. "Naw. Not really necessary."

Baier sighed and swatted a mosquito on his cheek. "Then I'd say it will be a real loss."

CHAPTER FIVE

"**S**o, the guy all but confirmed it." Crockett said. "You mean there have been other reports about a potential coup?" Baier asked. He was incredulous.

"Oh, hell, yes. Those started almost right after Minh was installed. But we've come to expect as much in his place. Those ARVN guys spend more time conniving against each other than they do fighting Commies."

"What's the sourcing like?"

"A lot of it is barely above the rumint scale. You know, corridor gossip. You can have a look at it, if you like. It might touch off something if any of it matches up with what Nguyen Van Trongh told you. He's been a pretty reliable interlocutor for us, though, so that does give the other stuff more heft."

Baier fell back into a chair across from the Chief's desk. "So, who's supposed to be the next great savior?"

"I don't think it's certain yet, or that it will even come off. It's still pretty early in the game to be calling in another relief picture. Minh's been in office for what, about three months?"

"Not even," Baier responded. "What's today, January 10th? It's only a little over two at this point."

Crockett nodded. He sat back in the swivel chair behind his desk and rotated slowly back and forth before responding. "Exactly. So, whoever the plotters may be, they probably haven't settled on a replacement yet. Hell, there's probably a good-size crowd competing for that inside track."

"Any name or names standing out?"

"There is one guy named Khanh," Crocket replied.

"And?

Crockett glanced out the window, then looked back at Baier. He smoothed a pile of paper at the center of his desk, then shrugged. He raised his right hand, holding it level with and about a foot above the desk, wriggling it back and forth. "Not all that great. If he does get the call, I'm sure Ambassador Lodge, Secretary Rusk, and the military command from General Harkin on down will be more than happy. The guy likes to give the impression of a real hard charger."

"And your opinion?"

Crockett laughed. It was actually more like a snort. "If it's who I think it is, the guy's more of an ambitious schemer than a real-life tough guy. I doubt the ARVN performance will improve all that much."

Crockett stroked his chin and gave Baier a puzzled look. "How did your talk with the Ambo go?"

"About what you'd expect. It didn't hold any great surprises for me. He's fully on board with the current strategy of maintaining our presence, even increasing it a bit..."

"Did he say by how much?"

Baier shook his head. "Not really. He just said something about some more advisors. Mostly, he talked about keeping the pressure up..."

"On who? Or I mean whom," Crockett pressed. "The Viet Cong or the local government?"

"I'd say both. He thinks we're here to stay because we need to be for a variety of reasons." Crockett started to speak, but Baier held up his hand. "For all the same reasons that you and I have heard before."

"The usual suspects?"

"Yep. Dominos, credibility, fighting for freedom, and so on. He's also pretty confident that we can win here with a little more effort."

"You know he was a strong supporter of the coup that tossed out the Diem regime last November? So, I'm not surprised that he is still a hard charger here."

"Yeah, I figured as much."

Crockett let a wide grin spread across his face before continuing. "All good fare for your report to the Director. Words from the very top."

"Yeah, I suppose so. We'll have to see what the DCM can add."

• • •

The following morning, Baier was back at breakfast in the Continental's restaurant when he received another visitor—another American. But this one did not work for the Agency. Or any other American organization, for that matter. The man stood at the edge of the table across from Baier, his feet planted firmly at the same width as his shoulders. His beard had about three days growth, and the eyes looked red and tired, as though he could use a good night's sleep. His hair was cut short but looked like it hadn't seen a comb in a week. He wore a white, cotton short-sleeved shirt that was also badly in need of a washing machine or a dry cleaner.

"Can I help you?" Baier asked.

"Yeah, you can definitely help me," a gravelly voice stated. "Me and my country. Yours, too."

Baier sat back, his hand still gripping his coffee cup. "Excuse me? Why don't we start with a name? Mine is Karl Baier."

The stranger nodded and smiled. "I know who you are. And I know what you're doing here."

"And that would be?"

A snicker escaped the rough patch of whiskers. "Oh, don't be cute with me. I know the business well enough to spot you guys. I used to be one myself."

Baier inadvertently scratched his cheek. "So, you must be that old OSS guy I hear has been hanging around." Baier pointed to the chair in front of his guest. "Take a seat. I was hoping to meet you eventually. I'm an OSS veteran myself."

"Thanks." He sat. "And, yes, I would like a cup of that coffee."

Baier signaled for the waiter to bring another setting and a second carafe of coffee.

"My name is Harry Pyle. I came here at the end of the war with the team led by Archimedes Patti to establish contact with the Vietnamese resistance. You know, the guys who morphed into the Viet Minh. Most of them were communists anyway."

"Excellent. I hear you're an old hand in these here parts, as one might say in a Western movie."

"Yeah, although most of my time—our time, actually—was spent up north. That's where the Viet Minh were active, as were the Japanese for the most part. So, this place down here is still kind of new to me."

"How long have you been 'down here'?"

Harry Pyle stared at Baier. When he finally replied, the stranger shrugged and shook his head. "A few years or more. Mostly on and off."

"What have you been doing in the interim? Or when you haven't been 'down here'?"

"I spent some time back in the States after the war. Couldn't really fit back in. So, I came back out here. To Indochina mostly."

"And?"

"Well, I feel at home here. More so than back in the States."

Baier waited to respond until the waiter had finished setting the new cup and saucer and extra coffee on the table.

"Okay. I understand you got to know Ho Chi Minh and his minions pretty well during your OSS service."

The stranger nodded. "Yeah, that's right. Real well, in fact. So well that we stood right by Ho's side when he read off his declaration of independence in '45. We even got him to add some wording from our own Declaration of Independence." Pyle smiled at the memory. "The crowd loved it. They went wild cheering us and the American plane that gave a nice fly-by." He looked up into Baier's eyes. "We represented the promise of a new world back then. One that would take those people beyond the colonial regimes of the past."

"Was Ho sincere? That wasn't all staged?"

Pyle poured a cup of coffee, his hand shaking slightly. "Hell, yes, he was sincere. If a bit naive."

"In what way?" Baier pressed.

"Hell, man, that was the American moment in this part of the world. All these poor colonial types who had been exploited for years by those pricks from Europe were looking to us to live up to our revolutionary legacy. You know, freedom, liberty, equality, and all that. I don't know about you guys in Europe, but those of us in the OSS here in Asia believed it, too."

"But it didn't help, did it? Ho got stiffed. I know the history."

"No shit. He also wrote some letters to Truman. No response, of course. Pretty much the same reception he got at Versailles in 1919 when he rented a morning coat and tried to call on Wilson to argue his case for an end to colonial rule in Vietnam. Inspired by the propaganda in the Fourteen Points. Ho didn't get anywhere near the clown."

"Wait a minute. Back up a step. Propaganda? In the Fourteen Points?"

Pyle leaned forward, spilling some of his coffee. His face had gone red at the cheeks and forehead. "That's right, goddamit. That was just a victor's peace for white Europeans who fought on our side. Those sacred points didn't apply to anyone else. I don't care what you learned in school."

"Is that why Ho Chi Minh went to Moscow? Is that how he came to suck up Lenin's bullshit about capitalist imperialism?"

"Of course. Who the hell else offered anything to those people? The victors in France or Britain?" Pyle sat back and blew out a breath that hadn't tasted toothpaste in days. If that soon. "Give me a fucking break."

"Well, it's too bad, because it marked him in the eyes of too many in Washington and elsewhere. Acheson himself said we had to realize that the man is in the thralls of Moscow. Nothing more and nothing less. That's a hard legacy to live down in these times."

"That's not Ho's fault. Those clowns needed to get to know the man. Like we did."

"Okay, the history lesson has been interesting and helpful. To a point. Is that what brought you here today?"

"I wanted to make sure I got the chance to open your eyes, Mister Baier."

"To what?"

"To the obvious fact that we're making the same mistakes the French did. As far as anyone here is concerned—the people who live here, I mean—we've just replaced them and are making the same mistakes. Both politically and militarily. And it will all end up the same."

"Now, just a minute, Mister Pyle. You have to admit that the global situation has changed considerably since 1945, and that Ho Chi Minh has shown his true colors. I can grant you that he was treated unfairly back then, and that mistakes were made. But he's shown himself to be a real Communist who will impose a Marxist dictatorship on the entire country if given the chance."

"You don't know that. We don't know that."

"Then look at the land seizures, the massive arrests that have crushed any opposition or dissent in the north. That makes it pretty plain to me. I saw it happen in eastern Europe after the war, and it would almost certainly follow the same pattern here. It's a typical communist m.o." Baier leaned in. "I'll admit that this crew trying to run things in Saigon is a pretty corrupt and hapless bunch. But we need time to try and set things right."

Pyle waved his arms in front him as though confronting a flight of locusts. "What the hell makes you think you can do that? This country has fallen onto a merry-go-round of feckless and corrupt leadership, regardless of who sits in the front office. We're just prolonging the suffering. Theirs and ours. Ho and his boys are going to win because they're the ones associated with the national cause, the one that is pushing for freedom from colonial rule."

"Well, what would you have me do?"

Pyle smiled for the first time since his arrival. "Just listen to me once in a while to make sure you get another perspective. The right one, I might add." He glanced around the dining room. "And maybe come with me now and then to meet with someone besides government officials, who are just going to give you the lines that they hope will keep you here."

"I'll give it some thought."

• • •

"Ah, he finally found you." Crockett exclaimed. It was later that afternoon, the time that seemed the least productive for westerners like himself and the chief, the time when the enervating heat of the place wore you down and made you feel like your steps had slowed to a crawl. Baier noticed that Crockett was wearing the same casual clothes as the day before, although he had changed his beige linen shirt for a long-sleeved white cotton one with the sleeves rolled up to his elbows. Baier had finally relented on the suits and left his ties and jackets in the closet...where they would probably stay.

"Finally?" Baier asked. "It doesn't feel like a whole lot of time. I've been here what, half a month? No, actually less now that I think about it."

"Oh, believe me. That guy gets around. Kind of worries me at times."

"Why is that?" Baier continued. "I mean, he doesn't appear to pose much of a threat. Actually more of nuisance, if you ask me."

Crockett laughed. "Oh, he's a nuisance alright. The threat lies more in him upsetting our hosts. There's enough distrust and resentment growing already. I'd hate for that old fart to make our jobs here any tougher."

"Where does he live? And more to the point, how does he support himself?" Baier asked.

Crockett instinctively scratched the back of his head, then ruffled his short brown hair. "You know, I'm not really sure. There are rumors that he comes from money on the East Coast, somewhere around Newport. You know, that old playground of the rich in Rhode Island. I've never seen anything official, though. Like a lot of those guys in the OSS—sorry, Karl—he supposedly went to Yale or someplace ritzy..."

"I did not come from some Ivy League princeling factory, Frank."

"I know, I know. You're an ultimate Yankee from Notre Dame."

"Yankee?"

Crockett nodded and chuckled. "Hell, yes. All you Northerners are Yankees. And you're a Catholic, to boot. And from Chicago. You can't get much more Yankee than that."

"Spare me your Confederate bullshit." Baier smiled and shook his head. "But back to Pyle, he did not impress me as some kind of blueblood. I've never known one to need a bath and a clean set of clothes before."

"Hey, I'm just passing along the scuttlebutt on the guy," Crockett protested. "He does not appear to want for money, although he is clearly not extravagant. Maybe there's a hidden trust fund or something."

"Or he's on someone's payroll. Has anybody bothered to check that out?"

"He's a private citizen, Karl. Not a pressing CI concern for us."

"Okay, so there's no obvious counter-intelligence issue, but does he have an address we know of?" Baier pressed.

Crockett shrugged. "Not that I'm aware of. Not anything permanent, anyway. I think he maintains a hovel or locker somewhere to store his belongings—whatever they may be—and sleeps wherever he can. Most of the time rumors place him at a brothel run by a Frenchman in town. I hear they're kindred spirits."

"You've never seen the need to run any of this information down?"

"Come on, Karl. You've seen how busy we are with real work here. Until the guy proves to be a serious threat to our operations I'm prepared to live and let live. From what I understand, he's earned the right from his war service to live in peace. Even if he is a pain in the ass at times. His views may be uncomfortable for us and our bosses in Washington, but so what. I'm not in the business of running some kind of a thought police unit here. Especially for American citizens."

"Okay, okay. I know you're right, Frank. But have you ever thought about possibly using him as an access agent. He offered to take me around to meet some people at some point."

Crockett's eyebrows rose, and he blew out his breath in a sigh of amusement and exasperation. "Any names?" Baier shook his head. "I really doubt that would be a good idea, Karl. I think that might be stretching the parameters of your assignment a bit."

Baier sighed and looked out the window before turning back to the COS. "Yeah, maybe you're right. But I do find the old coot kind of interesting."

"Has that 'old coot' also impressed you as all that dependable?"

Baier laughed. "You do have a point there, Frank. Still, it might be a good idea to gather some input and information from other venues, so to speak."

"Karl, you know damn well we are not depending solely on the Saigon government for our information. If we did, we wouldn't be doing our job. We've got a pretty good presence and feel for what's going on in the countryside. In fact, there are probably people in Washington that think we rely too much on information from sources in the villages and hamlets. It's why we've been reporting on the growth of VC control and influence, contrary to what the military and the Ambo keep telling that crowd around LBJ back home."

"Oh, I know that, Frank. And so does the Director. I did not mean that as any kind of criticism. But from what I've seen and read, there are a wide variety of views and perspectives in this place, most of them in that gray area between the black of Communism and the white of liberal western democracy. Who knows what nuggets we might find?"

Crockett laughed again. "Okay, fine. But don't waste too much time on the old OSS guy. Maybe when you two are reminiscing about how you won World War II and then got screwed by Truman—at least initially—you can pick some pearls of wisdom from the old guy and whatever friends he may have in town. I do have a bad feeling about the guy, though. Just be careful."

"Fair enough. I'll be discrete in my conversations and sparing with my time."

"Good. Because I think it's time to get you familiar with some of what we're doing in the field as well. Ever been to Laos?"

"Not yet. But Hartnett thought it might be a good idea for me to visit there."

Crockett nodded. "He's right."

"How do I get there. I don't plan on driving."

Crockett laughed. "Hell, man we'll fly you there on our own airline. Air America." He laughed again, louder this time. "And you'll get to meet Tony Purvis. The guy's a legend in his own time. And his own mind."

CHAPTER SIX

No, he had not been to Laos—not ever—and he had hoped he would not have to go there—ever. Vietnam was already a step pretty far in Baier's mind, and Laos was even further, even if right on the Vietnamese border. And that's what made it so important now.

Not that the country wasn't beautiful. He had seen it mostly from way high above, and now with a brief spell on the ground—hopefully, brief—and from what he had seen so far, Baier would have to admit that the scenery was nothing short of spectacular. The country appeared to be covered in lush, green vegetation, with hillsides rolling upwards and bordered by mountains of rock that erupted from the ground on nearly every horizon. The wooden huts that ran along the river banks and deeper into the bush looked like something out of a tourist brochure with their thatched roofs and stilts for support and elevation.

Baier had gotten what one might call a bird's eye view of Laos as the Air America Pilatus PL-6 Porter swept in from Vietnam and landed at the CIA base at Long Tieng. He had spent nearly the entire flight with his forehead balanced on the window, his face frozen in an open-mouthed smile at the wonderful landscape below.

But it was mostly the lush green vegetation of the surrounding jungle that seemed to overwhelm the earth that left the strongest impression on Baier. It was almost too much, especially given that there was little else, unlike the landscapes he remembered from growing up in the American Midwest. It was truly awe-inspiring. Baier had a sense of being overpowered by the tropical atmosphere that seemed to encroach on the base camp from every side. Like a verdant flood of vegetation that would win out in the competition with humanity in the end, regardless of what mankind might do to try to leave its imprint, or who might be leading that crusade.

In spite of the natural and untamed beauty of it all, Baier knew he was and always would be a Europeanist at heart. Spoiled might be a more appropriate word. And now, after a week at the Agency's headquarters for its secret war in Laos and humping through the thick jungle foliage, he was ready for a return to the semi-civilized environment of Saigon. There were plenty of officers at the Agency who loved this sort of paramilitary adventure, most of them graduates of the Special Forces or other unconventional and counter-insurgency units in the American military. But Baier wasn't one of them. He was a tried and true operations officer of the civilian sort: recruit and run human sources that would hopefully produce worthwhile reporting on plans and intentions for the analysts and policymakers back home.

"Don't be such a pussy, man." Tony Purvis had become almost legendary for his fighting prowess among the Hmong tribesmen and many Agency colleagues. "This is where the real action is. This is where we're going to teach those Commie bastards from North Vietnam and China what they're up against. You can forget those ARVN sisters down south."

Baier wasn't sure if Purvis and his two other Agency colleagues, plus their buddies among the Hmong, would ever get that far. They would probably inflict a lot of damage and loss on the North Vietnamese units operating in Laos, if it came to open warfare. His reputation suggested as much. What one could never be sure of with someone like Purvis, however, was where the legend ended and the reality began. It was like so much in this country, where that grey zone between the black and the white remained large and indistinct. Purvis reportedly took few prisoners and was even known to behead a few and then drop those heads on suspected PAVN, or North Vietnamese, and VC camps operating in Laos as a warning. "Scares the shit out of those bastards," he had bragged. Baier didn't doubt it. But he did doubt that it would keep them at home or from moving on with their mission to support the insurgency in the south. They had already demonstrated a remarkable capacity and willingness to absorb extensive losses and then retire and regroup, then try again…and again.

The U.S.—and all other foreign powers—were restricted from having troops operate in Laos by the terms of the Geneva Accords from 1962, which established the sovereignty and neutrality of Laos, reaffirming its independence granted by the French in 1953. Although the North Vietnamese had never withdrawn their forces from Laos—there must be between five and ten thousand of those pricks here at any given time, Purvis had assured him—Washington did not want to give Hanoi, Moscow, or Beijing any excuse to return the country to a full-scale civil war, or from pouring even more regular troops into the country. Laos was simply too important for the North as a friendly territory to use to support the insurgency in South Vietnam. However, memories of the Chinese invasion of Korea a little over ten years ago remained strong in Washington.

From his discussions and readings on the seventh floor, Baier knew that the budding CIA presence in Laos was intended to serve two purposes: create as much of a disturbance and loss for the PAVN units operating in the country to force Hanoi to divert resources away from the fighting in South Vietnam; and to monitor the buildup of a transportation network that was transforming the dirt paths through the Laotian jungle into what had become known as the much more ambitious Ho Chi Minh Trail that fed into the South. From what Baier had seen since his arrival, the latter appeared to be this group's primary mission. And Washington was now considering elevating that mission to one of interdiction and destruction—maybe not completely—but to do as much damage as possible, something for which officers like Purvis and the mountain tribes of Laos, who harbored no love for any Vietnamese but especially not for the regime in the North, were admirably suited.

"That's why I want you to spend some time there," Crockett had said. "Some of those guys we have there now are always itching for a fight. Shit, they'd probably like to organize a march on Hanoi."

"Folks in Washington are scared shitless that that kind of thing might draw the Chinese in and give us another Korea," Baier said.

"They're probably right, although I think Mao has enough on his hands right now trying to establish his revolution. Anyway, I want a cooler head to give me a more complete picture of what the North Vietnamese are up to, and whether the juice is worth the squeeze for us to make a major effort to disrupt and sabotage that traffic flowing south."

He studied Baier for a moment. Baier waited for more. "And it's probably something the people in Washington should appreciate as well. I know the decision won't be made here, so it's even more important to keep those people back home well informed." Crockett smiled. "And it's something I'm sure the Director will want in your report."

"Our assessments thus far have emphasized the southern nature of the Viet Cong insurgency," Baier had responded. "You know, the vast majority of the VC fighters and militia are southerners, and the bulk of their equipment, supplies, and support are southern-based. Lots of it material captured or purchased from ARVN units. What makes you think that's changing?"

Crockett had given Baier another long, hard stare before replying. "Karl, you know damn well what a political whirlpool Washington has become over this place. The principal advisors around LBJ are convinced that this is a war of aggression by the north against a free and democratic south. We need to give our own unbiased opinions and assessments as to what is really going on here. I just want to make sure we're looking at all angles. And keeping our eyes open."

"And you think you'll get that from me after a short spell in the Laotian countryside?"

Crockett nodded. "I sure as hell hope so. At least that's what I told our Ambassador in Laos, Bill Sullivan. He pretty much runs the war effort there, and he does not take kindly to interlopers. I assured him and our Station Chief up there that you are nothing of the kind. That we needed an independent view of what the North is up to there and how important it is. Sullivan eventually relented. The COS, as you might imagine, was not about to block an emissary from the seventh floor."

"Emissary?" Baier had asked.

Crockett nodded. "Hell, yes. That's how I sold it. Of course, it might affect how the paramilitary types up there look at you." He smiled. "You know, some kind of bureaucratic sissy."

Baier paused and returned Crockett's stare. "Well, thanks for that. But I'll do what I can in such a short time. I probably won't be able to say much about the importance of the supply chain for the VC operating in the south, but I'll try to get a clear view of just how much effort Ho and his boys are putting into it."

• • •

His first glimpse had come on the ride out to Long Tieng. The pilot—a Marine seconded to the Agency for resupply missions in the Laotian campaign, had not stopped talking for almost the entire trip.

"I'd never get this kind of action back home in Arkansas, or even Lejeune or Paris Island," he had gloated. "And I love this plane."

"What is it," Baier asked. "It doesn't look like one of ours."

"Oh, hell, no," the kid enthused. "This is a Swiss machine. We like to minimize the U.S. footprint wherever possible. This one's a Pilatus PC-6 Porter. They make a real fine airplane, they do."

"Like their watches, I guess."

"Yes, Sir." A moment's silence intervened. "Whatever."

He banked low over the jungle canopy when he spotted a clearing in the tree line. Baier had noticed on the way in, not more than twenty or thirty miles away, what looked like a full-blown construction crew at work building a bridge over a mid-sized river. The short road leading to and from the bridge abruptly disappeared in the trees and bush roughly twenty or thirty yards from either bank of the river. Baier also saw smoke from several fires under the canopy, suggesting that there were more encampments supporting work crews or supply trains presumably heading south.

He soon got to see a lot more.

"Let's go, Mister Washington Head. Time to get up, because there is no better time than the present," Purvis said as he shook Baier from what had been his best slumber of the trip. "You shouldn't need all that much sleep anyway. It's not like you joined us for the whiskey session around the fire last night."

"No," Baier said, rubbing his eyes and staring at the small mountain of manhood squatting next to his sleeping bag. "And I won't be after that first night when you all talked me into entering that stupid drinking contest." Baier shook his head in memory of the night spent drowning his gut in the local hootch and the time throwing it all back up in the latrine.

"Shucks, Mr. Washington Head. That was a celebration, not a contest."

"Whatever it was, I lost."

"Well, you should be rested. And you won't need one of those dark suits and white shirts you wear back in Washington."

"What the hell is up, Purvis?"

"We're going to raid the Trail." He pointed outside the hut where Baier had been sleeping. "Scouts have found a supply column. Or maybe part of one. Pretty small. But still… There's a path that will let us get real close, where we can set up an ambush. But it's a bit of a hike, so we need to get moving."

"Has this raid been approved? I wasn't aware that interdiction was now a part of the policy."

Purvis shook his and snorted. "Hell, Mister Washington Head, have you seen any commo gear for us to communicate with Langley that quickly? Consider this a probe, a taste of what's to come for those assholes." Purvis stood. "You've got just about enough time for a pee and a dump, if you need it. Get your boots on and grab some gear and a rifle. We'll meet you outside."

The last sentence trailed behind Purvis as he marched out the door of the hut and toward a group of about twenty Hmong tribesmen gathered at the edge of the runway at the camp's southern edge. When Baier emerged from the outhouse, he found a backpack had already been prepared and an M14 carbine propped against the side, plus a satchel with extra magazines for the rifle. Purvis, standing with the group, kept rolling his arms in a huge circle, signaling for Baier to hurry over. As soon as 'Mister Washington Head' joined the party, the group set off for the jungle.

He soon realized that Purvis had been right. It was a bit of a hike. In fact, it was a bit more than that. After two hours slashing their way through the jungle foliage that was often as thick as any wooden barrier Baier had encountered, the group came upon a small clearing that provided ample coverage from what was now a decent-sized road wide enough to carry a truck in either direction, but which also gave Purvis and his Hmong friends an excellent view of the highway below. They were able to set up their ambush—if the caravan ever showed—about twenty feet above the road and maybe fifty yards back.

"The guys found this spot about a week ago," Purvis explained. "We haven't used it yet. Once you use a spot like this those buggers mark it on their maps, and it's usually cleared whenever another convey comes by. Unless they're building other routes south." He sighed. "I hate those guys, but they are pretty damn effective and well organized."

Three tribesmen immediately got to work setting up a mortar emplacement, while others spread out in the woods to protect their flanks and add to the fire on the convey below. When it appeared. Which happened after about twenty minutes.

It looked to be a fairly small group, around fifteen to twenty trucks, that were accompanied by a host of porters and what looked like a small detachment of infantry. After the first three trucks in the column had passed, the mortar crew went to work. Round after round exploded along the road. Baier remarked at their accuracy—clearly these guys knew their business—as they shredded several trucks that were following. Secondary explosions rocked the area further, indicating that the convey must have been carrying ammunition.

Small arms fire ripped through the foliage in every direction, and Baier joined in, pummeling the road below with rounds from his rifle. He had no idea if he hit anyone or anything. He soon realized he was firing far too rapidly, and he was shooting almost blind from the smoke. He could see next to nothing of the road below, but he still had a pretty good idea of where it ran just below his posting.

But, goddammit, sight or no sight, he wanted to do his part. He found the urge to join the fight irresistible. His adrenaline had kicked in with the first shot, and it never let up as Baier felt himself plunge into the firefight and all that it represented. And he did it without a second's thought of hesitation or anxiety. The emotional blocks and barriers that would normally hold a man back all evaporated in a moment of intensity and exhilaration.

He felt like a man possessed. It was almost as though he was taking aim at the jungle itself, firing back at the dense foliage and all the primitive dangers it represented. The heat under the boiling sun, the humidity that continually drained the fluid from his body, the wildlife, and now the Viet Cong or North Vietnamese, all of them were hidden and lurking, ready to end his life in so many horrible ways. Fuck, Purvis, he thought, I'll show him what 'Mister Washington Head' can do.

He never saw a single target. He simply aimed at the noise and the suspicion that someone from the other side might be where he was shooting. He had no idea where the horizon stood, where the goals and objectives of the operation lay, but it no longer mattered. His most tangible connection to the world enveloping him came from the empty shell casings and ammunition clips that sprinkled the ground at his feet.

Screams ripped through the air, which only generated more fury and more excitement. Baier wondered for only a moment if the screams came from their side or his own. He never really paused, though, or stopped to listen. Only to reload his carbine, which he thankfully remembered how to do from his WWII training and the refresher course the Far East Division had insisted he take before departure.

Sweat poured down his forehead, and Baier had to pause periodically to wipe the moisture off his forehead and away from his eyes. He couldn't tell if it was the heat, the excitement, or the fear. But he didn't care. And through it all the mortar kept up its steady pop and thump.

After what seemed like hours, but was probably more like fifteen minutes, the firing died down and Purvis shouted an order that sounded like a cease fire and retreat. The tribesmen set a line of booby traps to cover their withdrawal, and the group gathered at the designated meeting spot for the long walk back to the base.

"Damn," Purvis cursed when he stepped in line with Baier. "We lost two guys back there. But we still caused a helluva lot of chaos. That's one convoy that will arrive a lot lighter than when it set out."

"You're not going to just leave your men back there, are you?"

Purvis grimaced and spit into the brush. "Have to. Too many PAVN types—the porters also carry on these trips—to stick around. Can't let the dead guys slow us down either. Don't know if they're pissed enough to organize a pursuit. Wounded would be another story. But there's nothing we can do for the others."

Purvis recognized the look of disappointment that covered Baier's face like a shroud. He rested a hand on Baier's shoulder. "I'll get some of the family members together later, and we'll return to see what we can find. Have to be careful, though. The PAVN, if they find the bodies, are likely to booby trap them, or maybe even hang around for a while to set up an ambush of their own."

"Yeah, I see."

"It's a dirty fucking war, man. Now you know."

"I had a pretty good idea already," Baier said.

• • •

That was not the last time Baier humped his way through the jungle with Purvis and his group of Hmong warriors, but it was the only time they engaged in a firefight. There had been one attempt to blow up a bridge, but when they returned two days later to check on the damage and its impact, the bridge had been repaired and looked ready for full operation.

Mostly, they took advantage of opportunities to sight and monitor construction work and supply trains heading south, which struck Baier as steady but not overwhelming in the amount of men and material moving along what was clearly an expanding route. He was able to take numerous photographs for Crockett to peruse back in Saigon and the analysts to study in Langley. Let them sort it all out, he figured. They would know best how much material was moving and how significant it was. All he had found on this trip was a snapshot of a bigger and changing portrait.

He had also become remarkably impressed by the skill and daring among the Hmong fighters. They were operating on their home field and clearly did not relish the prospect of living under Vietnamese or Communist rule of any sort. Whether that prospect was a realistic danger was not for Baier to say. But it was definitely a danger they believed to be real and were happy to fight against. It seemed everybody had their own worries about somebody else's imperialism and colonial ambitions.

"Okay, Mister Washington Head, I think we can get you home in time to send a Valentine's Day message to your wife. In fact, a whole lot earlier. Hell, it's still January."

"Well, I certainly appreciate that," Baier said. He was sitting on a crate of mortar shells to keep his butt off the rough ground. "I've been out of touch for a while."

Purvis sat on the open corner of the crate, slapped Baier on the back, then grabbed his shoulder and gave him a shake. He passed a mug filled to the brim with black coffee. A tad splashed over the edge and spotted Baier's bare leg and the cuff of his khaki shorts. "You've done well, especially for a Langley desk-sitter. You held your own in our little firefight…"

Little? Baier thought.

"Mostly you fired high, which is not unusual for someone in your spot. And I doubt your rifle helped much. Those wooden stocks can warp some in the heat and humidity here. But they're still pretty reliable. I guess they're still working the kinks out of these babies."

Baier studied the rifle in Purvis's lap. "I hear the Marines are going to introduce those pretty soon as their standard weapon here. It's one of those M16s, right?"

Purvis nodded, cradling his weapon. "Yeah. Has a tendency to jam, which is why I left you with one of those older boys. I got this one from some Marines, and I like how it handles in the jungle here, but I'm used to the jamming and can work it out pretty quick. A steady supply of ammo can be a problem, though. That's when I pick up one of those older babies."

He nodded at the M14. Then Purvis studied Baier for a moment. "I don't suppose you saw much combat in the big fight…"

Baier shook his head, then sipped some coffee. "No, I was a desk guy, doing analysis and hunting German scientists and industrialists. Ever hear of Operation Paperclip?"

Purvis shook his head and laughed. "Nope, not really. I suppose that's a good thing, though. The other day you were primarily a threat to the vegetation and not so much to the PAVN. But that's okay. You helped scare the shit out of them and didn't hit any friendlies."

"Well, that's good to know."

"You might have heard of some of the other stuff going on…"

"Like what?" Baier asked.

"Well, the other guys up here have been off with larger groups of our Hmong friends engaging in some real firefights—battles even—with those North Vietnamese pricks and their Pathet Lao brothers. You know, the local Commies. The assholes keep trying to raid the villages here to seize more territory and pressure us to leave the country to them. But we thought there was too big a chance you'd get shot if you went along on one of those trips."

"Too much paperwork afterwards?"

Purvis shook his head and laughed. "No, not that. But we figured the seventh floor would come down pretty hard on us if we let you get punched full of holes."

Purvis sat silent for a while, sipping his coffee. After about a minute he looked into his mug and frowned. "Look, Karl…"

"Karl? Not Mister Washington Head?"

Purvis smiled. "Oh, Hell man, not anymore. That was just a nickname we gave you. Everyone has one here. "I'm Moby. You know, like the whale."

"Okay. I can see that."

"But what I want to say is we appreciate your support here, especially during our little skirmish a little over a week ago. But I want you to know that checking on the Trail is no longer our main assignment. It was originally, but that's morphed now. You may be aware of all that, given your job back in Langley, but we were just responding to a quick request for an update on developments on the Trail. We're really here to help build a local tribal force that can hold its own against North Vietnamese efforts to control this country."

"Yeah, okay," Baier replied. "And you're telling me this because…?"

"Because you probably won't be hearing from us again. We're working here under the supervision of the Station in Vientiane and our Ambo there. And that mission may change again at some point."

"Sure. I know the parameters out here."

"Yeah, of course, you do. But you'll soon be swallowed up by the intrigues and politics of Saigon once you're back. Not to mention those in Washington. And I do not envy you. Our job is actually easier."

"Easier? How so?"

Purvis paused. When he resumed his lecture it was almost as though he was speaking to the trees. "Hell, man we just follow orders. Go there, shoot here. You know. It's simpler and more direct." He paused again and sipped some more coffee, then poured the remainder onto the ground. "Tastes like shit at this point." He turned to Baier. "Can I give you some advice?" Purvis asked.

Baier smiled. "For me? A Washington civilian?"

Purvis returned the smile. "Oh, hell, that probably means you need it more than ever." He tipped his empty coffee mug against Baier's in an informal toast. "First of all, there's a great whorehouse run by a Frenchman in Saigon. I don't want to tell you how to handle your love life, you being married and all. But you might find it could help relieve some tension."

"Thanks for the insight, but I'm good. A nice chat with my wife will do for now. Anything else?"

Purvis sat back and set his mug on a level patch of dirt. "As a matter of fact, there is. I mentioned that whorehouse for another reason as well…"

"I have heard of it."

"Well, good. But in some ways it represents a lot of what you'll encounter in Vietnam." Purvis spread his arms wide and looked around the camp at the countryside beyond. "This is one helluva complicated place, man. If there's one big lesson I've learned it's not just about Communists and freedom-loving democrats. Hell, the gray area is a whole lot bigger than the black and white parts. And you'll see that in the whorehouse as a microcosm." He smiled and shrugged. "Kind of. As it were."

"Seriously? All that in a brothel. You must have had some great sex there."

"Aw shit, man, I'm not trying to get too deep here. I just want to give you a warning to watch your back. Man-to-man. Wherever you go down there. There's all sorts working in that city, and their agendas aren't always clear. Even to themselves. Things are a lot simpler up here. You've just got to remember to be real careful where you're going. And real flexible." He slapped Baier on the back again and stood up. "I just want you to go home to your wife in one piece. You've earned that much with us."

"Maybe I should simply stay away from the whorehouse."

Purvis shrugged. "Easier said than done. Easier said than done. And not just because of the sex and the beautiful women."

• • •

He got back to Saigon the following day. Still in plenty of time for an early Valentine's Day call. Baier was sure Sabine would appreciate the effort, even if it was several weeks early. He had a call patched through to home from Crockett's office.

"It's good to hear your voice, Karl. I miss you."

"I miss you, too, Sabine. I'm already looking forward to coming home."

"Do you have a date? Already? You must be working pretty hard."

"No," Baier said. "Nothing that quick. There is actually a lot going on here. There's talk of us Americanizing the war soon…"

"But the President claims he won't be sending American boys to do the job Vietnamese boys should be doing."

"Well, not before the election. We'll see what happens afterwards."

"Well, I hope you won't be there that long."

Baier tried to laugh into the phone. "Oh, heck no, Sabine. But I did want to wish you a Happy Valentine's Day."

"So soon? Is this your way of telling me you will be gone that long at least."

"It's really hard to say. You know how things can go in this business."

"Of course. Take the time you need to do the job right. Just don't stretch it out too much "

"Well, I do think I can wrap this thing up shortly after that, though. If not before."

"That would be wonderful." Sabine paused, then jumped in with what sounded like a prepared question. "Have you seen much of the country? Outside of Saigon, I mean."

"No, not much really. Some sights from the air. It's pretty dangerous out there, despite what our leaders are saying. Hell, it's even dangerous here in Saigon at times."

"Karl, that is not what I was hoping to hear. I know I don't need to say this, but please be careful."

"It's not all bad, Sabine. It's not a constant thing. Plus, you know we are trained to survive in these kinds of areas."

"Yes. It does help to know that."

"And I've got lots of colleagues and company," Baier said. He immediately regretted having worried her.

"And the women? I've heard their beautiful."

"Oh, it's like anyplace else. Some beautiful and some not so much. Besides, I'm really too busy to pay much attention. Too busy and too tired."

"And the weather?" Sabine pressed.

"Now, that is rough. But I'm getting used to it. I am not looking forward to the monsoon season, though."

"But you should be home then. Right?"

"Yeah, of course," Baier agreed. He decided then and there that he would hold himself to it. He would finish this damn assignment, and then get the hell back home. He also knew he had little control over what this country and this budding war had in store for him.

CHAPTER SEVEN

"We've got to stop meeting like this," Baier said. "I mean it." His new American friend—if one could call him that—glanced around the Continental dining room. Sun shone through the large plate glass windows with hardly a shadow cast across the linen tablecloths and small bouquets acting as centerpieces. Not many patrons either. Just a handful of guests were at scattered tables, a blend of Westerners and Vietnamese, sitting mostly against the windows and away from Baier in the center of the room. Apparently, the view was much better there. That, however, was less important to Baier than the need to stay away from any potential glass debris should the VC launch another bombing attack in the city.

Pyle turned back to Baier. "Nobody here gives a shit. And it's the one place I know I can find you." He gave a superior smile. "Have you thought of varying your routine?"

"Thanks for the reminder." As though I needed that from some washed up OSS veteran, Baier thought, momentarily forgetting his own roots in that organization. "Now, what can I do for you?"

Pyle grabbed a seat across the table from Baier, but this time he did not appear to be interested in Baier's breakfast. His eyes never left Baier's face. "Do you think the Station can spare you for a little excursion this morning?"

"Why? What did you have in mind?"

"I'd like you to meet someone. A Frenchman."

"Is this someone with that differing perspective you think could be so enlightening for me?" Baier asked.

"Well, there is that. He's a former Legionnaire. Fought at Diem Bien Phu actually, and was one of the few—very few—who escaped. Headed to the mountains in Laos with some of the Tai warriors who fought for the French. Kind of like the Hmong you guys are so enamored with."

"I already know what the French have to say. That asshole de Gaulle reminds us almost every day about how futile our efforts here will be." Baier shook his head and frowned. "He should have thought of that back in '45 when he insisted on restoring France to her 'colonial glory' in Indochina."

Pyle waved Baier's complaint away like a bothersome insect. "Oh, this Frenchman can you give more than that." The superior grin returned. "A lot more. Why not give it a try?"

"You know, I do have work to do," Baier complained. "I am on an assignment from Washington."

Pyle stood and started for the exit, as though he had not even been listening. Baier cursed softly, stood, and threw his napkin on the table. He followed Pyle into the street.

• • •

People flowed past the two Americans, who offered little more resistance than pebbles in a stream. Pyle signaled for a rickshaw, one towed by a bicycle rider. "It's too far to walk. These guys can be pretty quick, especially since they know the best routes to take and don't really give a shit about anyone, or anything else, in the road."

Baier had to admit that it was a more pleasant means of travel than trying to navigate your way on foot through throngs of human flesh crowding the sidewalks and streets as they moved from one market or one café to the next. The movement of the vehicle even brought a nice, welcome breeze to the ride.

After about thirty minutes, they came to a small clearing in what appeared to be a residential section with large—by Vietnamese standards—houses on tree-lined avenues. Most were white and built of wood. Several even had pillars in the front enclosing a porch with lawn chairs or a bench or two; they generally sat on tree-lined lots ranging from a quarter to half an acre. It was clearly one of the more prosperous neighborhoods in the city, probably,

Baier guessed, the area where former colonial lords and rubber barons had settled in comfort and conspicuous prosperity.

The rickshaw stopped in front of one of these mansions. Pyle jumped out, paid the driver, and waved his arm for Baier to follow. Only then did Baier notice the sign on a stand in front of the right-handed corner of a brick patio. 'La Maison des Reves.'

Seriously? Baier thought. The House of Dreams? Don't tell me this clown brought me to a whorehouse. He wanted to scream at the old OSS veteran and ask if he had lost his mind…or spent too much time in the fetid southeast Asian sun.

Instead, he checked his anger as they met on the porch. Maybe this was the place Purvis had recommended. "Just what did you have in mind for this morning, Pyle?"

"Oh, don't worry your little puritanical mind, buddy. We're here to talk to the Frenchman, not his workforce."

Pyle led the way through the front door and foyer to an office at the rear of the house. Business appeared to be light this early in the day. Baier glanced at his wristwatch: 9:30. Women lounged in chairs or on sofas in the rooms that lined the hallway, most of them attractive Vietnamese who looked to be no older than women in their twenties. A few might possibly be teenagers. Baier had to admit to himself shortly after his arrival in this country that he found it almost impossible to come up with an accurate estimate of the age of Vietnamese women in Saigon. To his Western eyes they could be anywhere from 16 to 60, with most looking as though they were somewhere in their twenties or thirties, and many of them younger than that. The villages were no doubt a different story.

Baier saw several women he guessed were Eurasian as well, all of them stunningly beautiful. None of the women in La Maison could be classified as anything less than pretty, in Baier's estimation, but these few Eurasian beauties were a cut above the standard. A big cut, in his eyes, combining what appeared to be the best physical elements of both cultures. Maybe he had been too quick to judge and too dismissive when he spoke with Sabine.

Not that he planned to do anything about it, which wasn't easy as he surveyed the workforce. They were either dressed in silken pant suits that hung from their breasts and wrapped around their rear ends or in body length gowns with splits almost to the crotch to showcase legs that would easily grace any modeling runway in New York. It was like each outfit had been designed to pull your eyes to the bodily delights that awaited your choice. He was sure that had indeed been just what the owner had in mind.

"Come on, man, don't dawdle. We've got other business to pursue," Pyle said.

He led Baier past the female attractions and into a spacious office at the back of the house where a large glass table in the center of the room served as a desk for an older man seated there. Baier guessed he was somewhere in his forties, or early fifties at the most. Oil paintings of Vietnamese peasants at work in the fields and rice paddies covered the walls, along with an occasional nod to the French Alps. The man rose, his hand outstretched towards Baier. He was dressed in a blue, long-sleeved silk shirt with the sleeves rolled midway to his elbows. The shirt was untucked and draped over a pair of white slacks that ran loosely to his ankles. Leather loafers over bare feet completed the ensemble.

This must be the French guy, Baier guessed. He took his host's hand, then pointed to the walls. "You've got an eclectic taste in art and office decoration," Baier said.

The Frenchman's gaze followed Baier's. "Ah, yes. My first and second loves."

"Which is which?"

"First, let me introduce myself. My name is Henri de Couget. And as you might have guessed already, I come from France, Normandy to be exact. But the region I always liked the most was the southern part of the country not far from the Italian border. Since 1954, however, I have chosen to make Vietnam, and the southern part in particular, my home."

Thinking back on his breakfast conversation with Pyle, Baier asked, "Did Dien Bien Phu have something to do with that?"

"Actually, quite a bit." He sat. "But you must excuse my poor manners." He pointed to a chair opposite the desk. "Please. Be seated. Would you like a coffee or tea? Or perhaps something stronger?"

Baier shook his head. "No, thank you. I doubt we'll be staying long. I do have to get to my office."

"Ah, yes, at the American Embassy. Such as it is."

"Excuse me?"

"Oh, please, I do not mean to insult. But your country's presence here has come to be so much more than simply diplomatic. For better or worse, you practically run this country now. And I do not mean to comment on your actual job, such as that is."

"Well, let's hope it's for the better. After all that is certainly our intent." Baier shifted his weight on what were extremely comfortable and hard cushions in his armchair. "But just what did you want to discuss? I assume that Mr. Pyle here," Baier waved in his compatriot's direction, "brought me here for a reason."

The Frenchman shrugged. "He did not ask for an appointment this morning, so I cannot say for certain. But he has expressed an interest in introducing us."

"To what purpose? I hope it's not just to reaffirm your President's complaints and dire predictions about our efforts and role here. That man hardly has any credibility with us."

"And why is that?"

"Because he's the one—along with the Brits who were worried about their hold on Malaysia—who got us into this mess in the first place. He's the one who insisted on restoring French rule here as you all groped for a renewed global role and world prestige after getting your asses kicked by the Germans."

The Frenchman laughed. "Well, my friend, that certainly puts things in a nutshell, as Mister Pyle likes to say." He sighed. "I may be a former Legionnaire, but I am no fan of President de Gaulle. In fact, I do not even consider him my president. But I do agree with his forecast for your country here. You are likely to suffer the same disastrous results that we did. I do wonder why you have not learned the obvious lessons from our defeat."

"Maybe they're not so obvious. At least not in Washington."

"That is probably because you have not studied the history of this region enough. Or the true nature of the national revolt here. We had not either, but came to learn the hard way, as you Americans say."

"I think there's more to it than that. It's also because we had so little confidence in your efforts here. And we can think we can do better."

"Because you are bigger and stronger militarily?"

"Something like that," Baier said.

The Frenchman paused and ran his index finger over his lips. His eyes rose to meet a very attractive and petite Asian woman who brought a cup of tea and set it on his desk. He smiled and thanked her, then turned to the Americans. "Are you sure you won't have something to drink? An espresso perhaps. Or a cappuccino? It is the right time of day, you know."

Baier looked at Pyle, who shook his head. "No. No thank you." Baier watched the young woman saunter out of the room. He assumed it was for the benefit of the men who provided an audience.

"Do you find her attractive?" de Couget asked.

Baier nodded.

"Yes, I agree," de Couget continued.. "She is beautiful. I am very lucky to have her as my wife." He stopped stirring the tea and set the spoon back on the saucer. "Well, perhaps not legally my wife. But I became deeply attached to her when she nursed me back to health in her tribal village in the Laotian mountains. I believe she developed a similar attachment to me. She is Tai, a tribe close to the Hmong people your organization works with. She accompanied me to Saigon and has remained by my side ever since."

"My organization?"

The Frenchman laughed. "Oh, come now, Mister Baier. We do not need to play those games. Your friend here has confirmed it."

Baier turned to his American companion with a look that he hoped would shrivel the bastard in his seat. "Thank you for that," he said to Pyle.

"Ah, but you see there is a benefit in that," de Couget continued.

"Really?" Baier asked. "How so?"

"Your friend stays here often. In fact, I'd say it is more than a home away from home. It is probably his main residence."

"Yes, I saw why on our way in."

"But he has endeared you Americans to me. Of course, I already liked your countrymen, so different from us stuffy old Europeans in many ways. But he has reinforced that affection. His own experiences mirror mine in many ways, although his ties to this place are even deeper than mine. And he has convinced me that I can be of assistance to you during your stay in this— and now my—country. And I can also assure you that I will do nothing to jeopardize or endanger you or your mission here."

"Interesting," Baier said. "But I'm sure you can imagine my skepticism. Just what sort of help can you offer?"

"We shall see. Let us let time reveal that."

"And in return?"

The Frenchman shrugged. "Who is to say. I may need your help as well in the future. This is a very uncertain time for us all."

Baier leaned forward. "I can offer you no assistance with the local government or the local police."

The Frenchman followed this with a light laugh and a knowing smile. "I can assure you that I need no help on that front. All I need to do in that regard is ensure that they are satisfied customers."

"I see." Baier and Pyle rose to go. "That is an unusual offer. I'll have to think about it."

"Please do. I would like to help your country. If I can."

"Yes, if you can," Baier replied. "But you'll have to excuse me if I am still skeptical as to just what you can do for me or for us."

The Frenchman shrugged while his smile slipped away. "Mr. Baier, you have not been here long. Do not presume too much too soon."

As Baier strolled from the room, the Frenchman held the teacup to his lips, his eyes focused on one of the paintings on the wall. Baier was surprised that the man's focus was not on one of the spectacular views of the French Alps, but on a Vietnamese peasant woman, the pool of water in the rice paddy up to her knees as she bent to pull stalks from the earth.

The two Americans drifted through the hallway on their way to the front door, and Baier noticed two Vietnamese army officers in full uniform, medals running down the front of their jackets like a minor waterfall of silver metal and colored ribbon. Two women hung on the arms of each officer. In another room by the front door, there also stood a Westerner, a European, Baier guessed by his heavily accented English. He was rubbing two heavy, hairy paws together as he surveyed the offerings on the sofa set against the front window. He must have heard Baier and Pyle on their way out, because his head swiveled and stopped to study Baier. The man's nose had been flattened, giving Baier the impression of someone who had spent too many rounds in a boxing ring. His eyes were dark and nearly hidden under a ridgeline that formed a wall below his forehead. His eyes narrowed and settled on Baier like a challenge, before turning back to the women in the room.

• • •

"What the fuck were you thinking, Pyle?" Baier was almost shouting.

Pyle waved at his companion. "Oh, relax. For Chrissakes. That man has been in the game long enough. Hell, his profession alone requires discretion. So, he's not about to go blabbing that about."

"But that is my decision. If you tell anyone else, I'll have the Army throw you in the brig and keep you there until I go home. I am not going to let someone like you put a fucking target on my back."

Baier glanced at the street and was surprised to see the rickshaw there waiting for them. "Has he been here the whole time?"

Pyle nodded. "Yes, he has. It's pretty standard practice. Especially at a place like this one. Most customers don't stick around all that long." Pyle reached out to touch Baier's forearm as they approached their taxi. "Look man, I'm sorry. But I thought this guy could provide some good intel, given the kind of traffic that passes through his place. Can you imagine the pillow talk that goes on here?"

"Maybe. And maybe not. It depends on how much the customers are willing to talk about with a hooker. I can't imagine that those officers we saw in there are going to be real chatty this morning, or that they'll stay for very long."

Pyle considered the house a moment before replying. "Yeah, maybe. But you never know."

The Americans climbed aboard the rickshaw, and Pyle gave the driver directions to the American Embassy.

"Hey, did you get a look at that Slavic bruiser when we left," Pyle asked.

Baier sat back and crossed his legs. "Why do you think he was Slavic?"

"Oh, hell, didn't you hear him? That accent was dripping with eastern European tones. I'd guess Russian. Maybe Ukrainian or White Russian. I'm surprised you didn't pick up on that."

"Why? I mean, why those two places?" Baier shook his head and studied the street and pedestrian traffic. "Anyway, I wasn't really listening. I was too pissed off." Baier turned and glared at Pyle.

"Can't say for sure. But the accent sure sounded that way. I've heard that there are a few of those types around Saigon nowadays."

"Heard? How? And what do you mean by 'those types'?"

"Just street gossip," Pyle answered. "And by types I'd say KGB. Who the hell else would they be? There's no Russian businesses here or an Embassy. I wouldn't be surprised if those guys aren't here to help the VC or Hanoi in some way."

"What way?" Baier pressed.

"The way of providing their own intel. Or helping with some kind of counter-intelligence work. Especially in training. I mean, now that you guys are showing up in such force."

Well, Baier thought, that would make my job a lot more familiar. Interesting, too.

CHAPTER EIGHT

"A French whorehouse, you say?" Crockett's smile was as bright and wide as Baier had seen during his short time in Vietnam.

He nodded. "That's right. Apparently, a home of sorts for our American friend in town…"

"Pickles? Or whatever his name is."

"Pyle. And yeah, that's him. He took me out there yesterday, where I received more than just some eye candy. I got a very interesting proposal." Baier relayed the essence of de Couget's suggestion.

Crockett's smile stayed in place while he seemed to ponder the possibility. "I'm just imagining how I might phrase the cable back to Headquarters. That could be my most interesting challenge since I've been here. Do you think it's worth considering? I mean, is it really going to help you in your reporting back to the Director?"

"Well, yeah that last point is certainly one I need to consider. Although, I surely don't mind helping you guys out on more mundane operational stuff while I'm here. As long as it doesn't take up too much of my time."

"So, just what are the possibilities?"

"You know, I spent all day yesterday and this morning thinking it over. At first, I was pretty dismissive. I mean, how much do we know about the guy, much less trust him? Sure, we could try to explore his background, but how available would that material be? It's not like we're going to swing by the French Embassy and ask for information on a countryman who runs a local brothel."

"Although they might be steady customers there. But I'm sure there's stuff back in France that our folks in Paris could check on."

"Yeah, but what about the last nine or ten years, when he's allegedly been living here? And then, I thought about the kind of business the guy gets out there. There were two military officers visiting when I left with some pretty impressive medals on their uniforms. Now, I can't say how they got them and certainly not whether they earned them..."

"Yeah, no shit. Given what I've seen and heard about the ARVN performance thus far, I'd bet they got them through political connections, not battlefield valor. Or picked them up in a market stall."

"Okay, but I'm willing to bet that they're not the only ones patronizing that place."

"Are you suggesting we recruit some of the girls out there or bug the rooms?" Crockett asked.

"Not necessarily. We may not need to go in that heavy. Maybe we let the Frenchman run the show in his own house. I doubt we'd be able to do anything there without him finding out in any case."

"And the benefit?" Crockett pressed. "It's got to be big. Worth the risk. Just imagine how this would look if word got out in the American press."

"Aren't we worried about the Minh Government's staying power now? We've discussed what an enigma this guy is, just like the rest of them. And the same would go for whoever might replace him. I'm already hearing about how any possible replacements are pretty much like all the others who think this government—no matter who's in charge--needs to put some distance between themselves and the Americans. They supposedly need to respond to the general war weariness among their people and the growing interest in a negotiated settlement and possible neutrality for Vietnam." He paused. "Who else have we got talking to us about this stuff? How much do you trust our liaison partners on this?"

"You mean on the inner workings and deliberations of the military and government?"

"Yeah. Do we have controlled assets in their service?"

"As you might imagine, Karl, it's easy enough to recruit people on the inside as long as we pay them, and there are lots of 'em willing to share their thoughts with us. In addition, they want to make sure they stay on our good side and bring us into their planning. That's what happened during the Diem overthrow. But it also comes down to their real access. Besides, I'm not sure how much I trust our contacts there to give us a full picture. It's more like they want us to know what they want us to know."

"So, some pillow talk might prove useful?"

"Oh, sure. There's always some potential in that stuff. But back onto that neutrality thing. Hell, Karl, you know that won't work," Crockett protested. "It would only be a matter of time before Ho Chi Minh and his boys took over down here."

"I know, I know. That's the picture in Washington, and it's why our own government has been working so hard to undermine efforts to start peace talks. It also fits with my experiences in Europe. But I wonder, Frank…"

"Wonder what, for Chrissakes?"

"Well, it's worked so far in Austria. We were able to negotiate the end of the Four-power occupation of that country, and the Soviets have played along so far."

"Okay, fair enough. But that also fits with Khrushchev's desire to ratchet down tensions in Europe and address the Soviets' need to get out from under the cloud of Stalin. And it didn't stop him from rattling his nuclear chains in Cuba, did it?" Crockett glanced out the window before turning back to Baier. "And the Soviets are not the only ones making decisions up north. And I also wonder how much influence they have, given the Chinese presence. In fact, I wonder how much pull any outsider has over planning up north."

"Oh, I'm not saying that it would bring peace in our time. But it might be worth considering, given the continued success of the VC in the countryside. The one thing this government and army here needs is time."

Crocket shook his head the whole time it took him to circle his desk and settle into the chair behind it. "I'm afraid that that horse may have already left the barn. McNamara is coming here for a visit to get an on the scene appraisal of what's going on here. I'm also hearing that it may be too late, that a decision has already been made to escalate."

Baier retreated to the sofa against the wall and dropped onto the cushions. "When and how? And the rationale?"

"LBJ's advisors—like Mister McNamara—apparently believe that this is the way to buy the government and the army time. You know, take over and run the show until these guys can do the job themselves."

"And when is this supposed to happen? And how far are we going to go?"

Crockett shrugged. "I haven't been privy to those discussions, but there's been plenty of talk about turning our Air Force loose, even bombing the north. But I doubt any of that will happen before the election."

Baier nodded. "I've been getting the same impression. But I was hoping that more seasoned observers like yourself might know differently." He did not mention that he had said as much to Sabine a few days ago. "I have to admit, we are running out of options beyond escalation and withdrawal. I mean, the strategic hamlet program is a mess. We aren't winning any loyalty in the countryside. At least, not from what I've been reading in our own reporting from there. Hell, I understand that the Diem regime replaced elected village counselors with appointees from the central government. Then Minh just made things worse. And those guys are just out there—when they do show up—to rob the peasants blind. Or so it seems. No wonder the VC looks so much better."

"Plus stronger. Yes, all that's true. But we should get a chance to give our side of things when McNamara comes to town. He's already requested a briefing from the Station. I just hope Ambassador Lodge and General Harkins don't insist on sitting in. The Embassy and MACV usually like to control the message."

Baier nodded. "Good point. We're already getting pushback on our reporting and analysis in Washington as it is."

• • •

Baier spent the next two days updating himself on the proverbial lay of the land with Station officers, especially those who got out into the countryside, while also reading up on the Station's reporting and the analytic pieces from Langley to make sure he could give the Secretary of Defense a comprehensive assessment of the agency's views from the field. Crockett had asked Baier to join him in the working breakfast McNamara had requested in the Station. It wasn't until afterwards that he realized that it had all been more of a set-up than an attempt to acquire more information from those closer to the ground. In fact, when he heard about the other meetings McNamara had had around town, especially with members of the Government, Baier recognized the true purpose of the trip as one high-placed attempt to buck up a flailing South Vietnamese government that was faltering in its attempts to combat the Viet Cong insurgency and expand its own support and legitimacy.

"Gentlemen," the Secretary of Defense had asked shortly after everyone was seated in the Station's secure meeting room, "give me your honest assessment of the strategic hamlet program."

Baier could see why the press and nearly everyone else had formed the impression they had of the man: tight-lipped, austere, but brilliant and almost brutally efficient. Of course, some of that came with the reputation as a 'whiz kid' of American industry, especially after his appointment as the president of Ford Motor Company. The man looked as though he was willing the climate to remain as far as possible from him as he sat there in a cotton, navy blue suit, a white shirt buttoned to the top, and the regimental tie—blue and red, of course, to compliment the white shirt—tight against the collar. His signature eyeglasses betrayed no hint of humidity, nor did his clean-shaven face and immaculately coiffed hair.

Crockett jumped right in. "Sir, it's a failure, and a pretty abysmal one at that."

"Excuse me?"

"Well, sir, you'd have to expect as much. You take the peasants away from their ancestral lands, stick them in new villages removed from their holdings, and fail to provide them with the security that's been promised. Once night falls, a large chunk of that territory reverts to VC control."

"And yet, I recall hearing some glowing reports on progress in that program earlier."

Crockett nodded and leaned forward. "Yes, Sir, that is true. I haven't been here all that long. But I also recall reports about progress and expansion of the strategic hamlet program. That, however, was under the Diem regime. Since then, the new governments have taken steps backward, and things have continued to slide downhill."

"In what ways?"

"Well, the new government has replaced most of the people who had been running the program here in Saigon and out in the provinces. Just like they've kept up a merry-go-round in the Army and elsewhere. It's hard to get consistent and competent leadership in that kind of environment."

"What are the ARVN and local militia and police doing?"

"Keeping low, Sir, and real quiet. Otherwise they're dead." Crockett paused for effect. "That is, if they stick around, which few are willing to do."

"And most of the administrators appointed by the government are crooked as hell, Sir," Baier added.

"Can you elaborate?"

"Many continue to exploit the locals, at least when they're there and often when they're not. They and the ARVN commanders are more aligned with the landlords than the local peasantry. They also pad their rolls so they get pay for a lot more people than actually show up. It's almost like a mafia operation."

"I'll have to make sure I raise that with my interlocutors on this trip," the Secretary responded. "I understand, Mister Baier, that you were also in the field with some of your organization's paramilitary units not too long ago. Up in Laos, I believe."

"Yes, Sir. We observed some of the construction and transportation lines along the Ho Chi Minh Trail, among other things."

"Well, it's the former that I am most interested in now. What was your impression of what's going on there?"

"To be honest, Sir, we—or at least I—did not see enough, and I wasn't there long enough to get a clear picture of the volume and pace of material flowing south. But the North Vietnamese are clearly doing a lot of work on the Trail. They may not be moving much in the way of men and material now, but my guess is that they want to be in a position to do so at some point in the future, if it becomes necessary."

"Do you think an interdiction by air would be possible?"

"No, Sir I do not. A good deal of the Trail—in fact, probably the majority of it—is unlikely to be visible from the air at any time. And whatever you bomb, those guys will rebuild or redirect in a matter of days. If not sooner."

"Then what do you propose?"

"I would have to say that if you're truly serious about halting the supplies running south, you're going to need to create a permanent presence there. And that will require a lot of men and money."

"Our military leadership believes you are wrong, Mister Baier. Granted, there are those who would like to see a U.S. military presence on the ground to halt supplies coming down from the north. But we are not prepared to put our own troops in place. Barring that, the Pentagon has confidence in the ability of air warfare to have an impact on just that sort of thing. Besides, your solution would also require a violation of the Geneva Accords that established Laotian neutrality…"

"But the North Vietnamese are already in violation," Crockett interjected. "They never even pulled their troops out of there."

McNamara turned his focus back to the Chief of Station. "I'm aware of that. And that's why, as I understand it, you have your paramilitary program with the Montagnard communities there."

"That's one of the reasons. Which leads me to a question of my own for you, Sir," Crockett said.

"Yes?"

"When can we expect to see a revival of the covert operations program against the North, and what role do you see the Agency playing."

"As you are no doubt aware, Mister Crockett, President Kennedy was unhappy with the Agency's performance in running the covert operations against the North previously. That is why he decided to move control and authorization of that to the Pentagon. President Johnson has chosen to continue that same policy. Your people simply did not take the effort seriously or devote enough resources to it. That will change now that the military is running things. And your Agency's role is to provide the support and expertise to the military when they need it."

Which apparently is right away, Baier thought, and not a minute later.

Crockett just stared at the Secretary of Defense for about half a minute. "Well, I wish you luck, Sir."

It went on like that for about an hour. Thankfully, neither the Ambassador nor the chief of MACV, General Harkins, had bothered to show up. But it probably wasn't even necessary, Baier figured. McNamara appeared to be firmly in their camp, and they were obviously not worried about the Agency upsetting the proverbial apple cart of policy and statistics.

There had been one good thing, though, about the morning's meeting, Baier concluded. Crockett had ordered up a breakfast of bacon, eggs, and sausage, as well as toast and cinnamon rolls, all of which erased for a day at least the memories of the continental breakfasts Baier had been surviving on at his hotel. He had thought that with all his time living in Europe, he would have acclimated his taste buds and stomach to the light breakfast selections so common on the continent. And this was one area of French culture the educated Vietnamese elite—certainly those who patronized his European-style hotel—had absorbed. But Baier only realized that morning how Americanized he had become and how much he missed that hearty, calorie-loaded meal that fueled the American farmer and working man.

CHAPTER NINE

By late afternoon, Baier had had enough. The working breakfast with the Secretary of Defense had been frustrating, to say the least, as his mind appeared to have already been made up. From what he had gleaned from State Department colleagues who had accompanied McNamara on his discussions with officials in the South Vietnamese Government, his initial guess about the main objective of the Secretary's trip had been to buck up the faltering and incompetent Saigon government in its war effort and reform programs that were designed to win greater loyalty and legitimacy among the population, rural and urban. And that's just what it was.

The Secretary's message had also been that a negotiated peace and military neutrality were not the way to go about that—not yet, anyway, not when the Viet Cong and their North Vietnamese allies or masters, or whatever, held the upper hand. And not when nearly every indicator pointed to a willingness up north to elevate the conflict whenever necessary. It would be better to allow the Americans to deliver a solid military defeat to the Communists, and then negotiate from a position of strength.

That frustration turned instantly into anger when Baier entered his room at The Continental.

"What the hell do you think you're doing in my room? And how the hell did you get in here?"

Henri De Couget stood awkwardly, his arms outstretched towards Baier. "Please, Mister Baier. Please remain calm. I come to you for assistance this time."

Baier stepped into the room and slammed the door shut. Although it had been several days since he had seen the Frenchman,

87

de Couget did not look as though he had changed his clothes, nor slept much, for that matter. His hair was slick and matted, as though it had not felt a comb in weeks. His shirt and slacks were wrinkled, and the collar and cuffs of the sleeves lined with grime. There was even a food stain on one of the thighs of his slacks.

"What has happened? You look like crap."

"Not to put too fine a point on it. Typical of you Americans."

"Besides, I do not remember coming to you for assistance when we met. That was an idea Pyle had."

De Couget stepped forward, slowly, taking two, maybe three steps. "Yes, yes. It is because of him that I am here. He has disappeared."

Baier stepped forward. "What? Disappeared? How? I thought his movements and residences varied and were, well, basically irregular." Baier stopped, almost in mid-sentence. He glanced at the ground, then back up at the Frenchman. "What's different now? What has happened?"

"That's why I need your help. I do not know. But he has never stayed away this long before…"

"How long has it been?"

The Frenchman looked flustered. "I…I believe it has been three days now. Maybe four. In the past he might stay away for one, sometimes two days. But never this long."

"Yeah, well, one day extra is not exactly cause for alarm." Baier said. "Why are you so worried about some eccentric American? I never realized you felt so strongly about the man. If indeed you do."

"He is my friend, Mister Baier. Yes, he is eccentric, and at times he can be a burden. But we have a shared history of sorts. You know of his background in your former organization, the OSS. And you know of mine in the Foreign Legion. I fought in the north with many of your countrymen, you know."

"You mean to tell me there were Americans up there? And 'many'?"

De Couget smiled and shook his head. "No, no. Not Americans. But Germans. We had many recruits from the former *Wehrmacht*."

"Listen, Mister de Couget, I am sorry to inform you that I am an American. My ancestors may have been German, but I am not. And I most certainly did not have compatriots among the *Wehrmacht*. Distant relatives, perhaps, but no one I would consider a compatriot."

"Ah, but you can see, can you not, how my affections are not limited to French people. And your friend and I have a very strong connection to this place." The Frenchman's arms swept the space around him, as though they could encompass the entire country in this one small hotel room. "We have spoken for many hours of the beauty and wonder of Vietnam, its people, and its uncertain future. Which it does not deserve, I might add. And since he is your compatriot and from your predecessor organization, surely you will want to help him."

Baier cursed to himself. He did not want to spend any of his time chasing a phantom like Pyle, especially considering the rabbit holes he and this Frenchman might lead him down. His assignment from Langley was clear, and pretty clear, for the most part. Also it was limited, definitely limited. But he knew he could not just walk away, that he could not simply abandon a fellow American, and one who had served his country well in the last war. He just hoped Crockett would agree.

• • •

Roughly two hours later, the sleek, gray Citroën sped through the outer environs of Saigon and on its way to the countryside. Crocket had agreed to Baier's request and his rationale, which surprised Baier.

"You're right, Karl. We can't just walk away. The guy does not work for us now, and he's actually a pain in the ass. But he did do his service against one of our principal enemies in the last war. The big one, I mean. And in some pretty harrowing environments. He deserves better." He paused. "I doubt this little affair will keep you from your real mission here. Just make sure it doesn't last too long, though. You never know what the Frenchman might pull you into. And don't get stuck out there overnight. Regardless of what the US military night say or the powerful people in Washington might think, our side does not control the countryside when it's dark."

Which was just when they would be out there, considering how late they got underway. Their party was driving toward one of the strategic hamlets about fifty miles from Saigon, an area that had reportedly been secured by the ARVN and local militia half a year ago. Theoretically, they could all sleep tight there if need be. Theoretically, that is.

They did have a security team with them. De Couget had seen to that. Baier, sitting in the back seat with his newfound French ally, studied the driver and his beefy companion riding shotgun with an actual 12-gauge in the passenger seat up front. Another dark blue Citroen followed closely behind with four more security guards in tow. He had no idea if that was sufficient, but he figured it was better than driving out there alone. And he did have to admit that the used and battered French sedan handled the rutted, dirt roads pretty well. He wondered if it had been re-engineered, or simply reinforced, to handle the tough challenges of rural driving in the Vietnamese countryside.

"You do not need to worry, Mister Baier, these men are extremely capable. Even the Viet Cong avoid them whenever possible."

"How is that?" Baier asked. "Where did you find them?"

"They, and others, work for me at La Maison. They were formerly members of the Binh Xuyan gang."

"The what?"

"It was the most powerful criminal organization in Saigon. They controlled the gambling and prostitution trades. Most of the opium market as well."

"How come they work for you now? Aren't you worried about their former colleagues protesting you poaching their soldiers, as it were?"

De Couget smiled and patted Baier's leg. "Not anymore, my American friend. One of the first things Diem did when he resettled his government in Saigon was to push that gang out of the city. In fact, he crushed them militarily. It was one of things that endeared him to your government."

"Why was that? We may be descended from the Puritans culturally, but we're not that puritanical."

"It made him look tough. Like someone who would be willing and capable of preventing a Communist takeover in the south. And it helped him establish his government when things looked very uncertain and not at all stable." De Couget stared out the car window to his left for almost a minute, or so it seemed, before continuing. "That also made it much easier for me to establish my own business. I did not need a capital infusion to pay off the gangsters who already controlled that particular industry. Of course, I did need some to pay off the new government masters. I still do, as you can no doubt imagine."

"Okay, but tell me why we are heading to this particular hamlet first? Because it's safer? A good place to start?"

De Couget nearly laughed, but no sound came out of his wide grin. It was nothing more than a breeze of humor. "Oh, it is a good place to start. But not because it is safer than anywhere else. There is no such place, Mister Baier."

"That's not exactly reassuring."

"No, it is a good place to start because your friend Pyle has come here before. It is where certain needs and desires of his can be easily satisfied."

Baier was perplexed. He turned to the Frenchman. "But can't that sort of thing be taken care of back at *La Maison*?"

De Couget stared straight into Baier's eyes. "He has other needs. Not all of which can be satisfied by my employees."

"But then why am I here? What purpose does it have to bring me along if you already know where to look?"

"As I said, it is a good place to start. There is no guarantee that we will find him here. And for whatever we do find, you are my insurance."

"Against what?"

"Against whatever we may find here. And from either side."

• • •

In the end—or at the start, really—de Couget had been right. It was a good place to begin the search. It was where Pyle had gone, just like so many times before, apparently. The local village headman met the party at the village gate, built by the locals on the orders of the police chief appointed by Saigon. It was supposed to provide security and protection from Viet Cong marauders, or so he had called them. Baier doubted, though, that the patchwork of wood, bamboo, and barbed wire would stand up to much in the way of firepower or a good solid rush of men. He doubted it would even resist musket fire, for that matter.

That, however, was not the first thing that struck Baier. It was the smell—or stench, really—that filled the air as the cars approached the hamlet through open fields lined with irrigation canals of muddy water that supported rows of rice. Water buffalos and Vietnamese peasants moved through the rows, many with their backs bent near the water level as their hands roamed the fields for stalks of rice.

"I see you have picked up on the local scent, Mister Baier."

Baier turned to de Couget, his face split by a grimace that left his entire face in a frown, surrounded by wrinkles. "How can you tell? And what is it?"

"I can tell by the way you have crunched your nose to avoid it. But that is hopeless. Believe me."

"And the cause?"

De Couget waved his hand, as though to ward off the scent. "It is the village's toilet. They try to keep their human and animal waste outside the village, and it does help some. You will see. But it also works as a fertilizer, as you can no doubt imagine."

Baier could imagine. He remembered his trips as a child to the Illinois countryside outside Chicago that were dotted with large farms raising corn, soybean, and hay, much of it to feed the cattle and pigs stuck in the barns or grazing the fields of stubble and grass. The spring planting season had always been ripe with the smell of natural fertilizer.

"Oh, I can imagine it all right."

In any event, it was where the local village chief knew immediately what the newcomers wanted. He led them to a hut at the back of stockade, where they found a slumbering Pyle, his left arm wrapped around a young woman from the village. She looked to be no more than a teenager, but then Baier could not be sure. He had found the Vietnamese women in the countryside to be almost as ageless in their appearance as the women in Saigon, only older, worn down by lives of hard toil and deprivation. Whatever the case, he really did not want to start a guessing game on the ages and occupations of the local women in Vietnam's rural villages, especially not this one and not now.

Pyle mumbled something in his sleep, then rolled over onto his side. The arm that had encircled the woman fell to the ground. His clothes—the same ones he had worn when he led Baier to de Couget's whorehouse--looked as though he had spent the better part of his missing days in a similar spot and position. Small crease lines from the straw mat marked one side of his face, and a thin stream of saliva dripped from his chin.

Baier bent down and shook Pyle by the shoulder.

"Do not bother, Mister Baier. He is in an opium sleep. It will do no good. I have no idea how much he has smoked. Nor does the headman here. The young woman, of course, will say nothing to us."

Baier turned to the Frenchman. "Goddammit, de Couget, why do I have the feeling that you knew all along?"

The Frenchman simply stared at Baier.

"You did, didn't you?" Baier pressed.

De Couget shrugged. "I thought it was a strong possibility, but I could not be sure. Like I told you, he had never been away this long."

"How long has this been going on?"

"You mean the opium or the visits here?"

"Both, goddammit."

The Frenchman shrugged again, as though something like this was almost fated to pass. "This time, perhaps two to three days, as I said before. In general, for several years, would be my guess. At least almost as long as I have known him. But you needn't worry…"

"Why the hell not?"

"Because he has it under control."

The frown on Baier's face was unmistakable. "It sure doesn't look like it."

"No, really. We will take him with us, and he will be fine tomorrow. I suggest we clean him up some if he is going to ride in one of our cars. The woman, though, we will leave here."

The headman approached and whispered something in de Couget's ear. The Frenchman looked over at one of his security guards, who nodded in agreement. De Couget sighed.

"Alas, Mister Baier, we have been advised to stay here for the night. The roads are no longer safe."

"I thought I was supposed to provide some insurance for that."

"I am afraid that at this point, no one will be aware of your nationality. In fact, at this point, you might even provide a tempting target if they do know who you are."

"Goddammit, de Couget, you owe me one now," Baier cursed.

It was the Frenchman who now looked confused. "One what?"

"A favor. And I intend to call it in when we get back to Saigon."

De Couget smiled and shook his head, as though he would never fully understand America and Americans. "Never mind. Just relax and be happy we found your American friend," de Couget had said.

"How long do you think he has been like this?" Baier replied. "I mean this time around. And how much longer will he need to recover?" His hands clenched and unclenched, an outlet for his anger. "And the woman? What will become of her? Shouldn't we take her with us when we leave? Haven't you and Pyle done enough damage here already?"

De Couget shook his head as he glanced back at the hut. "No, that will not be necessary. I very much doubt if she slept with him. I'm quite sure she only prepared his pipes for him. She will be fine back here in her hamlet with her family." De Couget shrugged. "Besides,

I am sure our American friend paid her well for her assistance." He paused to give Baier a direct and solemn look. "And only that."

"And how did Pyle come to be here, of all places?"

"As I told you, he has come here before. You will have to ask him why he returned, and why at this moment. But like I said earlier, he has a mild addiction. It is not uncommon here. So, no, I am not surprised." De Couget smiled. "I am sure you are also asking yourself another question now, but no I have not succumbed. Oh, I was tempted. But my wife prevented that. It is one of the many things for which I am indebted to her."

Remembering the scent from the field earlier at their arrival, Baier had skipped an evening meal. He was too tired to eat much in any case. He simply disappeared into a deep sleep in a strange world unlike any he had known before.

Later, on the ride home, he would remember with surprise how easily he had fallen asleep that night. But then, the ride out and the confrontation over Pyle's discovery had been more exhausting than he realized. His adrenaline had fueled an excitement and anger simultaneously that had driven him from the hut in a fury that was just steps short of a rage.

• • •

It started just after midnight, or even a little before. It was a guess Baier made in the midst of the overwhelming noise and chaos set off by explosions, screams and shouts, and the rush of humanity. Baier never did get around to checking his watch.

Instead, he was thrown from his bed as the world around him exploded in a fury that brought back faint memories of his time in the Laotian jungle. But this was different and so much more frightening.

His first thought was that he had stumbled into the middle of an earthquake. The earth shuddered and rumbled and shook him loose, then tossed him from the straw mat on which he had fallen into his deep sleep. It was almost as though everything, every explosion was directed at him alone—the sole target—and the world was collapsing around him.

Baier rolled across the earthen floor and struggled to stand on shaking ground, his limbs weak with sleep and fear. Slowly, his mind awoke, and he realized that the thuds and spreading explosions were coming from the incoming mortar rounds that had broken the night's silence. The scent of explosive residue drifted across the compound. The ground and air around him shook with each explosion.

He froze, stranded in an atmosphere of shock and struggling to get his bearings. He guessed maybe ten or a dozen rounds had landed in the first onslaught, but after those first explosions there must have been at least twenty, probably more, that followed. Whatever the number, they were too fucking many, and most seemed to be falling too goddamn close to him.

He glanced back at the straw mat, then rushed to the open doorway. All he saw was the night outside. Baier realized that the space stood open, as the darkened air and dust rushed in. One blast must have blown the door away.

Baier immediately examined his body for any signs of a wound. He probed with his fingers in the dark and tried to look closer. He found nothing: no open wounds, no bleeding. Then he noticed that the walls had been shredded as well. The temptation to drop to his knees and thank the Lord for his survival was almost irresistible. Instead, he stumbled out from the hut and scanned the village.

One salvo had pulverized the gate and blown large holes in sections of the surrounding barricade. Baier assumed he would have only moments to throw on the rest of his clothes and recover his Browning in order to defend himself and others against the assault that must surely come.

He had little hope that his pistol alone would make much of a difference, especially since he was only carrying two extra clips of ammunition. That would last what, maybe a minute, or two? Maybe five or even ten, depending on how many VC rushed the perimeter. Hopefully, de Couget's security team would be able to put up stiffer resistance.

He guessed survival would depend on the size of the attack. Then again, the Viet Cong would surely not expend that much of an effort to seize this small hamlet. They could have it for their own in any case, once the strangers from Saigon had departed.

Yet the dreaded assault never happened. Isolated mortar fire continued for the next few minutes, but oddly, very few landed inside the hamlet's perimeter. In fact, when Baier scanned the area around his own hut, very few rounds appeared to have penetrated the hamlet's borders at all. No more than half, was his guess, and those all circled his own quarters, which was ominous.

Baier dashed through the streets and among the huts to assess the damage and help treat any casualties. But there was very little of either. A few stray rounds had done some damage to huts near the compound walls, but Baier noticed that there were no screams of the wounded. Several chickens had been slaughtered, and one hog was badly wounded. He felt a sense of relief that no women or children had been injured. But then, anyone wounded in the village, any civilian casualty at all, would be completely unjustified. Hell, this hamlet—even with the presence of the strangers from Saigon—posed no threat.

Baier turned back toward the path that led to his quarters and only then saw how closely some of the rounds had landed to his hut. One had come right next to it. That must have been the one that took his door away. Suddenly, a powerful sense of luck and grace burst from the darkness and overwhelmed him. He finally dropped down on one knee, cradling the unused Browning.

After a moment he glanced up, unsettled by the sudden silence. Baier rose and wandered the streets looking for a sign of de Couget's presence, or any members of his security team. Pyle, he figured, would have slept through the whole affair, at least based on what Baier had last seen of him. But there was no sign of Pyle or any villagers for that matter. Everyone seemed to have left for the night.

Baier searched for the two Citroëns to make sure they had not been hit by the mortar fire, and to be sure that his company had not departed without him. At this point, his mind was a muddle of panic and uncertainty, anger and relief. At that moment, Baier would not have put it past the Frenchman to abandon him. Not out of spite, surely, but perhaps to allow the American more time and reflection in a hostile countryside.

He shook off the thought. Baier was thinking primarily of his survival and Pyle's return. Later he would find the time to focus on de Couget, a man who became more of a mystery every time Baier met him.

Eventually, Baier found both cars parked next to one another, a spray of dirt and some broken pieces of wood scattered over their hoods. Well, we should be able to get the hell out of here at first light, he assured himself, as long as this was the extent of the attack.

On the way back to his hut Baier saw a handful of villagers who were returning to their homes from the surrounding fields. The young woman who had been lying with Pyle trotted along a path at the back of the village. He stopped to shout to her, but then realized she probably did not speak any English and that it would be of little use. He was also too tired to try, as his body began to cool down from the night's excitement. He decided to try to get what sleep he could from what remained of the night.

When he returned to his broken shack Baier noticed an older woman in the doorway of the hut across from his. She stared at the American with a look of confusion that quickly gave way to one of disgust and disappointment. She glanced in the direction where the young women had disappeared and shook her head. Baier started to explain that he had not spent the night with the young girl, but he waved his meaningless English words away. Then she looked to the heavens and pointed at the sky above. Baier followed her finger, but he could not find anything on the horizon, nothing beyond the edge of the hamlet's stockade.

• • •

"What do you make of that little assault last night?" Baier asked de Couget.

The two men were riding in the back of the lead Citroën with the same driver and his security partner who had accompanied them during the ride out from Saigon. Their tailing Citroën followed at a distance of about twenty yards, also as before. Only this time, Pyle sat propped up between the two men in the back of that car. He looked as though his eyes were open, but Baier could not tell if the man was truly awake. Or even on this planet.

"What assault? You mean the mortar fire?" de Couget asked.

"Yes, exactly. There wasn't any other excitement was there?"

De Couget shook his head. "No, not that I am aware. And I would not characterize it as an assault. It was more of a warning."

"A warning?" Baier said. "A warning for whom? Us or the villagers?"

"Probably both," de Couget replied. "Us to be sure we recognized their presence and control of the area. And for the villagers to remind them of the extent of their knowledge of everything that occurs there."

"I see. Was there any ARVN presence in the area? And what about the local militia? It seemed like the VC had a pretty leisurely time of it. I don't recall any return fire."

"Oh, those people were probably out helping the Viet Cong direct their fire or hiding in the fields with their families. They had no doubt been warned of the attack. If anything, those people would have wanted to be sure their homes would not be destroyed."

Baier thought back to his sighting of the woman who had been with Pyle running through the village after the attack. "Do you think they had help from inside the hamlet?"

De Couget nodded. "That is almost certain. If the Viet Cong had not seen us arrive, someone inside probably informed them of our presence." De Couget thought for a moment. "I do hope, however, that no one inside helped with the targeting. Unless it was to deflect damage away from the villagers. Did you not say that at least one of the rounds landed close to your hut?"

Baier sighed. "Yes. My door and one wall got a whole new ventilation system."

"Remember, my friend," de Couget resumed. "I said it was more of a warning than an actual attack. You noticed that no assault followed the bombardment." He thought for a moment as he watched the countryside slide by their windows. "But they apparently wanted to make sure you received that warning in particular."

Baier nodded in agreement. At least one of the warning shots had certainly been more direct. He doubted that was mere chance.

"One other thing," Baier said. "No one informed us or the village authorities of the VC presence outside. Instead, you said the people in the village probably informed the Viet Cong of our presence. That is, if anyone did say anything."

"That is correct. It is usually that way," de Couget concluded.

"Wait a minute. Did you just say that that sort of thing is not unusual?"

The Frenchman studied Baier's face. "It would have been unusual if no one had said anything."

This was certainly a strange war, Baier thought. And he found his position and observations stranger still. He had been relatively certain of US policy and the need for our presence in Vietnam. He had seen enough Communist duplicity and the resulting oppression during his time in Europe, sitting, as it were, on the front line of the Cold War. But this was new and different for him. As it almost certainly was for many back home. No wonder few in Washington seemed to understand the nature of this conflict, which was evolving beyond the impressions he had built back home.

"You know," Baier continued, "I never did see any provincial administrators. Nothing to represent the government in Saigon. Not during the fighting or before or after. Nothing during our entire stay there."

De Couget shook his head. "I did not either. Then again, I never have. It probably wasn't time to collect the taxes."

They rode in silence for another hour. Baier continued to ponder the aim and purpose of his presence on this excursion, asking himself what de Couget had really had in mind, what Pyle's disappearance and drug-soaked sojourn in the hamlet meant, if anything, and what his role was supposed to be in all this. The anger started to build again, and he turned towards the Frenchman. But before Baier could speak, de Couget interrupted his thoughts. It was though he had been reading Baier's mind from the expressions on his face.

"You mentioned a 'favor' yesterday, something you planned to 'call in,' as you put it," de Couget said. "What did you mean by that?"

Baier studied the Frenchman for several moments. He wasn't sure just how long he waited to reply, but he wanted this damn French fellow to understand the depth of his concern and his anger.

"Oh, there are several things behind that. But you can start by telling me about that Slavic creep I saw at your brothel the other day as Pyle and I were leaving. My bet is he's Russian. I want to know where he's from and what the hell he's doing here."

CHAPTER TEN

The next morning Baier sat in one of the back pews—a habit he had developed during his days as a student at the University of Notre Dame to avoid getting called on in class—of Saigon's own Notre Dame Cathedral. He was, at best, an occasional Catholic, at least in terms of practice and observation. But after the harrowing experience in the hamlet, Baier thought he might as well take up the practice he generally followed at Christmas and Easter: actually attend Mass and maybe even take Communion. He remembered the words of one of his parents' close friends who had stayed behind in Germany and survived six years in the *Wehrmacht*. He claimed that once the firing started there were no longer any fascists or communists in the trenches or on the attack. At that point everyone was a believer, and they prayed fervently to survive. That is to say, when they weren't too frightened to think of anything other than burrowing as deeply as possible into the resisting earth. So, Baier figured he could at least offer some form of thanks to the Big Spy in the Sky for his survival. Maybe even light a candle on the way out.

As the priest droned on with his sermon in French, Baier passed the time reading the pamphlet he had picked up just inside the entrance. The cathedral may not have been as large and ornate as those he had visited in Europe, but it still held a subtle elegance in the arched columns that lined the main aisle and the impressive stained-glass windows, reputedly built by a firm from Chartres, home to what many considered the most beautiful Gothic church in the world. This one may have been smaller, but Baier found the red bricks—all imported from France, allegedly—

that encompassed the church and double steeples understated yet effective. The church had been completed in 1880 and had seen several changes and additions over the years, the most impressive one being the statue out front of the Blessed Virgin, labeled Our Lady of Peace. Nice try, he thought, and good luck.

Struggling to keep his mind on the sacrament of the Eucharist, Baier's gaze roamed the walls of the chapels lining the side of the church by the nave. He was struck once more by a confusion that accompanied him nearly everywhere he went in this country. It was that of a world in its own space, but not really comfortable there. This cathedral, like so much else about the country, seemed to wander between the worlds and histories of Europe and Asia. He studied inscriptions in French and Vietnamese, and the latter in both Latin and Vietnamese script. The parishioners represented a mixture of Vietnamese and French *colons,* and although the priest was French, the altar boys were Vietnamese. Looking through the stained-glass window with the portrait of John the Baptist, Baier struggled to find a focal point for the service, and the church itself—aside from its universality, typical of a Catholic ceremony from a religion that considered itself just that: universal. But now it was a church and a service that left Baier in a daze of shifting and uncertain horizons.

• • •

"Russian, you say?" de Couget asked. "What makes you think that?"

Baier had called the Frenchman and asked him to meet over coffee the morning after they had returned to Saigon—just after he left Mass, in fact. It was now a day later. The speed of de Couget's response had actually surprised Baier, who still was not sure how far he could trust the man, especially after their jaunt to the strategic hamlet that had invited a VC mortar attack during the night. They were seated at one of two tables that rested on the sidewalk in front of a café not far from the Embassy, another concession on the Frenchman's part in Baier's mind. In addition, he had even been able to order a cappuccino and a *pain de chocolat.* Nothing wrong with a mid-morning snack, he reassured himself.

"A number of things," Baier replied. "Like his accent, his looks…"

"His looks? Now you sound like some of those ex-*Wehrmacht* soldiers we had in the Legion."

"His were close enough to cast him as a fucking Russian."

"You say that last phrase as those it were one word. Have you had some bad experiences?"

"It's a long story. I'll tell it to you one day if we ever do become collaborators," Baier promised.

"Well, my friend, what would you like to know? I believe I do recognize the man, but I have never met him. I can always see what my ladies can find out."

"Who he is, what he's doing here, how long he's been here. The sort of things that will help me pin him down," Baier said. "As to his purpose and goals, I mean."

"I'll look into it. Although if his purpose really is as nefarious as you suspect I doubt he will be that forthcoming."

Baier smiled. "*Monsieur* De Couget, I am sure you are well versed in the indiscretions that can escape before, during, or after a moment of passion. Not always, of course. But things can slip out every once in a while."

"As I said, *Herr* Baier, I shall see what I can do."

"And you can knock off the "*Herr*" stuff. Baier stood. "That's from another time and another adventure."

• • •

Baier returned to the office for his appointment with the Deputy Chief of Mission, or DCM, later that morning. Afterwards, Baier immediately dropped in on the Chief of Station to bring him up to date on the recent events and Baier's concerns over the possible presence of a foreign intelligence cell in Saigon, especially one that might include a KGB officer. There could even be more, given there was a war on and one with enormous strategic implications. But for now he would work on the assumption of there being just one cell. At least one with a fucking Russian.

Crockett held up his hand. "First and foremost, fill me in on what our DCM had to say."

Baier chuckled. "It was almost one hundred and eighty degrees from what the Ambo told me. He was, to say the least, a lot more skeptical about the path we're on."

Crockett nodded. "That's my impression as well. You know he's leaving soon?"

"Yes, he did mention that. He's also preparing his own report, which he plans to send back through the Department's dissent channels expressing his skepticism."

"What's his bottom line going to be?"

"That our chances of winning a full-blown military conflict are fifty-fifty. At best. And that's only with a large infusion of additional resources and manpower."

"That's not going to win him many friends in this Administration. Probably very few at State as well." Crockett blew out his breath. "Okay, so tell me about this Soviet spy ring."

Baier explained his suspicions and his most recent conversation with de Couget. "I have to admit, it's still pretty fuzzy. But I think I can still balance this issue and my broader assignment. At least for now."

"Well then, you definitely should follow up on that," Crockett said. "But don't get sucked in. I know how you can be, Karl, when it comes to the Soviets and a possible operation against whatever they might have here. Although, I'd have to say I'd be surprised. It's not like the VC or the Northerners need any help from those guys. There have been some reports of a Chinese intel presence in Hanoi, but I wonder what use they are as well, given the historical animosity between the two cultures." Crockett paused to consider another line of thought. "Then again, Ho Chi Minh and his pals have said some very nice things about their northern neighbor."

"Well, that's to be expected, given how the northerners could use the help. But, you know, I could be overly suspicious, given my past experience," Baier admitted. "There's always the possibility that whoever is here is pursuing a completely different agenda."

"You mean something unrelated to the Communist insurgency?"

Baier nodded.

"Like what then?" Crockett persisted. "Hell, I'd think the insurgency here would bring in work enough. And it would certainly fit with an agenda to keep us occupied and draining our resources in this swamp."

"Well, I can't really be sure at this early stage. But possibly something related to broader Soviet policy. We're just out of the Cuban missile crisis, which most people around the world see as a win for our side."

"True," Crockett continued. "I'd say it was also a win for the world, since we avoided a nuclear war."

"Oh, I agree, Frank. But our analysts get the feeling that there is some dangerous discontent in the Kremlin over how Khrushchev played that particular game. And the Chinese were not at all happy at how things turned out and how the tension subsided so quickly."

"Okay, but I'm not sure how being in Saigon plays into that scenario."

"It would be nice to find out," Baier replied. "Then again, I could be chasing a chimera. It wouldn't be the first time. But I'd still like to know for sure."

"Whatever. I would advise checking with our Vietnamese friends first to see if they've seen anything. They try to keep a close watch on the foreign presence here as well." Crockett looked Baier in the eyes before smiling and shaking his head. "Just remember, you are still supposed to be preparing your overview and report on the potential prospects of the U.S. involvement here for the Director. Is this all really relevant to your report?"

Baier chewed his lower lip for a moment while he studied the floor as though a first draft of his missive for the Director could be found there at his feet. "I can't really say until I've had a chance to check it out. I guess if I do find anything I can kick it over to one of your teams in the Station here."

Crockett shrugged. "Whatever you say. It's your career. But if you stir up a hornet's nest, the Director might think twice about sending you out to a war zone again."

"And that's a bad thing?"

• • •

Although he had been in Saigon now for roughly a month, Baier still felt like a newcomer. Understandably. It was after all, a whole new world for him. His contacts were limited, so he turned to the one Vietnamese official he knew, Nguyen Van Trongh. It did make sense, though, seeing as how Van Trongh was highly placed in an office that dealt with counterterrorism, a topic of deep concern shared by the two allies.

Baier had turned down Crockett's offer to have Hartnett accompany him again. It wasn't that he did not appreciate Hartnett's help. It was just that he wanted to keep this particular investigation close to his chest. Especially if it didn't lead anywhere. Lord knows he didn't want to look like some seventh-floor nincompoop out chasing his own shadow. But if there was some substance to his suspicions, Baier could always call others, like Hartnett, in to help. In fact, he would probably have to.

"It's just as well," Crockett had said. "It turns out he's going to be in DaNang for the week."

Baier was struck first by the beehive of activity that swarmed over the hallways and offices at the National Police headquarters. That was probably to be expected, since just days earlier General Khanh had finally moved to remove Minh from office and take control of the South Vietnamese government with a coterie of allegedly likeminded officers. January 29th. Baier had been in country for a little under a month, and the place had already changed regimes. How many more times before I leave, he wondered.

To his surprise, Baier encountered no delay at Nguyen Van Trongh's office. This time, Baier had not even been asked to wait while the secretary typed. Instead, he was ushered immediately into Nguyen Van Trongh's office. An Orange Crush was waiting on the end table next to the sofa. There were even ice cubes floating in the glass. Baier wondered how long they would last.

"Ah, thank you," Baier said. "I regretted having left before I could enjoy one of these the last time I was here."

"Yes, when my secretary brought in the bottle after you departed I realized that my hospitality had been wanting." Van Trongh paused to give Baier time to take a sip. "So, Mister Baier, what can I do for you this time? Do you have questions on General Khanh and his prospects? His intentions?" Van Trongh paused to consider his next words. "Undoubtedly, you have heard that General Khanh has just taken over from Minh."

Baier set the glass back on the table. He noticed that a ring of moisture had already settled on the glass top. "That is interesting. There is certainly no shortage of surprises here." He thought of Crockett's prediction a few weeks ago. "No, not this time. Our Secretary of Defense was recently in town…"

"Yes, I was part of a group the met that with him to discuss our progress against the Viet Cong cadres in the countryside."

"Good. I'm sure that was a great help to him. But my interest today has to do with other intelligence services operating in Saigon."

"Do you mean the North Vietnamese? I am sure you are aware that is a major focus of our work here. Not this office per se, of course, but our organization's for certain."

Baier took another sip of the Orange Crush. It was surprisingly refreshing, given how rarely he drank the stuff at home. Then again, anything wet and cool would be nice in this climate. He glanced up at the ceiling fan, which labored to shift the air above their heads. For some reason the floor fans were not moving today. He wondered if his host was trying to keep their meeting short.

'It's not them I am wondering about. I believe I came across a possible Soviet officer a few days ago, and I thought I'd see if you have any information on other services here, especially Eastern European ones."

Nguyen Van Trongh rose from his desk chair and walked to the door. When he opened the door, he leaned through and spoke to his secretary. Then he turned and walked back to his desk.

"I have asked to have Le Duc Vien to join us." He waved his hand when Baier shot him a look of curiosity and was about to speak. "My colleague has been in his position as chief of the Counter-Intelligence office for over a year now. And I believe he is likely to remain there for some time yet."

Baier was in the middle of another sip of his soda, and raised his eyebrows as he set the glass back on the table.

"No, he is no relation to General Khanh, nor a family friend. I know that Khanh, now that he has seized power, will almost certainly replace many officials formerly associated with the Diem government, as well as appointing a good number of his own and other Cabinet members' family relatives to high office once he takes over. But Le Duc Vien does come from the south, in fact the Mekong Delta, like Khanh. However, unlike Khanh, Vien is Catholic but obviously not a refugee from the North. Nonetheless, he has proven himself to be a competent and very useful officer. He will be able to answer your questions much more thoroughly than I can."

The two men made small talk for the next half hour while they waited for their new participant. It did not take Nguyen Van Trongh long to bring up Baier's visit to the hamlet and the Viet Cong attack, such as it was.

"I heard of your misadventure in one of our strategic hamlets," Van Trongh said. "I believe it occurred a few days ago."

"Yes," Baier agreed. "Five to be exact. When did you hear of it?"

"Four days ago."

Well, now that was interesting, Baier thought...the day after. Not only had they learned of it immediately after, but no one from the liaison service had bothered to inquire as to his well-being. He was pretty sure there was a message here. He just wasn't certain what that might be.

Van Trong did not wait long to give him that message. "I am sorry that your life was endangered, but when people wander unescorted into the rural areas, they have to expect some trouble. Not always perhaps, but sometimes."

"But I was escorted," Baier replied.

Nguyen Van Trongh simply smiled.

Okay, Baier thought, message received. Baier doubted there was only one.

Those thoughts were interrupted by the arrival of Le Duc Vien, who, like his colleague, was dressed casually in khaki slacks and a linen, short-sleeved shirt, this one colored a light blue that matched the sky outside the window. He approached Baier and held out his hand. Baier stood and shook the hand. Then the two men took their places at opposite ends of the sofa. Nguyen Van Trongh remained seated behind his desk throughout the exchange.

"I understand you have some questions for me," Le Duc Vien said. "Something about European services operating in Saigon."

"Yes, that's right," Baier said. "Are you aware of any? And if so, which ones and how many people do they have here?"

Le Duc Vien thought for a moment, as though he was preparing a careful answer. He brushed some imaginary lint from his slacks before speaking. "Where did you see these people?"

"There was just one. I believe he was a Soviet, although I can't be sure."

"I see. Are we excluding the French?"

Baier nodded.

"Where was this?"

Baier hesitated. "At a brothel, several miles from the city center."

"The French one? *Le Maison* something or other?"

"Yes."

Le Duc Vien smiled, condescendingly. "Enjoying some of what our country has to offer in the way of entertainment, Mister Baier?"

Baier did not reply. He did not move, and his facial muscles felt as though they were set in stone. He glanced over at Van Trongh, whose own face seemed to be just as hard.

"I am sorry," Duc Vien said. "I did not mean to be flippant. Or disrespectful. But that is a common attraction for westerners like yourself, Mister Baier. We occasionally hear of a suspicious presence there and investigate. But as you can imagine, we must do so carefully. One can never be sure what or whom one might find there."

Baier thought of the two ARVN officers he had seen there that same morning.

"I understand," Baier said. "What about elsewhere in the city? Perhaps at other embassies."

Le Duc Vien sighed. "There are no Communist Bloc embassies in Saigon, as I am sure you know already. So, no one would be operating under diplomatic cover. There are some commercial and press establishments those services could use. But we have not seen or heard of anything underway at those beyond the usual commercial or journalistic activities." Vien nodded. "However, I will ask to have some resources placed to investigate those more closely to see what we might turn up. If they are active here, we can be certain that they are up to no good, Mister Baier. And we would be eager to help."

Baier stood. He noticed that his own white cotton shirt was plastered to his back by sweat. "Thank you for that."

He drained the rest of the soda in his glass, then refilled it and drank most of that. He turned to Nguyen Van Trongh and winked. "And thank you for that as well."

CHAPTER ELEVEN

Pyle had never looked so sheepish. At least, not in the short time Baier had known him. Hangover or guilt, Baier wondered. Probably both. Baier had been in contact with his fellow American and intelligence veteran through de Couget, who always seemed to know where to find Pyle. Most of the time anyway.

"I think you've got some explainin' to do, Mister Pyle."

This time, they were not meeting at the Continental during the breakfast service. Yet the American still stood riveted in place in front of Baier's table at a café down the street from the Continental. It was almost as though his shoes were glued or screwed to the floor, keeping both legs solid and stiff. The meeting had been Pyle's suggestion, and Baier realized that, given its location so close to his hotel, it was probably the last time he would use this place for a business meeting of any sort. The great advantage of the place, however, was that it was never crowded—like this morning. You never had to worry about being overheard, as long as you kept your voice low. Baier sat one row in from the window looking out on Tu Da Street, formerly the Rue Cantinat, and right in the middle of a small pond of empty tables.

Pyle nodded with a slight movement of his head that was almost imperceptible. If he hadn't spoken, Baier probably would have missed it.

"What's that your eating? It looks like a Pho dish."

Baier smiled and let a grunt slip out between helpings. "Oh, hell, ya. This stuff is delicious. I went for the chicken. I thought I'd help myself to an early lunch as long as we're here." He motioned toward the plate with his fork. "Would you like some?"

Pyle's lips twitched, and his eyelids fluttered. "Sure. But I think I'd rather have some Banh xeo instead. That's my favorite. It has a blend of pork, shrimp, and bean sprouts." He pointed at Baier's fork. "I won't need that, though. Just some chopsticks."

Baier signaled for the waiter and gave him Pyle's order. The waiter looked suspiciously at Baier's fork. Baier shook his head, which brought an immediate nod of assent—and, it seemed to Baier, approval.

Pyle had put on a clean set of clothes and even smelled as though he had showered and washed his hair. It still hadn't seen a comb, but Baier didn't want to ask too much of the man at this point. He also really didn't care about his fashion sense or cleanliness. Pyle finally shuffled his feat for several seconds, then plopped down into a chair at Baier's side without any ceremony, or coordination. Baier reached out to steady the man before he fell over.

"Whoa there, pardner. Relax. Move as slowly as you feel necessary," Baier said.

"I'm…I'm sorry about the other day…"

"And night."

"Yes, that's right. I certainly didn't mean to put you in any danger. How can I make it up to you?" Pyle asked.

"Well, the first thing you can do is to try to get and stay sober. How long has this been going on?"

"Oh, some years now. Seven or eight. A bit after the French pulled out and after the country was split in the Geneva Treaty. I guess I hung out here too long and got bored. I also got in with a bad crowd."

"A bad crowd? What are you, some kind of a teenager?"

Pyle looked at Baier with genuine pain and hurt in his eyes. "What's that supposed to mean? You know what it's like after going through the kind of stuff I did during the war."

Baier waved his hand. "Forget it. I'm sorry I even made that crack." He had realized on the drive back to Saigon trailed by an exhausted and slowly sobering Pyle that he would not be able to ignore or even escape this American's presence during this temporary assignment in Vietnam, or TDY in Agency parlance.

The man had issues, and living alone in an alien environment and far from family or his personal roots in what had been his home did not help. Baier had no idea what the man might have gone through during the war. He would not be the only one to suffer some kind of consequence. Whatever repercussions he carried with him would not go away easily. Baier realized that his best bet was to try to limit the damage that might await Pyle, and what he might cause in turn. Baier might even be able to find some use for the man, maybe give him a purpose, however small and minor, that could help him escape his current opium-addled prison in exile.

"How frequently do you fall into these episodes?" Baier continued.

Pyle looked out the window and shrugged. "Oh, once every few months. They usually aren't that bad."

"What happened this time?"

"I'm not sure. I guess the girl mixed a pipe that was too strong for me. Several of them."

"Had she helped you before? Do you know her well?"

"No, not really. Someone sent her over when I arrived. It was her first time with me, in any case."

"Okay, maybe we can look into that. Or perhaps de Couget can help there. He does seem to care for you."

"I hope so. I care for him. We share a lot about this place..."

"Yes, I've figured that much out all by myself."

"And he has been a big help to me over the years," Pyle finished.

The waiter brought Pyle's dish then disappeared. Baier leaned forward, resting his elbows on the glass tabletop. "What can you tell me about the man. You clearly trust him, or you wouldn't have taken me to his business to meet him."

Pyle studied Baier for about half a minute. Baier wondered if the American was alright. He looked as if he was about to fall asleep. The eyelids slid lower, slowly, and Baier reached over the shake Pyle's shoulder. Maybe he should have suggested an afternoon meeting, but Baier figured the man would be sharpest earlier in the day and probably not much longer. Pyle straightened and leaned in towards Baier.

"I told you that I trust him. And you know that he's my friend. I owe him a lot. One helluva lot."

Baier glanced around the room before focusing back in on Pyle. "Yes, I already know that. And I know you're dependent on him. So, I'm not about to suggest anything inappropriate or potentially harmful. But I'm trying get a better sense of the man if our paths are going to cross again. Which I believe is likely."

Pyle sat back, more relaxed. "Okay." He paused to gather his thoughts. "I think Henri is genuinely committed to the West. By that I mean us and our allies who see a need to halt the spread of communism here in Indochina. I mean, how long do you think his business would survive if Ho and his mandarins up north succeeded in replacing the government down here?"

"Not very long." Baier replied.

"Nope. He doesn't think we're likely to achieve our dream of defeating the Communists with our present military-focused strategy. And certainly not with the current leadership down here. But he's not going to do anything to undermine it. Not actively or willingly."

"Is he in a position to do so unwillingly? Are there any possible pressure points that you're aware of that could put him in a position where he has to cooperate with the insurgency? Or others opposed to our presence here?"

Again, Pyle paused to consider his answer. "No, I don't think so. Look, the guy's been around for a long time. He fought the Viet Minh for about four years before the French pulled out, and he's been living in Saigon ever since. I think he's only gone home to France once. That was to settle up some family business when his parents died. This is his home now. And his situation isn't all that bad. He lives in the house of a former French rubber magnate, has a beautiful and devoted wife, whom he also loves."

"Just what is their story? He once told me they are not officially married."

Pyle waved his arm over the table. "Oh, that. No, not in the eyes of the Church. The guy is nominally a Catholic, although I've never seen him go to Mass or eat fish on Friday. I think there was some kind of ceremony in the Tai village. He never bothered to register it with the authorities here either." Pyle paused, and his eyes focused long enough to zero in on Baier. "They are really devoted to each other. I think she pretty much saved his life after Dien Bien Phu, which she thinks has given her some kind of responsibility for de Couget."

"Okay, okay, I'm convinced," Baier said.

"Why? What did you have in mind?"

"Oh, nothing bad or dangerous."

"Just about everything is dangerous around here right now." Pyle spoke those words with a conviction that set his jaws tight and his eyes hard like small stones. It was as though he wanted to make sure Baier understood what he had to say. Plus the implications and obligations that came with that.

"Well, it's not my intention to endanger anyone here, and least of all an American expatriate and his French friend and patron. First, though, let's see about getting you off that fucking drug. I think my first project for our brothel owner is going to get him to help you in that area. In fact, I have to ask myself why he hasn't done so already."

"Maybe he has," Pyle said.

"Well, in that case, he hasn't done very well." Baier nodded in the direction of Pyle's bowl. "You'd better get started before your food gets cold. You also look like you could use a good meal."

"Thanks. But this stuff is great in any temperature."

• • •

This time, Baier visited de Couget and *La Maison des Reves* alone. He even drove himself out later that afternoon in an Army jeep the Station had, getting lost on the way only once. Fortunately, everyone he asked appeared to know the way to *La Maison des Reves*.

The house was not very busy, only a few more visitors than during his previous visit. At least from what he could see in the first-floor rooms, which served as lounges, of sorts. Of course, Baier had no idea how crowded the rooms upstairs were. It was already the middle of the afternoon.

"Russian, you say?" de Couget asked again. Baier couldn't be certain it was not a rhetorical question.

"That's right. That was certainly Pyle's impression. Neither of us speak Russian, but we weren't about to engage the guy in conversation."

"But you've had experience with Russians before, I take it? It would surprise me if someone in your profession had not."

"Oh, absolutely. And I would say 'Soviets.' There are numerous Slavs, especially those within the Soviet Union, who are not Russians. Or 'Great Russians', as they like to describe themselves."

"Yes," de Couget agreed. "Such as the White Russians or 'Little Russians', as the Ukrainians are known to many in Russia proper." De Couget rose from his desk and walked over to the sofa where Baier had taken a seat when he arrived. "And I must ask myself if this is also a case of mistaken identity."

"How do you mean?" Baier stiffened at what looked like an attempt at diversion.

"You see, I asked one of the girls who has seen this customer on several occasions..."

"How many and for how long?" Baier pressed.

De Couget held up a hand. "And she claims that he described himself as Bulgarian."

"So what."

"Excuse me?"

"That means nothing. The same questions remain. What is he doing here? Did he share that with your prostitute?"

"No, he did not. But that does not mean he is lying."

"It also does not mean that he is Bulgarian. Are you aware of any Bulgarian diplomatic or commercial presence here in Saigon? Or anywhere in Vietnam, for that matter?" De Couget was silent. "In my mind that all makes his presence here even more suspicious. It's like he came out with the first nationality he could think of without ever bothering to establish a credible back story. I don't suppose you could have your girl ask some questions along those lines."

"That would be unusual and would almost certainly make the man suspicious. I believe you would prefer to avoid that."

"Yes, for now anyway. Did she say anything else about the man?"

"Yes, in fact, she did. She rather likes him?"

"Whoa. She likes him? Does he tip well?"

"If he does, she has not mentioned it to me. But she finds him cultured. At least that's what she said once."

"Cultured? In what way? And which culture?"

"Well," de Couget continued, "he reportedly enjoys classical music. He even brought a record player for her room so he can listen to Tchaikovsky."

"Anyone else? Say, Beethoven or Mozart?"

De Couget shook his head. "No. She claims he refuses to listen to anything by a German composer."

"The more I hear about this guy, the more Russian he sounds," Baier concluded. "Do you have any other suggestions?"

De Couget stood and moved back behind his desk. "I can see how important this is for you. Although I cannot see why."

"Maybe I'll explain it some day. As I said before, it's a long story."

"In that case may I suggest an alternative? I could have a microphone placed in this girl's room. I mean, as a listening device. That would give us two benefits."

"Which are?"

"Well, in the first place we would be able to listen to their conversations. And perhaps Monique—that is her name; people here prefer European names—could discretely ask for some background. She would have to be very careful, however."

"Of course. And the second?"

De Couget held up two fingers. "The second would be that then we would have a recording of his voice. You must have someone fluent in Russian or another East European language in your office. Then, we might be better able to place the man's origins."

"I see. But how long would something like this take?"

De Couget waved a hand in the air. "Oh, not too long. The man comes here at least once a week. Sometimes more often."

"Does he always choose Monique?"

De Couget shook his head. "No, not always. But more often than any of the other ladies. She is one of our Eurasian employees. Some people prefer those women. Russians, I understand, can be terrible racists."

"Okay, let's try that." Baier nodded, satisfied. "There is one other matter, though."

"Yes, of course. What else can I do for you?"

Baier shifted his weight on the sofa and settled back against the cushions. "It has to do with Pyle. He told me you've been a big help in his battle with this opium addiction."

The Frenchman smiled and shrugged. "I have tried to help. His is not that bad a case, however. I have seen much worse."

"Well, he looked pretty bad in the village the other night."

De Couget nodded, a look of concern spreading over his face. "Yes, that was unusual. I think the girl with him may have given him several doses too many or made pipes that were too strong."

"Intentionally or by accident?"

"That is an interesting question. If it was intentional, I cannot think of why. I mean, what purpose would it have served for the girl to do such a thing?"

Baier thought back to the nighttime bombardment and the image of that same girl scurrying through the village streets. "How well do you know the people in that hamlet?"

"Not well at all. I have only ever travelled there to find our friend Pyle. And that has only been on several occasions before the other evening."

"Then we can't rule out that it was intentional."

"But again, to what purpose? I fear you are already becoming overly suspicious, Mister Baier. It can happen in this atmosphere here. A sort of mild paranoia. You need to be careful that you do not succumb."

"I'll do my best. It is also a matter of caution. But more to the point, Pyle may have become a target because of his association with you or me. Or someone may have wanted to be sure we visited the village, which they might have suspected was a strong possibility if Pyle became debilitated and you needed to return to retrieve him," Baier explained.

"I'm afraid I do not follow your point. Again, what would be the purpose of that?"

"Well, there isn't much of a path to follow. I'm simply thinking out loud to see if I can find an explanation. And we are both Westerners…"

"Yes, the former and current colonial masters," de Couget added. He stood. "Well if you do find an explanation, please let me know. In the meantime, though, I will stay with my belief that it was accidental." He paused. "Accidental, that is, in terms of a target. Perhaps not in terms of a message."

"A message for…?"

"For anyone like us. Representatives of foreign powers."

"And the message would be?"

De Couget smiled and shrugged. "That we do not belong here and must be careful where we go and what we assume."

"Fair enough," Baier said. "But in the meantime if you would also try to keep Pyle off the opium. I fear that more evenings like that last one will only lead to more trouble."

"Ah, but Mister Baier, I have kept your compatriot alive. And I plan to continue that."

"That's a pretty low bar. That doesn't seem to offer very much to aim for."

De Couget came around his desk and escorted Baier to the door. "In this country and at this time, that is quite an achievement. I hope you will enjoy as much success."

● ● ●

He could not be certain, but when Baier got to the jeep, he could have sworn that the car had been searched. It had not been locked, of course. Without a roof or sides, access was pretty damn easy. But some of the material inside had been shifted, or so it seemed. Baier had made a mental note of the arrangement of the books and paper inside, and that was different now. What really pissed him off was that his copy of Graham Greene's *The*

Quiet American was gone. It had been a weathered and beaten-up paperback copy, but he hadn't finished the damn thing. When he glanced back at the guards by the door, one of them smiled and nodded towards the driver's seat.

The book was not there. He wondered why else the guard may have motioned toward the jeep, and the driver's seat in particular. Just to be safe, Baier did a quick inspection of the undercarriage and engine to make sure no explosives had been attached. He was glad he did. A dangling wire led to a twin packet of dynamite under his seat.

Baier carefully peeled the tape away and disconnected the wiring from the starter. He carried the package inside and dropped it on de Couget's desk. The Frenchman looked up in astonishment.

"My God, where did you find that?"

Baier let it sit on the brown leather blotter for about ten seconds before responding. "Underneath my vehicle. You need to increase or find some way to improve your security here. That was not in my car when I drove out here. One of your guards must have seen whomever it was plant the damn thing." Baier sighed. "I'm lucky your man warned me. And I'm thinking that a healthy dose of paranoia is probably a good thing in this country."

"Yes, yes, of course," de Couget stuttered. "I will look into it immediately. And I will get an answer for you." The Frenchman paused, then glanced up from the bomb to Baier. "You see? I told you that staying alive in this country is no small victory in itself."

CHAPTER TWELVE

February 3 already. Baier noted how the time was moving along pretty swiftly. He sat at his desk, scribbling his thoughts alongside a rough outline that he hoped would help him organize those thoughts for the Director. He wasn't having much luck. That's probably why the days kept slipping by.

"Let's go get a coffee," Crockett suggested. His shadow loomed over Baier's desk and left Baier's notes in temporary darkness. "I'm tired of sitting in this damn office."

"What's the matter, Frank? The paperwork getting you down? You can always pay a visit to the boys in Laos, or head out to a 'strategic hamlet' to check on the progress of the hearts and minds campaign. I've got this damn report to do."

Crockett didn't move. Baier sighed, then stood. "To hell with it. I could use a break, too."

Crockett led the way down the hall.

"You know damn well that when the season for the Personal Assessment Reports rolls around, we have little else we can do. If you want to destroy morale, just forget to send any PARs back in time for the promotion panels. I'm sure you've written more than a few in your time."

"Oh, hell, yes. And I don't envy you that job in a Station this size."

The two Americans strolled down the stairway at the back of the Agency quarters that connected their offices with the rest of the Embassy. When they got out into the street, Crockett grabbed Baier's arm and steered him towards a café several blocks away from the Embassy compound. Baier took advantage of the noise and bustle on the streets of a crowded Saigon to fill the Station Chief in on the misadventures at the hamlet where he and de Couget had found Pyle. He also included the most recent discussion with the Frenchman at his brothel. Baier finished with a description of the surprising welcome package he had discovered underneath his jeep.

Crockett passed through an opening in a thin white railing that encompassed a handful of metal tables and chairs that lined the sidewalk along Ham Nghi Boulevard. Baier could see the curve of the Embassy building where it dominated the broad intersection at its front.

"That's actually a very interesting building. How old is it anyway?" Baier asked.

"I'm not really sure. We took it over in 1889, when we established a commercial office here to represent our interests to the French colony back then. It was elevated to a legation in 1950 after we recognized the Bo Dai government, and in '52 Congress made it a full embassy."

"That sounds kind of old for us. For a building, I mean. At least for an embassy. I do recall us having an even older consulate in Istanbul, which still operates as such. And I think the Embassy in Vienna works out of some old Habsburg training school for its now-defunct imperial diplomatic corps." Baier shrugged. "There are probably a few more around the world."

"Yeah, well, there are plans afoot to build a new one. I guess as we expand our presence here, we're going to need a bigger building to house all the people we'll need to bring in to run this place. And it could easily use a more modern wiring system." He paused to catch the attention of a waiter. "Not to mention better security arrangements." Crockett studied the building for a few seconds. "With that location so close to the street, the security challenges are huge."

"Any idea of the timing?"

Crockett signaled the waiter to bring a cannister of coffee. "As usual, that all depends on when Congress authorizes the funds to purchase the property and build the damn thing. But enough of that. Where do things stand with your report for the Director?"

"Oh, that. I've got some thoughts and an outline down on paper. You might have noticed the mess back there on my desk. And I might add that your folks have been helpful and forthcoming—not to mention patient—with me. I still don't have any well thought-out conclusions, though."

Crockett nodded. "Good. Good enough, anyway. Those will come in due time. You're still relatively new here." Crockett stirred some cream into his cup after the waiter dropped off their cappuccinos. "Then again, you always will be. But at least the rough edges will be replaced with some genuine insights, even if gradually."

"But it's not like my time here is unlimited," Baier said.

Crockett nodded. "True enough. But you'll get it done. You always do. Somehow. How about our poor American drug addict and his French buddy? And just what did you have in mind for both of them?"

Baier sighed. "Right now, I'm not sure how much I can trust either one, or what use they might be. Especially Pyle."

"Why is that?" Crockett asked. "You sounded more open, optimistic before."

Baier sighed and studied the crowd strolling by before responding. "You know, it's been really hard to figure Pyle out. Okay, so he's developed an opium habit. It's sad. But it's not that unusual in this part of the world, as you are no doubt aware. And both he and de Couget claim that it's a mild case, one they've been able to control. Pyle claims he's had it for years."

Crockett paused to take a sip of his coffee. A healthy sigh escaped from his lips when he set the cup back down. His hand rested on the rim. "It's amazing how you can find some of life's little pleasures in the oddest places."

Baier smiled while he took in the pressed white shirt and seamed black cotton slacks of the staff working the tables. "You could almost mistake yourself for sitting at a French café in some of these places."

Crockett nodded. "I see what you mean. As for Pyle, though, I'd say that's fair enough. But his addiction does kind of limit his usefulness."

"I still don't know how he finances his life here. I doubt at this stage that he has anything worthwhile to sell or market. Maybe people keep hoping that his OSS background and some connections—which I doubt exist anymore—will lead to something more profitable."

"And there is the question of his reliability," Crockett added.

"Yeah. No shit. And the Frenchman is an even bigger enigma. I thought we might get some useful information from customers that liked to talk in their sleep or brag about their importance."

"That still might come true."

"But only if de Couget is willing to use the access his *Maison* and the working girls provide. I really had to push for his help on identifying and filling in the gaps on the Russian character. If he is Russian." Baier sipped his own coffee. "Which I'm pretty certain he is."

"What about de Couget himself? Does he have any connections you could exploit?"

"I'm not sure. I haven't seen any as yet. The excursion to that village did suggest that he has some connections to people in the countryside, or perhaps people who know people in the countryside. I'm just not sure how deep or strong they are." Baier drank some more of his coffee. "Or who has the leverage."

"That's okay. I think we're pretty well plugged in there. Although more information is always useful. Our analysts can be insatiable, as you well know." Crockett stirred the foam around in his coffee. "As for the Frenchman, however, I was wondering what he might be able to tell us of the residual French influence here. It goes beyond coffee and pastries, you know."

"You mean political influence? With ARVN and or the government?"

Crockett sipped, then nodded. Baier drank more of his own coffee.

"That's right. As you are aware, Washington is still pissed as hell over de Gaulle's continued meddling on the international front, telling everyone how foolish and misguided our policy is and how badly we need to reconvene an international summit—

like the one that allegedly solved the Laotian problem—to end the fighting. He keeps bringing up the 'n' word, too."

"The what?" Baier asked.

"Neutralization."

"I see. So? Do you think de Couget is in touch with Paris to promote de Gaulle's agenda? Political backing for some good PR and reduced pressure?"

"Now, don't be a smart ass, Karl. I'm not pushing the guy's importance. But he may be aware of some kind of French influence or contacts within the Khanh Government. There are people in Washington…"

"Who?" Baier pressed.

"Well, I'm not really sure, but I'm guessing they work in pretty close proximity to the Oval Office. Anyway, they suspect that the French are using some of that residual influence to push Khanh in that direction. They were not at all helpful in the years leading up and immediately after the Geneva Accords. In fact, they were downright obstructive."

"And the reason for that?"

"As you no doubt suspect already. They were pissed about losing this corner of the world to the Twentieth Century."

"You want me to see if I can get de Couget to spy on his own countrymen?"

"Karl, if there was anyone who could pull that off, it would be you. But it doesn't need to go that far. Perhaps he can find out if there is a Vietnamese contact or two the French are using. Didn't you say he owed you a favor, or several?"

"Yeah, but I was hoping to use those to run down what the Soviets or any of their East European friends might be up to here."

"Just add this to the list." Crockett finished his coffee. "And it would fit in more with your assignment from the Director. You know, a more complete picture of the diplomatic and security puzzle we're operating in here." Crockett paused. "But given what you found in your jeep the other morning, I'd say you also might get him to look into his security. Where does he get that?"

"He mentioned something about ex-gangsters on our trip to the countryside."

"You mean the old Binh Xuyen group?"

Baier nodded. "Yeah, that sounds right."

"Oh shit, man, those guys have a sense of loyalty that never goes beyond the next pay check. Be careful out there. My guess is that someone has gotten to them, or at least one of them."

Well, not all of them, Baier thought.

Crockett signaled the waiter for two more cappuccinos for the table. "I never find one cup to be enough. The portions are so damn small here."

• • •

La Maison was busier than on Baier's previous visits. That could have been because it was late in the afternoon. Did hormone levels rise in this part of the world as the day wore on, or were the various customers more confident that they would not be missed at work or home at this time of day? Whatever the reason, Baier had to thread his way through a collection of horny Asians and Europeans as he made a path to de Couget's office at the back of the main floor.

He had driven to the brothel alone again, and this time he did not get lost. Baier remembered the way from his last trip and made it in well under an hour. Closer to thirty-five minutes, actually. He also parked right in front of the entrance, hoping to deter another attempt at sabotage. He had practiced a rudimentary counter-surveillance run on the drive out, and he felt pretty secure. But one could never be absolutely certain that there was no tail, or from where the bomb had come…and from whom.

Baier also arrived uninvited and unannounced. When he strode into de Couget's office, his wife was there, massaging the Frenchman's shoulders with small hands and tiny fingers that made Baier wonder if she was really doing any good. That is, for the muscles. De Couget's head lolled to the side and his eyes were closed like a man in a deep sleep and a pleasant dream.

Baier stood in the office entrance for several seconds, then coughed to let its occupants know they had a visitor. De Couget's expression shifted from one of bliss to one resembling more of a nightmare. He caught himself quickly, however, and his familiar— if condescending—smile slipped into place. Baier was impressed at the man's quick thinking and diplomatic skills.

"Ah, Mister Baier, you must learn to knock."

"And you, Monsieur de Couget, must learn to close your door."

De Couget's wife stepped back and let her arms fall to her sides. She, too, wore a smile, but this was one that looked as though it was intended to hide an embarrassment more than anything else. De Couget still sat slumped in his chair as he considered his new and unexpected visitor.

"To what do I owe this unexpected pleasure? Have you found the name and purpose of our mystery visitor?"

"Not yet. But I do plan to keep trying."

"Well, that is good. Because I have had no luck on that front. Not yet anyway. Nothing definite."

Baier moved several steps closer to the desk. De Couget motioned towards a chair, but Baier shook his head. "No, but thank you. I appreciate the gesture and the hospitality. As always. I came to discuss something else." Baier nodded towards de Couget's wife. "Can we speak in private?"

De Couget gave a quick glance behind him. "My wife is privy to all my secrets, Mister Baier. We can talk openly."

Baier shrugged. "Suit yourself. How large is the French presence here these days?"

"In Saigon or all of Vietnam?"

"Let's start with the whole country."

"Oh, I cannot be certain. But I would estimate between 10 and 15 thousand. And as you might expect, the vast majority of those are here in Saigon."

"How much of that represents an official presence?"

De Couget leaned forward. "I am afraid that there you have me at a disadvantage. I really have no idea, although that presence cannot be very large. Not after the Geneva agreements. We do have an embassy here, of course, and some commercial interests that require a consular representation. But as you might imagine, that pales in comparison to what we had here before. My impression is that we focus our work on this half of the country now." He smiled. "The southern half, that is."

Baier nodded. "Yes, I figured as much. And our Embassy can give me a figure on that sort of official presence. But what about French civilians, as it were? How many stayed behind? I gather quite a number have retained their properties and plantations. Or at least some of those holdings. And they appear to have a pretty active social life here in Saigon, at least."

"Yes, that is true. But I have little contact with those people, at least publicly. My presence can cause some uncomfortable or awkward situations. I am sure you understand."

"Oh, sure. I understand completely. But what about privately?"

"What did you have in mind?"

"Well, before we go into that, I would also like to know if you have a relationship with elements of the French Sûreté who have stayed behind."

De Couget smiled once more and sat back. His wife's hands settled on his shoulders. "Ah, now we come to the heart of the matter, as it were. What is it you really wish to know, Mister Baier? Just what do you mean by a 'relationship'? Do I work for them?"

"Do you?"

"No, I can be quite honest about that with you. I do not work for them. Like you, they stop by every once in a while for information on a particular matter. It is not a regular practice, and I receive no money for this information. But I believe it would be unwise for me to ignore their requests. It never hurts to have extra friends. Especially in a country at war."

Baier leaned forward, his hands on the edge of the desk. "Do you know how to get in touch with anyone in your compatriots' security service here?"

The wife's hands were working de Couget's shoulder muscles again. "Perhaps. Let me ask around. I will try to arrange something. May I also ask the purpose of your request?"

Baier straightened up. "Let's just say I'd like to share some ideas on the direction and purpose of the Khanh Government. And I respect the French service's longstanding connections and expertise in that area." It was Baier's turn to smile. "I'm sure they'll understand."

"Very good then. I'll see what I can do." De Couget took his wife's hands in his own. "Oh, there is one other thing I forgot. You may find something out about this mythical Russian of yours after all."

"How is that?"

"Your compatriot, Mister Pyle, has taken it upon himself to investigate the matter."

"He what?" Baier stepped forward and leaned over the desk, his hands resting on the edge. "What the hell have you done, de Couget?"

The Frenchman's face displayed genuine surprise as he dropped his wife's hands and stood up. "I did nothing more than ask if he knew anything about the stranger you both saw here that morning. He became quite agitated and said he wanted to know more himself. He ran out of here before I could stop him."

"Goddammit." Baier felt his face turn red, and his breath came in short bursts. "If anything happens to him, it will be on your head. Goddamit it all. Why did you even say anything to someone in Pyle's condition?"

The Frenchman stood, his shoulders square and feet planted. "I meant no harm. I had no idea he would respond as he did. I think you have forgotten where you are and in whose house you stand."

Baier swung about and marched out the door. He slammed it shut behind him and trotted down the hallway, pushing potential customers out of his way as he raced for the door. Once in the jeep, Baier realized he should have pressed de Couget for more information. But he had been too angry to speak with that damn Frog any longer.

CHAPTER THIRTEEN

De Couget was true to his word, on one subject, at least, and it had only taken him a day to deliver. Baier had an appointment with a member of the Surete, one of a small group of French intelligence officers operating out of the French Embassy in Saigon. Crockett had told him that they were active mostly as a liaison service, providing what assistance they could to the Vietnamese. But, he assured Baier that, "that can't be all they're doing. Those damn frogs are undoubtedly up to no good on what is our patch now."

"How do you mean?" Baier asked.

"I mean that they are also proactively pushing de Gaulle's agenda here. At least that's my guess. The Vietnamese are pretty tight-lipped about what their old masters are up to, and there's still a lot of resentment against the old colonial bosses, especially against these guys from the French security service. They left behind a lot enemies and a lot of sore feelings."

"I thought you said a lot of the Vietnamese officers were trained and run by the French back in the bad ol' days. Hartnett claimed that a lot of them share a sense of superiority, or a different status in any case, from their colleagues."

Crockett nodded. "Yeah, that's true. But the resentment that the Vietnamese share is directed against their own government for forcing them into an organization where they believe they've lost their special status. And they still resent the French for their earlier behavior as well. As you have no doubt noticed, there's a lot of animosity in this country."

"Then what good can talking to the French do? Are they likely to have any assets or agents of influence with the Vietnamese?"

"Well, if you think about all the dissension and plotting going on within the government and military here, it wouldn't be hard to find an ally or two. Even if they are temporary and don't always pursue the same objectives."

Well, we'll see what they're willing to admit to, or even share, Baier thought as he approached the French Embassy.

His first impression of the building was one of former imperial splendor, maybe even glory. Crockett had told him that the building itself dated back to 1872 when it was constructed by some French naval engineers. They had clearly put a lot of effort into the design, since it became the seat of the French governor for all of Indochina and the home of the Governor General for Vietnam from 1945 to 1954. The Geneva Accords put an end to that pretention, however, and the site now served as Paris's embassy to South Vietnam. Unlike the United States, France had recognized the regime in the North and had opened an embassy there as well, a point that did not sit well with many in the South, especially the refugees from up north.

When he looked at the structure, the operative word for Baier was 'former.' It was, admittedly, the first time he had seen the building, but he had the distinct impression that the historical meaning and importance of the site had faded along with its décor and upkeep.

Perhaps the biggest reason for this insight was the presence of numerous Vietnamese police officers, ostensibly there to provide security; the reason that their presence was even necessary was the sense of abandonment, no, more like betrayal many of the locals felt towards their former colonial masters.

But the sense of betrayal in the sense had more complicated roots and reasoning behind it. From what little Baier had gleaned during his brief stay one thing he had gained was a clear understanding that there was definitely no love lost for the French. But many locals also believed, abetted by popular rumors, that Paris had decided that Ho's regime in the north represented the future. Even worse than that, many locals suspected that France had been advising and assisting the Viet Cong as a way to curry favor with the Communist regime, now that they—the French—had proven to be so incapable of stopping them militarily. These rumors, or the actual conviction, had become so strong and persistent that a mob had ransacked the French Embassy just last year. Looking at the diplomatic grounds and the crowds milling about, Baier suspected that that particular mob would not be the last. The police looked nervous enough to suggest they feared the same.

A tall, thin Westerner approached and broke Baier's reverie, waving his hand in Baier's direction until he was almost on top of the American. His long blonde hair and blue eyes could not have presented a greater contrast to the sea of pedestrians that flowed past him like he was a flagpole on the riverbank, buffeted by the wind.

"Mister Baier?" Baier nodded. "I am Jacques Schroeder." He held out his hand. "I am pleased to meet you. Shall we grab a coffee? There is a nice café down the street in front of the park."

Baier took his hand. "Likewise. And, yes, a coffee would be great. And thank you for finding the tine to meet with me."

"Oh, it is my pleasure. You see, I do not have that much to do these days. Our movements and access are fairly restricted. Ever since the riot against our embassy last year. You have heard of it, no doubt."

They crossed the street and found a small table just inside the park.

"Yes, as a matter of fact, I have. I gather there is still some resentment against your country here."

Schroeder shrugged and nodded.

"But that kind of thing—the attack on your embassy, I mean--strikes me as a bit more serious and, frankly, surprising," Baier continued. "I don't suppose the popular suspicions about your assistance to the Viet Cong and preference for the North are true." It was more than just a rhetorical question for Baier. He raised his eyebrows and gave off a wry smile to suggest he did not believe it himself. Although he wasn't truly certain, deep inside.

Schroeder shook his head vigorously and looked over at Baier as they settled into their seats. "No, no. Of course not. The Viet Cong are unlikely to ask us for our help. Or accept it if we were foolish enough to offer any." The Frenchman returned Baier's smile. "Can you imagine the complications that would present. For example, what would that do to our cooperation within NATO? And there we face a much more important challenge from the Soviet Union."

"Have you any indications that more is coming? Riots, or popular protests, I mean."

Schroeder ordered two espressos. "No, not really. At least nothing specific. But, let me insist again and state quite frankly, as you say, these suspicions of us helping the Communists in any way are ridiculous. How can anyone think we would even consider something like that, or that they would be willing to accept help from us? After what we went through? Our war with them lasted almost ten years."

"And there was all that colonial baggage from before the war as well. No, it does sound a bit far-fetched," Baier admitted. "But then your President has been pretty outspoken in support of peace negotiations and neutralization. And there can be little doubt as to where that might lead."

Schroeder held up a finger while the waiter set the two cups of espresso on the table. "Ah, but only if negotiations lead to a final result. That would be one possible end point, but there are any number of other possibilities. And hopefully, the government here would use the opportunity that comes with peace to gain some popularity of their own."

"But have you made that clear to the Khanh Government? What are their thoughts on this? Do they believe the Viet Cong and North Vietnamese can be trusted, that the fighting would actually stop?"

"Well, as you might imagine, our Ambassador has taken the lead on these discussions with the current government. I have not been privy to these talks."

"But surely you have heard something about how these discussions have gone. Have you discussed these things with your contacts in the local service?"

Schroeder smiled as he sipped his coffee. "I must say that you get right to the point, Mister Baier. You Americans certainly can be direct."

"Life is short. Or it can be. Especially in this country." Baier sipped some coffee of his own.

"An excellent point. Do you think we are pushing the Vietnamese in a certain direction?"

"Are you? It would only be consistent with the message your government is pushing from Paris."

Schroeder shook his head. "I am afraid they do not need us to push them. How long have you been here?"

"Well, it's early February, so I would say just over a month," Baier replied.

Schroeder nodded. "I have been here for two years. And if there is one lasting impression I have of the South Vietnamese government, it is that they are desperate for legitimacy. Not only are they unpopular, thanks to the massive corruption and the fact that so many of the prominent members are Catholics from the north, but they also realize that no one accepts them as the legitimate rulers of this country. Ending the war and bringing the two halves of Vietnam closer together would go a long way to secure both a sense of legitimacy and their popularity." He sipped some coffee from his tiny cup. "I also believe a ceasefire and negotiations would give the regime here an opportunity to demonstrate the difference between this kind of government and the Communists up north."

"Don't they want to establish the foundations of a democratic state first? The better to prevent a Communist takeover. I mean, Ho Chi Minh has an awful lot of popularity throughout the country, especially in the rural areas." Baier took another sip of his espresso. "One could say that that popularity is another legacy of his battles against your country."

"Perhaps. But how are they going to do that? Establish their democratic credentials, I mean." Schroeder asked.

"With our help. Hopefully."

"We already tried that," Schroeder said. "And we failed. I suspect you will as well."

"But you were trying in order to restore this place as a colony. We actually want this country to be free and democratic."

"When I see how you are expanding your presence here, I don't think the Vietnamese see much of a difference. What is the saying: a distinction without a difference?"

"Then let me ask this. Who does most of the talking when you get together?"

"Oh, we both talk a lot. We are, after all, diplomats…"

"Or intelligence officers," Baier corrected him.

"Touché." Schroeder lifted his cup in salute before finishing it. "But it depends on whom we are meeting. Some are more receptive than others. But they are all looking for a way out. That, at least, is my impression. But I—and I suspect my colleagues as well—do not try to convince them one way or the other. We do not need to. And in view of our past relations, I seriously doubt they would take our advice in any case."

"Let me ask this," Baier continued. "Is the Sûreté still active within the Vietnamese service? I've read where your organization—and others within the French Government, such as the military—remained as advisors and influencers in the South Vietnamese government for some time after the Geneva Accords were signed."

Schroeder appeared taken aback by Baier's question, even if it was placed in terms of past activity. He shifted his weight in his chair and glanced around the park before resettling himself and returning his gaze to the American.

"Yes, it is true that we kept a sizable French military force in this country after the Accords were signed, until about 1956."

"Yes, that seems about right. And it was more than sizeable, wasn't it? Something like 150,000 troops."

Schroeder nodded while he sipped some espresso. "I believe so. Yes."

"I also recall that the French advisors working with Edward Lansdale were…how can I put this diplomatically…less than cooperative," Baier continued. "At times they were even dangerously disruptive. Something about resenting Americans as the new powerbrokers on what had been a French patch for just under a century."

Schroeder smiled, having retrieved his calm exterior. "Oh, that. No, I believe that is all in the past, Mister Baier. Those officers were relics, really. We've learned our lesson, most recently in Algeria."

"The revolt against French colonial rule there, you mean?"

Schroeder nodded. "Yes, that's right. It was a very painful experience for us. And it remains so."

"So, nothing more here in Vietnam at present?"

"I believe I am safe in saying that while there may still be some connections, they are really no more than a nostalgic link to a past era for some. Nothing more, I assure you. And nothing our office here supports or encourages."

The two men passed the rest of their time exchanging pleasantries and discussing their respective roles in the last European war. Baier was surprised to learn that Schroeder's father and uncles had fought in the *Wehrmacht*. But like their countryman Schumann, they had taken that experience as a life lesson to promote rapprochement in Europe. He also invited Baier to visit his family in Alsace at his home just north of Colmar.

"Our food and wines are the best in France."

"Yes," Baier agreed. "I've heard that from others as well. I've also heard it described as 'French cooking with German portions.'"

Schroeder laughed. "Well, I would say that the food is a blend of both, but the portions definitely are more like those on the other side of the Rhine."

• • •

When Baier got back to the Station, Crockett's secretary told him to see the Chief right away. "And he said, 'right the hell away,'" she added. "He looked pretty angry."

Baier quick-stepped his way to the Chief's office. The door swung open as soon as he arrived, as though a rush of anger and exasperation was dragging Baier into an inner sanctum of frustration.

"Tell me, Karl, and don't hold anything back. What the hell have you done?"

Baier was momentarily stunned. He had never seen Crockett this agitated. The Chief was pacing back and forth in front of his desk, his right hand repeatedly brushing back the dark brown hair off his forehead.

"Maybe you'd better tell me what's going on, Frank. I went to see someone from the Sûreté, like you asked. What, is Paris sending the Foreign Legion back to help the VC this time? If so, I swear I had nothing to do with it. In fact, my contact swore there was no military cooperation between the two sides whatsoever."

Crockett stopped just long enough to point a finger at Baier and give him what looked to be intended as a death stare. "Don't give me any of your smart ass shit, Karl. This is serious. Very serious. Did you or did you not send Pyle out on a fool's errand to run down this phantom Russian of yours?" The Chief paced around his office, snorting angry rushes of breath and fury. "I was afraid something like this would happen."

"Goddammit, Frank, you should know better than that. I've been in this game too fucking long to pull some amateur's stunt like that. Where did you get that ridiculous idea?"

Crockett dropped into a seat on the corner of the sofa. He threw both arms wide across the back of the furniture. He pulled a slip of paper from his shirt pocket and handed it to Baier. "This came from a messenger, whom I believe was sent by your Frog pal. The guy who owns the whorehouse."

"A messenger? What did the guy look like? And how did he know to come here?"

"He looked like a fucking gangster's gunman, that's how he looked. Beefy and stupid."

"Come on, Frank. There had to be more than that."

"Yeah, there was. He said the note was from Monsieur de Couget. I think in spy novels they call that a clue. He must have sent the messenger."

Baier opened the note and read. He shook his head and exclaimed, "Motherfucker." It was all he could do to avoid laughing. He stared at the Station Chief with his eyes wide and his mouth open.

"Seriously?' Baier asked. "A kidnapping and ransom note?" He studied the envelope, then looked back up at Crockett. "Who is it even addressed to? There's nothing here. Not a name, not anything. It's just blank."

"It doesn't need an address, apparently. And it's not exactly a ransom note. They're not asking for money."

"No," Baier said. "But they are asking for me."

"But as a negotiator."

"Which will become an exchange."

"So, what do you propose? Do you plan to go?"

Baier handed the note back to the Station Chief. "I have to go, Frank. I can't just throw Pyle to those wolves, whoever they are. Like you once said, he may be a pain in the ass, but he's our pain in the ass. We can't just leave him to rot somewhere."

"But how do you know whoever has him are the wolves? And just what does your favorite Frenchman have to do with this?" He reached for the note. "I take it the note is not from him personally."

Baier pulled the slip of paper back, studying it while he spoke. "No, there's no way he would communicate like this, if he is involved. I'm guessing that whoever grabbed Pyle, knew of my link to de Couget and decided that was the best way to get a message to me." He looked up from the note again. "The first thing I should do is to see just what 'my favorite Frenchman' knows about this."

"Yeah, that sounds about right. But why would someone grab this poor old American fart? You didn't send him out on some harebrained scheme, did you? You never answered my question on that one."

"No, Frank, I sure as hell did not. The last time I spoke with de Couget he said something about Pyle getting wind of my interest in the Slavic guy we both saw on my first visit to *La Maison des Reves* and rushing off to see what he could find out. So, my next guess is that whomever he approached was the wrong person to do that to. I can't say if it even was the potential Russian or someone else Pyle approached along the way. Hopefully, de Couget will be able to shed some light on this. I also let that damn Frenchman know how pissed off I was that Pyle had been allowed to go running off on his own fool's errand."

Crockett stood up from the couch and walked behind his desk. "Look, Karl, I'm sorry I flew off the handle back there. But may I make a suggestion?"

"Sure. What is it?"

"Take a Browning with you this time. I don't like all the uncertainty surrounding this case. Your assignment cable from headquarters said you had been recertified for weapons use. You comfortable with that?"

Baier nodded, eagerly. "Yes, I am, and I agree." He paused. "I don't like all the uncertainty either. This could get pretty ugly, pretty quick."

• • •

De Couget was, if anything, only slightly less agitated than Crockett had been.

"I can assure you, Mister Baier, that I had nothing to do with this. I have no idea who might have grabbed my good friend Harry Pyle."

The Frenchman was also pacing in his office, and beads of sweat gathered along his forehead. It was the first time Baier had seen the man perspire. Large round patches of moisture had collected under his arms. Only then did Baier notice that the air conditioning was not running.

"Okay, okay. Have you checked that village again? I don't suppose he's off on another bender."

De Couget did not bother to stop circling his office when he waved his hands in the air. "Yes, of course. That was the first place we looked. They had seen no sign of my—no, our—friend."

"Was the woman who had been with Pyle there? Did you have a chance to speak with her?"

This got de Couget to halt and consider his American guest. "No. Why do you ask? I seriously doubt she had anything to do with this."

Baier stepped over to his host. "I wouldn't be so sure. I saw her running around the village on the night of the mortar attack."

"So what. There were probably others running around as well. It was an attack, after all."

Baier shook his head. "Not really. It was a demonstration. And there was no one else outside that night that I saw. Plus, she's the one who overloaded Pyle's opium pipes. It was almost as if she wanted us to come out there to retrieve him."

"You have a devious mind, Mister Baier."

"It must be the air around here. But did you see her?"

De Couget shook his and leaned against his desk. "No, unfortunately. I doubt she would have had much to say. In any case, Pyle was not there. No, I believe this is much more serious."

"Then who brought you the note? And how did they know it would get to me?"

At that moment de Couget's wife entered the room. She walked over to her husband and embraced him, her hands running down the sides of his face, along his shoulders, then around his waist. She pressed herself tight against the Frenchman.

"Thank you, my dear," de Couget said in French. He turned to Baier. That just about exhausted Baier's limited supply of the language. De Couget continued in English. "She always knows how to comfort and settle me. It helps me focus and think straight again."

"Then ask her or someone else who brought the note to you."

"Ah, I can answer that myself. It was one of my security guards. I'm sure you have seen him before. He is usually at the front door."

"Is he here now? If so, we can get a description at least of whomever brought the note here."

De Couget spoke to his wife, again in French. Those words were lost on Baier. She released her husband and left the room. "She will check to see," he said.

When she returned, she was shaking her head in disappointment. She spoke to de Couget, but in a dialect that, like the Vietnamese spoken in Saigon, was completely incomprehensible to Baier, but it was clearly a separate dialect. To his surprise, de Couget responded in the same language. Then he turned to Baier.

"My wife says that the man is not here at the moment. He has not shown up today."

"Well, that is interesting. How well do you know him? Where did you hire him?"

The Frenchman walked over and stood beside his wife. He took her hand, stroked it, then let it drop. He turned to Baier.

"He came to us with other former members of the Binh Xuyen gang. Many were looking for work after the Diem government crushed them to gain control of Saigon."

"And you trusted that bunch?"

De Couget shrugged. "We did not have a lot of options, you see. They were bound to be as loyal as anyone. As long as we kept paying them. Which has not been a problem, given our source of income."

"Do you think that there is an organized crime group behind Pyle's disappearance?"

De Couget thought for a moment, then shook his head. "There was only the one group that I am aware of. I doubt they have the resources or the organization for that sort of thing anymore."

His wife spoke to him in her dialect once more, which set de Couget thinking again. After a minute or so, he spoke to Baier.

"My wife has had a very good idea. She thinks it would still be possible for some former members of the gang to work together on something like this, but only if someone else is organizing and bankrolling it."

"Bankrolling it?" Baier repeated.

De Couget laughed. "Yes, that's right. We all watch American gangster movies, Mister Baier. But she also said that when the note was delivered, others noticed that the messenger knew exactly whom to approach. The two men seemed to know each other."

"Is there any way we can find out where they might be holding Pyle?"

De Couget looked at his wife and nodded. "Yes, I believe so. I will send some others out to look for him. Also former members of the gang. They will know whom to contact and where possible hiding places are."

"But can you trust them?" Baier asked.

"Oh, I will make sure they remain loyal. I will offer a bonus to whomever helps us bring Mister Pyle back. Alive."

"Good," Baier replied. "And thank you." He turned to go. "Another question, if I may."

"But of course," de Couget answered.

"Why is your air conditioning not running this afternoon? It surely doesn't help your business to have it so hot and humid in here."

"Ah, that," De Couget said. He blew out a breath with a touch of moisture and looked around the room. "Our power is out. Temporarily, I am sure. And we were not able to get enough fuel for our generator this morning."

"I see. But why is that? Some dissatisfied high-level customers? Or did you forget your weekly payoff?"

"Those are monthly, Mister Baier. And, no, we forgot nothing. We have been at this too long to make such a mistake."

"Then the government must be behind this."

"Yes, presumably so. Apparently, we have made someone angry. We will get it straightened out. Eventually."

"That long?"

"Mister Baier, things move at a different pace in this country."

CHAPTER FOURTEEN

It surprised Baier that de Couget needed only a day—less even—to locate Pyle's prison. On the surface this was good news. Yet, also raised suspicions in Baier's mind about the Frenchman's role in and even prior knowledge of Pyle's seizure.

The first step had been to identify the culprits and locate the safehouse. There the Frenchman's team had moved with surprising speed, coming to de Couget by noon the following day. Apparently, his ex-gangsters had run down the missing security guard through a mutual friend and former colleague, who had assisted with Pyle's kidnapping. The man had not wanted to give out the information on Pyle's location and the people holding him.

"How did you get it?" Baier asked later that afternoon. "The information, I mean."

"Ah, you see, Mister Baier, my men have learned some very useful and persuasive methods to extract the necessary information. But do not worry, they are also professionals."

Whatever that means, Baier thought. He did not ask for details. Instead, he was willing to chalk it up as part of the game here in Indochina. It hadn't exactly been absent in Europe over the years either.

"Well, that's always good to hear."

"Yes, it seems our friend is being held in Cholon."

"Cholon?" Baier asked. "Isn't that the Chinese part of town?"

"Yes, that is right," de Couget replied. "I suggest we hurry. There is no way of knowing what kind of shape our friend is in. I will have my people determine the exact location before we go. It may take a while, but no longer than a day. Perhaps less. We will also want to be sure that this not a trap."

That same evening Baier trotted to the sidewalk in front of the Continental, where de Couget and his good old Citroen were waiting. The Frenchman leaped from the back and grabbed Baier's arm, his jaw and eyes set with a determination Baier had not seen before. He led Baier to the car, where both men squeezed once more into the back seat of the sedan, accompanied in the front by the same team of security guards that had traveled with them to the hamlet some weeks ago. At least, Baier guessed they were the same men. What he really wanted to know was whether these two men were loyal. He studied their faces, both of which remained solid and as unemotional as the stone that covered the white art deco facades that lined the buildings along Tu Do Street.

"Is there a reason Pyle was taken to Cholon?" Baier asked. "That doesn't mean the People's Republic is involved, does it?"

"No, I seriously doubt that. I doubt there is much support for the Peoples' Republic of China, or PRC, in Cholon. Those Chinese who live there are overwhelmingly business people, not the kind who would follow Chairman Mao."

"But it might provide a favorable environment for any PRC agents to blend in."

De Couget nodded. "Perhaps. I see you think like an intelligence operative. But me, I think like a local entrepreneur who knows the history of this city and this country. And that knowledge tells me that Cholon was always the place where the underworld operated most openly and most successfully. You know, drugs, gambling, prostitution, and the like."

"You've never operated there?"

De Couget gave Baier a look of disappointment and condescension. "Please, Mister Baier. I do not operate my business like some kind of gangster." He paused and smiled. "Except perhaps when it comes to hiring my security assistants." He motioned with his head towards the front seat.

"I see. I feel so much more comfortable now."

"Ah, that sense of humor. I appreciate that. But it is also the section of town where the Binh Xuyen group was headquartered. So that is where anyone from that old criminal organization would feel most at home operating again. It is where people who were associated with the group would know their way around and feel most comfortable with the loyalty of others around them."

"But that loyalty frayed, didn't it?"

"Let us hope so. You must also remember, my security assistants can be very effective."

The Citroën crawled through the crowded streets of Cholon, at an incredibly slow pace. Gone were the broad boulevards that ran past the Continental and the American Embassy. In their place was a warren of small streets, some little more that blacktop pathways, in which what Baier assumed were where the true working people of Saigon hustled through the streets as vendors, carriage drivers, delivery men, hookers, street urchins, and all the others who battled for their daily survival in a hostile world.

It reminded him of the scenes in post-war Europe, after the collapse of the Nazi regime and the disintegration of its empire. Back before the Allies had been able to establish some stability and introduce the reforms and reconstruction that would give the continent a prosperity it had never known in all the years of Europe's long and storied past. He doubted that this country—regardless of how many allies it found, which were precious few at the moment—would be able to achieve the same here. Not with the current government at hand, and not with a war underway where the other side appeared to hold the better hand.

After what seemed like hours—but which Baier was surprised to learn had been more like forty minutes when he checked his watch--the Citroën arrived at the Binh Tay Market square, the heart of Cholon. They parked down a side street a block from the square and in front of a grocery store. The front window sat behind a barricade of fruit and vegetable stands, over which a host of Vietnamese women of ages ranging from ten to one hundred picked and pulled pieces of food, presumably for the evening meal.

De Couget's security team jumped from the car and held the back doors open, then followed the two Westerners through an alley at the side. The party stopped in front a nondescript, two-story brick building at the back end of the alley. The bricks had long since turned brown from the residue of years of smoke and dirt. The heat of the afternoon and the noise of the crowds that flowed through the streets of Cholon like a river of soot and sound made Baier feel as if they under an assault.

One of the guards stepped forward and pounded on a loose metal door with his fist. The other hand remained clutched around an AK-47, the weapon of choice, Baier noted, of the Viet Cong. The door shook under the beating, but it held until a thin Vietnamese man in shorts, sandals, and a loose, green, short-sleeve t-shirt that appeared not to have seen a laundry tub in over a year, swung it open, his voice breaking with an angry flow of words that Baier could not distinguish between Vietnamese or Chinese. Or any other Asian language. Led by the two security guards, Baier and de Couget pushed past the man and found themselves in a large open room that had probably served as a warehouse at one time. The little thin man hustled to a stairway at the back, waving his arms for the new party to follow him.

The entire group climbed the stairs to the second floor. Their guide swung around the railing and marched down a narrow hallway to another door at the back. Baier figured they had stashed Pyle here to keep him as far away from the street as possible. Then again, he doubted anyone would have heard him if he cried out, given the overwhelming noise and bustle in the streets below. The little man knocked, then pounded his fist when no one answered.

After about thirty or forty seconds, the door opened a crack. De Couget's team thrust themselves between the guide and the door, then smashed their way inside. The room was empty except for a cot in the middle, on which a prostrate Pyle lay silent and motionless. Two hulking Vietnamese sat in a row of chairs against a back wall. Baier glanced in their direction, then walked over to Pyle. His face was lined with grime and sweat. His shirt had been ripped down the front, the buttons gone. Baier could see that Pyle had also wet himself, his crotch disfigured by a large stain. He felt for a pulse but found nothing.

When he turned to demand an explanation from the two watchmen, one of them met Baier's gaze with a wicked smile of arrogance and superiority. He leaned back in his chair and shook his head. Baier marched slowly up to him, his hand on the Browning tucked into his waistband in the hollow at his back. Before he knew what he was doing, Baier had leaped at the man, smashing the side of his face with the Browning over and over again.

"You son of a bitch," Baier screamed. "You fucking sons of bitches. What have you done?" The Browning smashed into the side of the guard's face once, twice. "How dare you? Just who the fuck do you think you are?"

Baier did not know how long this went on. He didn't know later how far he would have gone, whether he would have beaten the man to death. All he knew was that at some point everything went black, and he slipped into a deep hole that no longer seemed like Viet Nam, or Saigon, over even Europe and America. It was a new place, a strange one. It was like nowhere he had been before. It was almost like Hell.

• • •

When Baier awoke, he found himself in the same warehouse-like room that he remembered. And that was about all he remembered. He now had a cot of his own. He assumed he was still in Cholon, which did not surprise him. That was easy enough. What did surprise him was that he had been left unbound. Nor was he alone. Pyle still lay on the cot, but now he was resting on his side, his eyes open and focused on Baier. His lips were moving, but no sound escaped. Pyle was not tied up either.

Baier shifted his weight from one buttock to the other, and an immediate and sharp pain ran through his skull. His shirt was soaked through with sweat, and his mouth was also dry. It took a few seconds for the room to come into focus. He and Pyle were alone.

"What the hell happened?" he asked.

Pyle did not answer at first. He simply smiled, weakly. Then he tried to speak, but the words came slowly and with a good deal of effort.

"I..." Pyle shook his head. "I don't know. I was out." He paused. It sounded to Baier as though he was struggling to catch his breath. "I heard them talking. You went crazy. Someone said they had to knock you out." A small, light laugh slipped out. "I think you hurt the guy pretty bad."

Baier held his head between his hands before speaking again. The pain was smaller now and the throbbing shorter.

"What happened to de Couget and his team? Where are they? And where is everyone else?"

Pyle shrugged. At least to Baier it looked like something that approximated a shrug. "Don't know." Pyle had a bout of coughing and some heavy breathing for about a minute. "I feel lousy. Just want to sleep."

Baier felt the same, although he recognized that he was in far better shape than Pyle, who appeared to have been heavily drugged once again. Baier sat up, slowly. Then he waited for the pain and dizziness to pass.

"Can you move? I think we should try to get out of here."

"No, I just want to sleep some more. I'll be better in a little while."

Baier stood, and he stumbled when he tried to take his first few steps. Once he felt like he was standing on solid ground, Baier walked slowly to Pyle's cot. "Come on. We need to try to get out anyway."

But it was too late.

• • •

When he heard the sound of movement behind him, Baier turned. Once again, he moved too quickly and stumbled, barely getting Pyle back onto the cot. Then he turned and found himself staring into the face of the creep he had encountered that first morning at *La Maison des Reves*. Baier nodded to himself. He still couldn't be sure. But at this point, he looked more Russian than ever.

If anything, he looked bigger than Baier remembered him. The broad shoulders and thick arms gave the impression of great strength, but the small waist and thin legs that extended from the khaki shorts made him look as though he stood on a weak foundation. He almost expected to see the man totter and fall when he moved. Baier wondered just what might happen if it came a fight, if he tried to make his move to get the hell out of this room and out of Cholon. Would he be able to use the man's weight to topple him over? At the moment, though, it was no more than an academic question. Baier doubted he could best anyone in his current condition. Certainly not a beefy-looking Russian who no doubt had help at hand.

"Ah, Mister Baier. I am so happy you took bait." The man looked over at Pyle. "He made it quite easy, actually. You should train your people better, especially in operation like this."

"What operation would that be?" Baier asked.

"The one to find out who I am and what I do here." He stood silent in front of Baier, not more than three or four feet away. Baier noticed the crooked, yellow teeth and a breath that stank of stale smoke and old fish. "Imagine my joy over knowledge that you were here as well. I had hoped your curiosity would overcome judgement. How you say, get better of you."

"And who told you about me? Just who do you think I am?"

"Oh, I know who you are. You work for CIA, of course. That is probably why you guessed correctly about me at outset. I work for KGB. My name is Vladimir."

"Vladimir what?"

He smiled again and shook his head. "No, never mind about that."

"And your mission here?"

The smile stayed in place. "Never mind about that either. Because for now that has changed. You are new mission."

"Me? Your superiors must not trust you with anything truly important."

This time the Russian laughed. It was a loud and hearty laugh that came from deep inside his chest. "Oh, you are important enough. At least to me. After all, you are prick who got Chernov to sneak out of Berlin and tell you about so much of operations in

Europe. You also killed perhaps best Ukrainian assassin."

"That wasn't me. That was one of your own. An East German."

The Russian nodded. "Nice try. I know it was you and that colleague Pittmann. He will get his, too. Just wait."

"No, really," Baier insisted. "You are mistaken. We wanted to bring your fat boy in. He was much more valuable alive. The Stasi prick shot him to prevent that."

"Never mind. I have you now. I will find out everything I need to know." The Russian clapped his hands together. "And more, too." He looked over at Pyle, who had fallen back to sleep. "How is your friend? We will move him now."

"No wait. He is very sick. He needs a doctor."

"Ach, no. We give him some more opium when he wakes. That will make him much easier to handle."

"If anything happens to him, you Russian bastard, I will see to it that you pay. In fact, I will personally deliver your punishment myself."

Another full-throated laugh rang through the empty warehouse. "Ha. Big talk for someone in your position. Maybe I give you chance to punish me. That would be fun."

"Fuck you. Where is the Frenchman?"

"Oh, him. He is gone. He is not coming back. I see to that. His team is gone also. Really gone." The Russian shook his head and glanced at the ceiling before returning his gaze to Baier. "You may not believe me, but I find such violence unfortunate. How you say, distasteful? It should not be like this between us." He shrugged. "But you brought weapons and attacked one of my men."

"Who hit me?"

"One of Frenchman's team. He was with us. The other one is dead. So no help there."

"And how did you discover that I was here in Saigon? Not many people knew."

The Russian waved his hand at nothing in particular. "Oh, that was easy. Our people in Hanoi found out. North Vietnamese tell them."

"And how did they know?"

Vladimir shrugged. "Who knows. Probably from someone in South Vietnamese service." The next smile was the broadest the Russian had used since he arrived at the warehouse. "You see, you really have no chance here. You will lose, and we will keep you tied up for years." The fat laugh burst through the air again. "You will waste away. Eventually. Easier for us then to win."

"But the Chinese will replace you in Hanoi's favor. They probably already have."

The Russian displayed his first bout of anger. He almost spit in Baier's face with a stream of obscenities that flowed across the space between them. "Those bastard pricks can try all they want. We are leader of revolution. Fuck them. Fuck them. We are true anti-imperialists here. The Vietnamese hate Chinese. Too much bad history between them."

It was then that Baier got a sense of what Vladimir's true mission was—or had been. But where did he himself fit in, Baier asked himself. And did this mean he also had a 'new' mission to go with his original one?

"Let's go," Vladimir barked in Russian. Baier understood that much. So did the guards, which was just one more surprise for the morning.

CHAPTER FIFTEEN

Baier and Pyle were still untied and free to move about the new room. Neither one had any idea where they were, not exactly. They knew they were still in the Cholon quarter, or at least Baier guessed that was the case because he could hear the Saigon River running just behind their building. He guessed that made sense, since Cholon, Pyle had informed him, was an old Chinese— Mandarin, he thought—word for 'embankment.' Or the modern version of the term.

Of course, the river ran for some length through the city. But their transport to the new site had been short and simple. Not a lot of turns, and not a lot of time in the trunk of the car. The blindfolds had not really been necessary, at least not for most of the drive. Apparently, though, their captors had not wanted them to see what the new prison looked like, or its exact location on the street.

Ropes to bind their hands and feet were also not necessary. Baier and Pyle had both tried the two doors at either end of the room, and they were definitely locked. Solid as Fort Knox, in Pyle's words. They were also pretty heavy, or they certainly felt like it when Baier had tried using his shoulder to force one open. The windows were also shut tightly, especially when one considered the nails that had been driven through the frames and into the walls. Their captors had also not bothered to beat either of the two Americans. A lonely guard stood watch, but he spent most of his time with a nodding head as he fought off a nap.

All things considered, their captivity had not been all that torturous, except, of course, when Pyle had been drugged and Baier had been knocked unconscious. That must have been a relatively light touch, though, because the pain in his skull had subsided quickly. In fact, the worst part about their imprisonment was the heavy, fetid air that hung in the enclosed space without a fan to help move it around. Forget any air conditioning. Baier doubted such a thing existed in this part of town. The smell didn't help either. Baier guessed they were sitting above a butcher's shop or maybe a fish stall. Whatever it was, the stench suggested the produce had been out in the open too long. Maybe their captors were going to force them to eat as a new form of torture.

Another surprise had been Pyle's quick recovery. Relatively speaking, of course. Despite Vladimir's threat, their captors had not forced any more opium upon the American. He certainly looked better than when Baier and de Couget had discovered Pyle in the 'strategic hamlet' outside Saigon. He wondered if Pyle's addiction had been long enough to allow him to recover and function relatively easily, or whether the Russian and his team had used the drug sparingly. If so, he doubted it was because the stuff was in short supply.

Baier still had his watch and wallet, so robbery was definitely not at play, even as a sideshow.

After about an hour, Vladimir returned with a former member of de Couget's security team. Baier recognized him from the trailing car on their last excursion. He hoped the thug was a 'former' member, since that would imply that the Frenchman had not been a part of the trap. One more thing to consider as Baier fought through the pain and confusion to figure out what the hell was going on.

Now, Vlad and his buddy were accompanied by two more Vietnamese, both of whom carried AK-47s and who greeted the other security goon like a long lost friend. Apparently, the bonds of gangsterism stood strong in Vietnam.

"I apologize for inconvenience and discomfort," the Russian said. "But I am sure you understand why is necessary."

"No, I don't. Why don't you tell me," Baier replied.

For the first time, Vladimir looked frustrated and even a little angry. "Because, Mister Baier, it is necessary for me to keep you safe..."

"Safe?"

"Yes, safe. Or perhaps I should use your word for safekeeping. I do not want you to get away before I am finished."

"And when will that be?" Pyle asked.

The Russian turned. "Ah, he speaks. I hope you recover from your accidental overdose."

"Accident my ass," Pyle nearly shouted. "You're making me regret all the aid and assistance we gave you back in World War II."

Vladimir walked calmly over to Pyle, then slapped him across the face with the back of his hand. "Now that angers me a great deal. I always suspect that you Americans preferred Nazis over us and were simply letting them bleed and weaken us." He turned to Baier. "Your country not understand what we went through at hands of Nazis."

"Don't be ridiculous," Baier shouted. His anger at the blow to Pyle grew even more intense by this blindingly stupid comment from the KGB officer. He had heard it before and considered it an insult to the sacrifices the United States had made to help defeat the Nazis. That included his own service with the OSS, as well as the sufferings and sacrifices of his parents and others like them. "Don't be such a stupid son of a bitch."

The Russian turned back towards Baier. "You are making this so much easier."

He signaled to the guards, who marched over to the chairs where Baier and Pyle sat. One of them struck Pyle first with an open-fisted slap to the face, then did the same to Baier. The other two then tied their arms and legs together, the arms behind the chair and the legs shackled at the ankles. Baier tasted blood, but he couldn't be sure if the cut came from his lip or his nose. Both hurt like hell.

"Just what do you think you're doing?' Baier asked. He was incredulous. "Just what do you think you're going to achieve with this? If you want information, you have the wrong people."

The Russian smiled. "We shall see." He laughed. "And even if you don't give me information. I can still pay you back for stealing Comrade Chernov. You see, you have added personal element to this."

"Stealing? He came of his own accord. He wanted to leave your godforsaken country and its bankrupt system."

"That's not what happened. Not from what I have heard. You will start by telling me where he is being held."

"He's not being held anywhere. He's living in America of his own free will. I realize that such a thing is an alien concept to you…"

Baier's words were interrupted by a fist from one of the Vietnamese goalers to his solar plexus that drove the wind from his body and left him grasping for air to suck into his lungs.

"Consider that as first of what will be many paybacks." Vladimir announced.

"You are an idiot. There really is no hope for people like you." The words struggled to escape in a mixture of breath and spit. When he finally caught his breath again, Baier motioned with his head toward Pyle. "At least let him go. He's not involved in our business anymore. Hasn't been for years. Decades really. He knows nothing."

"Ah so. Then what is he doing here with you? Why was he involved in your search for me?"

"He got overexcited about having something to do. I didn't ask him to get involved. That was all a mistake. He shouldn't have even known about you."

"We shall see about that. But back to you. How did you know my presence here. And who told you about me?"

"You must have a very short memory. Have you forgotten about that morning at the brothel already." Baier forced out a smile. "Then again, it did look like your attention was on other things."

"But how did you guess my background?"

"I didn't. You confirmed it by grabbing first my compatriot here, and then by grabbing me. I guess they don't teach you much about discretion in your service."

"'Discretion'? What does that mean?"

"It means knowing how to fly under the radar, as it were. You know, keeping your cover."

"Ah, I see. But no matter. You will not be telling anyone about me. Not if you do not cooperate." Vladimir's hands rose to rest on his hips, and he thrust out his chest in a moment of triumph. "Now tell me, what is your purpose in being here? What operations have you been involved in? And what contacts have you with Chinese?"

"The Chinese?" Baier was incredulous. No, he was beyond that. More like stupefied. He stared at Vladimir for several seconds, even longer, before speaking again. "What makes you think I've been in contact with any Chinese?"

"Because we know what kind of people you are. It is just like last war. You try to divide us and have us work against each other while you sit back. Watch."

"Is that what you think is going on here? You really are clueless."

"Clueless? What does that mean?"

"Without any idea as to what is really happening."

Vladimir stood and rushed at Baier. His index finger was jutting out like a knife that had stopped inches short of Baier's nose. "You are really making me angry. You are true son of bitch. When I return you will answer all of my questions, or we will beat you until you do. You will be sorry you came to this country. You will really be sorry you met me."

Vladimir paused to consider something that must have been percolating in his feeble brain ever since he had entered the room, or since he had first captured Baier earlier the day before. "And if what you say about Chernov is true, he will suffer same fate that will soon be yours. Think about that until we return." The Russian straightened himself, apparently hoping to make himself as tall and large as possible. "Believe me, I do not enjoy this. This is unfortunately necessary now because of your interference. You have one chance to live. To earn that you must talk. You must tell me what I want to know."

Vladimir stood and let his eyes roll to the ceiling and back to Baier. "I go out now to catch my breath and relax some. We have much work to do."

With that, the Russian turned and marched to the door. Baier almost expected him to goosestep his way out of the room. Vladimir motioned towards the door with his head, and the Vietnamese guards left with him. Baier heard the bolt slam shut once the door closed. Baier immediately turned his head in Pyle's direction.

"Let's find a way to get the hell out of here. I am not looking forward to their return."

"Me either," Pyle said. "Here, wait. I think I can get my hands loose."

"How's that?"

"It's a trick I learned in the OSS. When they tie your hands, try to keep some space between them while they're doing it. That lets you pull them together and wriggle one out. Don't they teach you guys anything these days?"

"Sure. But I guess I skipped the class on the hand-tying tricks."

It took a couple minutes, but Pyle eventually got his hands free, then he untied his legs. He stumbled over to Baier's chair and untied his compatriot. Both men stood shakily at first. After several minutes they got their blood circulating again, and the stinging sensation left their hands and legs.

Baier walked over to one of the two windows that looked out on an alley behind the building they were in. Their new prison was on the second floor, and Baier noticed a pile of trash on the pavement below.

"This looks like our only way out. Hopefully that trash is big and soft enough to break our fall. The fact that we're on the second floor should help as well."

"Do you want to break the windows out? They seemed pretty tightly locked when I checked them before."

"Yeah, the nails made sure of that. But I don't see any other way," Baier answered. "They can send us the repair bill later."

"Got it," Pyle said. "Let's go."

Baier slammed the glass and inner frame with his shoe, then he and Pyle picked the remaining glass shards out of the sides. By crouching nearly in half, both men were able to step through the window frames and leap to the ground below. The trash was a mixture of boxes, old food, and a crate or two. There was also some kind of feces mixed in, which they smelled after they landed. Baier sighed. This would make for an uncomfortable and very ripe trip home.

"Fuck," Pyle exclaimed. "I think I broke my ankle."

Baier helped him stand up and get free of the garbage. He noticed that Pyle's left ankle was indeed crooked and beginning to swell.

"Here, let me help. Swing your arm over my shoulder, and I'll get us to the street."

Pyle did as asked, but then stopped when he looked down. "Your leg is bleeding, man. You must have hit something sharp in there."

Baier followed the path of Pyle's eyes and saw that his right pant leg along the shin was indeed ripped and that a patch of red had begun to grow.

"Shit," Baier shouted. "Let's get moving. This may be a helluva a ride home, but it still beats waiting upstairs for Vladimir and his merry band of gangster thugs."

The two wounded Americans hobbled down an alleyway three buildings log and followed the noise to the Binh Tay Market, where they figured at least one driver would be willing to take them in his rickshaw for a grossly inflated price.

• • •

Crockett greeted Baier in the hallway near the entrance to the Station with his hand outstretched to offer assistance and a look of deep concern on his face. The forehead and eyebrows looked as though they been wrinkled for hours. "They called me from the infirmary and told me about your injury. Let's get you inside and resting."

Crockett stepped towards Baier and the Marine guard who had acted as a human crutch and started to lift Baier free. Baier shifted his weight and took Crockett's arm. Together they limped through the hallway until they reached the sofa in the Chief of

Station's office. "So, how many stitches did you get? And did they give you anything for the pain?"

"I lost count at a dozen. And yeah, I got some pills and a tetanus shot. But thanks, Frank. I appreciate your help. You should know, though, that Pyle is worse off than me."

Crockett sat down behind his desk. "So, he's alive?"

Baier nodded. "Yes, he is. But he broke his ankle during our getaway."

"Then where is he?"

"He asked me to drop him off at *La Maison*. I argued against that, since we don't know what de Couget's role is in all this."

"I really don't trust that motherfucker." Crockett almost shouted his judgment. He sat back hard against the chair, then rolled it forward until the arms hit the desk. "I mean it, Karl."

"Yeah, Frank, but we still don't know for sure how this all went down. There's a chance that his own guards, or at least one of them, betrayed him. In any case, Pyle is convinced there's nothing more to this than a simple betrayal by one of de Couget's men. And he's convinced that our Frenchman is as innocent as a newborn."

"So, tell me just what did go down. At least as much as you know."

Baier relayed the story of the arrival and search in Cholon, the discovery of the abandoned warehouse and Pyle's seemingly lifeless body.

"And you say you lost it when you thought he had been killed?"

"That's right." Baier nodded and glanced out the window. "I think this place could be getting to me. It's been what, a little over a month? And I've already acted like some thug from the Viet Cong, or ARVN even, from what I've been hearing. Not to mention that fucking Russian, who appears to be behind all this."

Crockett leaned forward at his desk. "Listen, Karl, you've been through a lot. And it sounds as though you were provoked pretty well. It happens. It can happen at home and in Europe as well."

"But not like this. This was really dangerous, when I think back on it. And you know that we're trained to control those kinds of emotions. They don't serve any real purpose. They only demean us and our work." He sighed. "And in this case it only made matters worse and more difficult." He pointed at his leg. "I've got the stitches to prove it."

"Okay, okay. I'll arrange for you to go to confession. You've probably noticed that there's no shortage of Catholic churches here. But tell me more about this Russian creep."

Baier sat up and repositioned his leg when it began to throb. "Now, that is an interesting part in all this. In fact, he appears to be the main player behind the events of the last two days. He claims to have engineered Pyle's kidnapping, as well as mine."

"But to what purpose? It's not like those guys are major players here. I'm surprised you've managed to smoke out a single one."

"Yeah, that is interesting. He spoke about colleagues in Hanoi, so they must have a station up there."

"That's not a big surprise when you think about it. I'm sure Moscow wants to give Ho Chi Minh as much help as possible. But I would have thought they'd do that in the comfortable confines of Hanoi. This town is a whole new challenge for those guys, and you can bet the South Vietnamese will be all over them now."

"But I'm surprised our local allies didn't know about Vladimir already. I met with one of the local guys working counter-intelligence, and he claimed to pull a blank when I brought this issue up."

"That's probably just incompetence, Karl. We are trying to help them build up their capabilities in that field as well. I can have you speak with one of the officers on our team that's handling that."

"Thanks, Frank."

"I'd also think the KGB would let the Red Chinese handle this part of the country. There may be a troubled history between the Chinese and Vietnamese over the centuries of Chinese rule and domination here, but the northern neighbors would still have a much better understanding of the Vietnamese than the Russians. I mean, those guys in Moscow are worse racists than we Americans." Crockett shook his head. "And from what I've gathered, the Chinese have been more than helpful to Ho's boys. Certainly more than the Soviets."

Baier started to stand but collapsed when the pain shot

through his shin. "That's just it, Frank. This Vladimir jerk talked as though his main enemy here was the Chinese, not us or the South Vietnamese. In fact, he wanted to know what sort of contacts I had—or we have—with the Red Chinese here."

"What the hell...? Does he really think we would get in cahoots with the Red Chinese after all the shit that's happened. Don't those people read the newspaper?"

"Oh, hell, Frank, they probably distrust our press as much as they do their own. The notion of a journalistic establishment free of governmental control is just too weird for them and the world as they see it."

"Did you disabuse him of this notion?"

"I never got the chance. And I'm not sure I should have. Let him chase these chimeras. It's not going to help them do whatever it is they've been sent down here to do."

"Do you think there's more than one? Just how big can this base be?"

"That's another interesting point. The whole time Vladimir was in there, he sounded as though he was working alone." Baier's eyebrows rose and dropped, then he shook his head. "I'll say this much for him, he did succeed in recruiting some pretty tough gangster types from the old organized crime group that used to run Cholon and its underworld businesses there."

Crockett stood. "He must have had help." He moved around the desk to help Baier stand. "Look, Karl, I've got a meeting with the Ambo. Lodge is getting ready to ship back to the States. No firm date yet, but I'm supposed to bring him fully up to date on our programs here before he goes."

"Do we know who his replacement will be?"

"As a matter of fact, we do. It's going to be General Maxwell Taylor."

"Well, that should be interesting. As I recall from my time in Washington—which seems like ages ago and worlds away—he was one of those who has been resisting the notion of putting US ground forces here. And he was swimming against a pretty strong current."

"Well, maybe he'll be able to do some good on that front from here. His advice should have a lot more weight and credibility coming from the front lines, as it were." Crockett paused. "One more thing. You said this Vladimir mentioned Chernov. Isn't that the KGB guy you brought out from Berlin? If so, that seems like old history. Why bring that up now?"

Baier shrugged. "Got me. I guess some elephants refuse to forget. Especially when you've kicked their asses. He definitely sounded like he wanted some kind of revenge."

"How do you feel about that?"

Baier smiled wide enough and laughed hard enough to forget the pain in his leg. "Fuck 'em, Frank. I say bring it on."

"Well," Crockett continued, "Why don't you give your wife a call before you take the Soviet Union on all by yourself. Sabine needs to know what you've gotten yourself into here. But try not to scare her to death. You don't want her holding a vigil out by the front gate on Route 123."

"Thanks, Frank. I'm way overdue for a call anyways."

"No problem. And you can use my office and phone while I'm with the Ambo. Give you some privacy."

• • •

"Karl, is that you?" Sabine asked.

"Yes, Sabine. It's me."

"It's wonderful to hear your voice again. But, tell me, is something wrong? Or are you calling to tell me you're on the way to the airport. I hope it's my second guess."

"No, Sabine. Unfortunately, it's not the latter. It looks like I'll be here for a little while yet."

"But shouldn't you be finishing up by now?"

"Normally, yes. But I've gotten into a bit of a mess here that I need to straighten out. Hopefully, it won't take too long."

"Karl, dear, that does not sound good at all. What kind of mess is this? And what do you mean by 'too long'?"

Baier shifted his weight in the COS's chair and swallowed hard. "Weeks, honey. Just a few weeks, I swear. It's not like Turkey. And I'll need to let my leg heal properly."

Baier could have sworn later that he had heard his wife's gasp sail through the telephone wire. "What…what has happened? How badly are you hurt?"

"It's nothing, sweetheart, I swear. I'd tell you more but since this is an open line it will have to wait until I'm home."

"Please tell me. You know you don't need to hide anything. I'll just worry endlessly if I don't know for certain what has happened."

"I cut my leg…"

"How badly? Stitches? How many?"

"I'm not sure. I guess a dozen or so. Maybe a few more. But I'll be all right. They took care of it at the infirmary here"

"Well, that's good to hear."

"I've also got some other things to sort out. There are people here who rely on me. It's something I need to fix. Please trust me."

Baier heard nothing for a moment. "Sabine, are you still there?"

"Yes, of course. I'm just frightened for you, Karl. This wasn't supposed to happen. Does the Director know?"

"No, but he will soon. I just need to make certain what is going on before I try to explain things to him."

"Please don't get yourself into another situation like Turkey, Karl."

"No, Sabine, I won't allow that to happen. You mean too much to me."

"It's not just that. You almost lost your life then. Not just our marriage. Please finish the work you were sent out there to do. I know how important that is. Then come home to me. Please come as quickly as you can."

Baier's heart began to rip open at the sound of his wife's voice. "I will, Sabine, I will. I promise."

CHAPTER SIXTEEN

Since Hartnett was still up north at Da Nang, or thereabouts, Crockett had Baier talk to Mark Melby, a fourth tour officer who had been in Vietnam for about a year and a half. As chief of the six-man branch working with the Counter-Intelligence, or CI, department of the South Vietnamese service, Melby was the Station's principal liaison officer for that topic, a job that appeared to be a full-time occupation. Baier was not surprised to learn that his family were a bunch of Swedes from Minnesota, but he was surprised to learn that they were also Catholic.

"Did someone in the past convert to Catholicism?" Baier asked. "I mean, you don't find many Swedish Catholics, except maybe in the movies."

"Which movies would those be?" Melby inquired.

"Well, I seem to remember Ingrid Bergman playing a Swedish émigrée nun in *The Bells of Saint Mary*. You know, opposite Bing Crosby, who actually was a Catholic, by the way."

"No," Melby replied. "I must have missed that one."

"No matter. I'd really like to know what your impression is of the people working CI issues for the local Vietnamese. I imagine the main focus for those guys would be Viet Cong and North Vietnamese infiltration of the Saigon government."

"Yeah, that is certainly right. And from what I've seen it's a pretty hopeless assignment."

"How so?"

Melby scratched his head, then ran his hands through his light brown hair. "Well, my contacts claim they've got a good handle on who they investigate—when they do launch an investigation.

But with the last two coups and the turnover those have brought in the government ranks, it's almost impossible—in my mind—to keep an accurate tab on all the people moving through the offices. Especially when you consider that they don't have the kind of record-keeping that someone like you might be used to working in places like Europe."

"Those places lost a lot of their records and other documentation during and immediately after the war, too, you know. An awful lot of people slipped through the cracks."

"Yeah, but at least the records existed at some point. So, there was always the chance you could find some useful information. On top of that, many of the appointees that come in with the regime changes are personal friends or relatives of the new rulers. Or at least their families are. And that, as you can no doubt imagine, limits what the service is allowed to do in terms of CI and security. Also what it's capable of."

"So, how do you cope?"

"We try to get them to highlight the obvious or really suspicious cases and run a thorough background check. As much as we can, that is. We also try to teach them to check on suspicious behavior, like new sources of wealth or odd hours at work or access to sensitive information they shouldn't have. And then there's the matter of political objectivity."

"Sounds like the kinds of things we look for in our own house or in other services we work with."

"Well, it's what we know. The big thing is to work on that last point, keeping political loyalties out of the equation, or personal vendettas. Accusations are easy to come by, we tell them. But proof is what really matters."

"Do any of your contacts investigate other areas besides VC or North Vietnamese activities?"

"Like what?"

"Like Soviet or potential agents from the PRC."

"You mean the Peoples Republic of China?" Melby thought for a couple seconds, then shook his head. "Naw, there's not much of that. Their resources are pretty well absorbed by the other targets closer to home. There is some concern about the Chinese, since they seem to be providing the bulk of foreign support. But that's all primarily in military aid and advisors. I suppose there is some suspicion about other Communist states, but basically, it's all about the Chinese. There is absolutely no love lost between them and the Vietnamese."

"Try to tell that to people in Washington."

"Really?"

Baier nodded. "Oh, yeah. That's one of the reasons the people around Johnson are so committed to winning this war, if you can call it that. They're afraid the loss of Vietnam to the Communists will simply be the first step in the expansion of a Chinese hegemony in the region. Hegemony with a red overcoat, of course."

"It doesn't sound like they've spoken to many Vietnamese," Melby said.

"No, they've spoken to the South Vietnamese who want to stay in power." Baier paused before redirecting the conversation. "There have also been comments playing on those fears about dominos from others in the region and beyond. Publicly, but not so much in private, from what I've gathered," Baier added. "So, I don't put a lot of credence in statements like that."

"And I haven't noticed much in the way of backup diplomatically or in committing their resources for the fight either," Melby added. "Then again, the Australians are a different matter."

"Back to our point, though, I suppose there's been no interest in or awareness of a KGB presence here," he said.

"Oh, Jesus, no. There's very little concern about the Russians, or any other Europeans for that matter. Except maybe for the French. A lot of these guys do not like the French at all," Melby explained.

"Part of the colonial legacy?"

"That, and the distrust of De Gaulle and his policies. They suspect he wants to sell them out to get in good with Ho Chi Minh and his boys. And this after he cried and whined after the war about restoring French grandeur in Indochina."

"Well, if it's any consolation, a lot of people in Washington feel the same way." Baier held up a finger. "One last question. What's your impression of Le Duc Vien?"

"The CI chief?"

Baier nodded.

"He's seems like a pretty capable and competent guy," Melby continued. "He can be kind of stand-offish. But I think he wants to do right by the government here. I would definitely not place him in the ranks of sympathizers with the VC. And he's certainly easy for us to work with. Almost like an American. I think he picked up some of the slang and mannerisms when he was in the States a couple years ago." Melby shrugged. "At least when he does talk to us."

"That's good to hear. The Greeks have saying, 'A fish stinks from the head first.' It sounds like we don't have to worry about that in this case."

"No. But why do you ask? Have you heard anything on him? If so, please let me know. I do run into that guy over at their headquarters. A stronger relationship would help, but I don't want to overlook anything."

"Just trying to get a feel for the lay of the land. I think I need to swing by and see him. Would you like to join me?"

"For sure. In fact, let's take the guy to lunch. There's a pretty nice French restaurant on Cong Ly, just up from the Gia Long Palace. It's not far from here. We can walk there together once we have an appointment. That should help relax things and get him talkative," Melby suggested.

"Great," Baier agreed. "Let's set it up."

• • •

Melby was true to his word, and quick. The lunch was set for noon, the following day. "I don't doubt that Le Duc Vien made himself available so quickly because of the restaurant," he said. "But it will probably be more like 12:30 once he gets there. You know, Vietnamese time, not like your German friends." And Melby scored a nice reservation in a room off to the side from the main dining room in *Le Montmartre*, where they could talk in private.

"Kind of obvious, isn't it?" Baier had suggested. "The name, I mean."

"Not to worry, Sir. The food is really good there, and they always provide nice and efficient service. It will remind you of Europe. And make you long for a return."

"I already do," Baier said. "Have ever since I got here. Although I have to admit, this place does grow on you." He thought of people like Pyle and de Couget. "It definitely has its attractions for some."

While the two Americans waited for their guest, Baier reflected again on how out of place a setting such as this felt. It was a feeling similar to the one he experienced in the Cathedral. It was a sense that he occupied a parallel universe, part of Vietnam but also separate from it. And one with only a tenuous connection to the real world of Vietnam and its dynamics and history. And he had to ask himself, as they sat in their comfortable cushioned chairs set around an immaculate white table cloth with sterling silver place settings, if the policy mandarins in Washington inhabited the same distant world.

As Melby had predicted Le Duc Vien showed up a minute or two shy of 12:30. He wore a light, beige linen suit with an actual long-sleeve cotton shirt and a bright yellow tie. Baier figured he was dressing up for either the occasion or the restaurant. Maybe it was both.

"I apologize for my tardiness, Gentlemen. Something came up at the last minute that needed my attention. I hope you will understand."

"Of course," Baier replied. "Believe me, we both know what that is like. In our line of work it happens all the time."

"Excellent," Le said. "And thank you for the invitation. This is one of my favorite restaurants in all of Saigon. You must try the *coq au vin*, Mister Baier. I am sure Mister Melby would agree that it is quite delicious here. It is a house specialty."

"Absolutely," Melby echoed. "It's what I am going to have."

"Good then," Vien answered. "That will make three of us." He spread his napkin over his lap as the waiter brought a dish of duck liver pate, which Baier had ordered before Le Duc Vien's arrival.

"So, tell me, what can I do for you gentlemen?"

Baier settled deeper into his chair and waited for their guest to reach for the pate before sampling some himself. Baier then gave the waiter three orders of the house chicken dish and a bottle of Sancerre for the table as well.

"Before we begin, let me express my condolences on the loss of your officer recently. I guess I'll have to blame the lingering effects of my jet lag and acclimation for that lapse in curtesy when we first met," Baier explained.

"Of course. And thank you. I take it you are referring to Nhu Van Kim."

"Yes, that's right. How is the investigation going? Do you have any suspects?"

Vien shook his head. "No, no one in particular yet. But we are certain it was the Viet Cong. We will eventually find out who was responsible. A reprisal will be coming in any event."

"Well, good luck." Baier sampled the pate on a slice of freshly baked French bread. He enjoyed it so much it took him a minute or so before he resumed his conversation with Le Duc Vien.

"That is not the main reason I wanted to meet here today, however. You may not recall from our first meeting at your headquarters that I was curious if your service was aware of any Soviet or Warsaw Pact intelligence work in your country, or in this city in particular."

"Yes, I do recall. And as I remember, I told you that I—or I should say we, meaning our service—was not aware of any such activity. I believe that remains the case."

"I see," Baier said. "What would you say if I was to tell you that I recently experienced such activity myself. It came in the form of a kidnapping and several threats."

Vien leaned in with his half-eaten serving of pate. "That is very interesting. Who was kidnapped, and who was threatened? And by whom?"

"I was kidnapped, along with a retired American, living here in Saigon. We were both threatened."

"Was the American this Pyle character?"

"Yes, as a matter of fact he was," Baier admitted. "Do know the man?"

"We know of him. He is a bit of a nuisance. He has a completely mistaken impression of Ho Chi Minh. I gather he met Ho during the war. I would even label him a bit of a troublemaker."

"That is unfortunate," Baier answered. "But that does not justify his treatment."

Vien nodded as he chewed. "Yes, you are correct, Mister Baier. And you believe it was done by agents of the Soviet Union or one of their Warsaw Pact allies?"

"Yes, I am quite certain of that. The ringleader of the group was a European and the only one in the group. He admitted that he worked for the KGB. He was also working with former gunmen from the Binh Xuyen gang."

"That would be an unfortunate alliance. May I ask where you were held?"

"Cholon."

"Ah, yes. That certainly makes sense. It would be nearly impossible to find you in that human maze, especially if former Binh Xuyen members were involved."

Le Duc Vien was quiet while he ate another serving of the pate, and the waiter brought the bottle of French white wine. Vien's eyes closed as he relished the food and a sip of the wine. "Ah, this is really delicious. I am truly grateful for the luncheon invitation. It is a wonderful courtesy."

Then his face grew serious as his mind returned to the business at hand. "Those bastards." Le looked around the room, not so much for information as to avoid Baier's eyes. "Excuse my profanity, please. But that criminal gang remains a sore subject with me. We tried to eliminate the group almost ten years ago. But they keep popping up, as you American say."

"That is almost an impossible task, if I may say so," Melby stated. "A group of that size and with the role and presence it formerly had..." Melby shrugged, "...you are likely to continue finding them embroiled in something unsavory at times. Probably whenever you look."

"Like now, you mean?" Le Duc Vien asked. "Hiring themselves out to an enemy security service?"

"Sure," Melby said.

"I have to say, though, as regretful as that may be, my primary concern is with the KGB operative," Baier said. "I hope this is the only one, but we cannot be sure, of course."

"Do they always travel in packs?" Duc Vien asked.

Baier smiled. "No, not always. In fact, I have encountered them in all shapes and sizes and configurations. And often alone. It is nice to be sure, though."

"What do you suppose his purpose or mission here to be?"

"Now, that is where it gets interesting," Baier added. "I would have assumed that just about any KGB mission would involve building and training a cadre for some Viet Cong and or North Vietnamese intelligence operations. And it would make sense that he would not restrict himself to the North but also work on that in the South, if possible, to achieve that."

"Yes, of course," Vien agreed.

"But I do not see how surrounding yourself with former gangster thugs contributes to that."

Two waiters arrived bearing their main courses on a large oversized tray. The second server held the tray, while their original waiter distributed the dishes to the three guests, with a curt bow. Baier paused while the waiter also refilled everyone's wine glass. Then, both men backed away from the table and disappeared

"In any case, he showed a surprising interest in any Chinese presence here," Baier continued. "Have you found much of that?"

"Yes," Le replied. "There is some. And it would make sense as well for him to be active in Cholon, if that was his concern. But I would assume that he would be already aware of their presence and plans here. They are, after all, allies."

"Yes, I would assume so as well," Baier replied.

"Well, whatever his interests, Cholon is a good place for him and his organization to start. And it is not a bad idea to find assistance from former gang members. As you are no doubt aware, Mister Baier, that is our own Chinatown. I have visited your famous Chinatown in San Francisco. This one, I assure you, is much more dangerous. Please be very careful if you decide to go there on your own. In fact, I would suggest that you let us know what your plans are for Cholon, so we may assist in providing security for you."

Baier sat back. "Thank you. I appreciate that. It's good to know I have friends like you in Saigon."

"Of course. Now, I suggest we dig in, as your countrymen say, before this delightful chicken gets cold."

• • •

On the way back to their offices, Baier made a sudden suggestion to Melby.

"Let's swing by the scene of that officer's murder."

"The Kim guy? Why? What do you expect to find there?"

"I'm not really sure," Baier said. "But something seems a bit odd about the whole affair."

"Like what?"

"Well, for example, the whole m.o. of the thing. Don't the VC usually make their hits in drive-bys on motor scooters, or even bicycles? Or bomb explosions, for that matter, if they want a bigger bang. No pun intended."

Melby thought for a moment. "True. But it's not like they're wedded to a rigid set of rules. They'll do whatever's most effective."

"Still, let's just check out the site. You know the way, right?"

"Sure."

The side trip lasted about forty or forty-five minutes, and Baier was actually more baffled than before. Kim's apartment was located not that far from *Les Maison des Reves*, but in a more provincial and traditional neighborhood. His place had been at the front of a two-story wooden building with a balcony facing the street. A spray of flame trees at the front added a nice touch of color in an otherwise solemn area, covered by a small lawn. A parking lot that was little more than a glorified alley sat at the rear of the complex, hidden from the street and any foot traffic passing by. A twin row of tropical almond trees set a natural barrier that enveloped the rear and sides of the building. Baier stared at the canopy, thinking that the shade it provided was undoubtedly a welcome benefit. The layout also created a bottleneck in any escape route, leaving only a single driveway between Kim's building complex and a neighboring lot shielded by a tall, wooden fence.

"It looks like it would be relatively easy to shoot Kim without anyone noticing from the street," Baier said.

Melby glanced around the lot and the parking spaces. "Yeah, it certainly does look like it."

"Okay, how did it go down?"

Melby pointed to a back corner behind several parked cars and motor bikes. "Apparently, the assassins were waiting for Kim to get into his car, a Ford, which probably helped with the identification and targeting of the victim."

"How is that?"

"Well, they could be sure they were waiting for the right vehicle. You don't see a lot of Fords on the road here. And the right passenger, if there was any doubt."

"Pretty unlikely," Baier added. "I'm sure they had the hit cased out and well prepared. So, they shot Kim when he climbed into his car?"

Melby nodded. "Not quite. From what I understand, the guy was shot as he sat in his car. We haven't pressed for more information, since it's an internal matter for the service. If we had any additional info, or if the Vietnamese asked, we'd be happy to help."

"But nothing so far?"

"Nope."

"And why this Kim fellow?"

"I can't say for sure. He must have set off some alarm bells within a local VC cadre in a case he was pursuing. I doubt the VC would sit idly by and let him his finish his work if it threatened to disrupt their own programs. Plus, he was known as a good friend of the Americans"

"By whom?"

"I can't say for sure. I gathered it was pretty much general knowledge."

"So, the VC would have known?"

Melby nodded. "Sure. Them and just about everyone else."

Baier studied the corner and the rest of the lot, then walked to the street where their jeep was parked.

"Still, that's a long time to be stationary. Or so I would guess. They must have been confident of a quick getaway. Even in a restricted space like this one. But something just doesn't seem right."

CHAPTER SEVENTEEN

Baier decided to follow up with de Couget the day after. Thanks to the uncertainty regarding the Frenchman's role in the events surrounding Pyle's and Baier's kidnapping and beating, not to mention de Couget's sudden disappearance, Baier wanted to develop a strategy for their confrontation. Given all the uncertainty, however, he never came up with one. So, he decided to drive out to *La Maison des Reves* on his own and launch into the interrogation when he got there.

It took Baier an extra two hours on this trip because he wanted to do a countersurveillance run first. Now that he knew he had become a target, Baier had taken a much more cautious approach on all his travel around Saigon. He had found proper counter-surveillance a tricky episode at best, given the lack of experience in working with the Vietnamese and other Asians and the overcrowded streets through which he had to drive and walk. On top of that, he got lost twice, thanks to his use of unfamiliar streets, all of which made this particular run longer than necessary.

"Jesus," Baier had once noted to Crockett, "I look one way and see thousands of Vietnamese. Then I look the other way and see a thousand more. How the hell am I supposed to pick possible surveillants out of a crowd like that?" Baier asked.

"Very carefully," the Chief had replied.

One advantage this time, though, was that he knew his principal antagonist and was pretty sure he could identify him once he saw him. It was the others the Russian might be working with that baffled him. Baier knew there was no way he would be able to keep track of people who blended into the crowded streets like leaves in a jungle. He would simply have to do his best to look for repeated sightings and hope the clothes or vehicles would give any tail away.

At least he believed he had less to worry about in terms of a bomb under his seat. Although the individual who Baier believed had placed the bomb was long gone, he still couldn't be sure that someone else would not simply replace him. But the front of *La Maison* would seem to be a much less accessible place to try something like that again; the more he thought about it the less certain Baier was that the bomb hadn't been little more than a warning. The placement was so amateurish and easy to spot. Still, he made sure to check his undercarriage and engine whenever he took a vehicle through the city.

When Baier pulled up in front of *La Maison*, he left his jeep parked by the front door, his favorite new spot. He also reminded himself to search the vehicle before he left.

De Couget was, as usual, settled comfortably behind his desk. That seemed to be the throne from which the Frenchman ruled his empire: aloof and separate enough to remind everyone of his elevated status, but close enough to keep tight control over what could become a loose and dangerous business.

"Ah, Mister Baier, you cannot imagine how happy I am to see you safe and sound." De Couget leaped from his chair and hustled around the desk to greet Baier. The Frenchman actually reached out and embraced Baier by the shoulders.

Baier did not respond to the hug. "I can imagine you are surprised," Baier said as the Frenchman released him. "But I have no idea whether you are actually happy or not.' Baier raised his pant leg. "As you can see I was wounded while escaping.'

"Yes, yes. Our friend Pyle showed me his broken ankle, and he told me of your injury. Hopefully, you are not in too much pain."

"It's not too bad. Not now. The doctor gave me some pills for that. But as you can probably imagine, I have a few questions for you."

"Yes, of course. I will help in any way I can."

Baier walked back to the sofa and lowered himself into the corner, resting his back against a cushion that felt very plump and well stuffed. He also recognized the new color, a dark green that almost seemed out of place in this city. Certainly in this establishment. "New furniture?"

De Couget nodded as he rested his rear end on the edge of his desk. "Yes. Business has been very good lately. War always seems to do that."

"Well, I'm happy for you. But tell me again how you knew where to go to find Pyle."

"As I mentioned before. My men still have some contact with former colleagues in the Binh Xuyen gang, and they were able to use those contacts to find out who was responsible for snatching Mister Pyle. They may have been a little rough, but sometimes that is necessary."

"Yes, well, apparently, they were not quite rough enough. You did not know of the traitor in your midst?"

"No, of course not. He is no longer with us, by the way. I mean on this planet, not just this establishment. I have seen to that."

"And how can you be sure there are not others here like him?"

De Couget shrugged. "Mister Baier, one can never be one hundred percent sure of something like that. It is one of the risks in this business, and especially in this country at present. But we are being more careful in whom we hire and the jobs they have. We cannot perform a completely thorough check beforehand. I am sure you will understand."

"Okay. What I do not understand, though, is what happened to you when I was knocked out. Why and how did you disappear from that warehouse?"

"Yes, that does look suspicious."

"I'll say."

"Well," de Couget continued. "Once the shooting started, I pulled out my own weapon—a Makarov pistol I took from a dead Viet Minh officer during the fighting around Dien Bien Phu—and shot at the other guards. I don't know if I killed anyone, or even hit anyone. But I am pretty certain I shot the man who hit you over the head. I slipped out of the building just as the Russian was arriving. I recognized him from his visits here and knew immediately that you had been right about him."

"I thought you said he was Bulgarian."

"No, that is what one of the girls here said. She later told me he admitted that he was a Russian and on a dangerous mission against the Americans. It was not the first reason he came, but that had changed."

Baier leaned forward. "That is an awful lot to admit to anyone, much less a prostitute."

De Couget shrugged. "I guess he was trying to impress her. It is something many men would do in the presence of a beautiful woman. It does not always matter if she is a prostitute. And this is his favorite woman. I think he is quite smitten."

"Are you worried for her safety?"

De Couget shook his head. "No, not anymore. The Russian will not be coming back here. My guards have orders to shoot the man on sight. Besides, he never impressed his favorite paramour that he was a violent person. She claimed he could be very sweet and generous."

"Hmmm, a man of contradictions."

"Most of us are, Mister Baier."

"So, where is Pyle now?"

De Couget's eyes rose to the ceiling before coming back down to Baier. "He is upstairs resting. He has been since he returned. I took him to the hospital and brought him back here, where my employees can take care of him. I feel responsible in some ways."

De Couget's wife entered the room and moved over next to her husband at his desk. She rested her head on his shoulder, and he patted her hand.

"From what I see," Baier said, "you are responsible in a lot of ways. Your people led us into that mess and never bothered to get us out."

"But Mister Baier, if you had not attacked that one man we would have been able to escape untouched. By the way, he was seriously hurt. He did not die…"

"How do you know that?"

"I heard some of my guards discussing it. In any case, you lost control of yourself. That was a critical moment."

"No, you are not going to get off that lightly, de Couget. You put us in that situation, and I will find out why. And I am holding you responsible for Pyle's further safety. If anything happens to him, you will have to answer for it."

"Yes, of course," de Couget answered. "I am happy to accept that responsibility."

Later, while he was bent over exploring the jeep's undercarriage, Baier swore to himself that he still did not trust de Couget. The Frenchman's answers had been too easy, too pat. And Baier wondered why Pyle was so comfortable with the man and felt so secure.

• • •

"You will have to give him more, you know."

De Couget's wife spoke to him in her tribal dialect. When she continued, she switched to French.

"He is too persistent. And this matter clearly means a great deal to him. He did not appear convinced."

Yes," de Couget said, "I believe you are right. I just hope it does not come to something more drastic."

"But it is all traveling down that very path right now."

De Couget stroked his wife's hand, then kissed her forehead. "I promise to be careful."

"We do not need to be involved with the death, or even injury, of an American," she added.

"I will see to it that nothing more happens to Pyle."

"And the other one? This Baier person?"

De Couget sighed. "He is a professional. He will have to look out for himself."

CHAPTER EIGHTEEN

When Baier returned to the Station, Crockett's secretary was waiting for him in the hallway. She wore a worried look, underlined by the movement of her hands which repeatedly swept from her hips to her waist, stopping only to clasp each other and then circle her wrists before starting the whole process over again.

"The Chief needs to see you now. Right away, he said."

"Of course," Baier replied. "Did he say what about?"

She simply shook her head. At least the hands stayed still after she had delivered her message, Baier noticed.

Crockett jumped up from behind his desk when Baier entered the office. "Good, Karl. I'm glad you're here."

"What is it, Frank? Not another kidnapping I hope." Baier remained by the door.

Crockett actually smiled. "No, no. Nothing like that. The Director just called. He wants to speak to you soonest. He instructed me to find you and call him back immediately."

"Any idea what he wants?" Baier stepped inside and stopped in front of the Chief's desk.

Crockett let a grimace slide across his face before it disappeared with a shrug. "I can't really say. Although he did not sound happy. Where do things stand with your report? I'm guessing that's what's on his mind."

"Well, Frank, you do understand that I've hit what you might call a bump in the road. The last few days have been rough. Kind of hard to concentrate at the moment."

Crockett stared at his colleague. "I'd find another way to phrase that, if I were you, Karl."

Crockett sat back down and lifted the receiver on the secure communications phone to Langley. Within the space of about thirty seconds, he spoke into the phone, apparently to the Director's chief of staff. He nodded several times, then passed the receiver to Baier, who remained standing at the desk. Crockett came around and pushed a chair behind Baier.

Baier raised his hand in appreciation and fell into the seat, speaking with the Director at the same time.

"Yes, Sir, I understand that." He paused. "Let me put this on the speaker phone, if I may, Sir. Frank Crockett is here and it would probably help if he listened in to our conversation. We're in his office and can close the door the door to keep our conversation private."

Baier nodded some more. Then he turned to the Chief and passed the receiver back. Crockett selected the appropriate button, then replaced the receiver in its slot.

"As I mentioned to the COS, Karl, I think it's time for you to return. We originally agreed on a six-week interim out there, although I do recall that we agreed we could be flexible. We're nearing the end of February—it is now the 20th back here—so your time in Vietnam has just about run out."

"Yes, Sir. But several things have come up, and I could use some of that flexibility now."

"Like what? I hope I do not need to remind you that we are in the midst of very important and very difficult conversations in Washington, and I would benefit greatly from your observations. Especially since Secretary McNamara told me of your rather negative outlook when you met with him last month."

"Well, Sir that is accurate. I've formed my opinion, but I would like to discuss them with Frank before I put anything to paper."

"One thing that is definitely on my mind is the state of the covert action program there. That will be the subject of a Principles Meeting this week. What have you gleaned on that topic from your time in country?"

"I'm afraid, Sir, that my opinion there will be even more negative."

"Why is that?"

"Sir, a Station officer I've been working with here just returned from a temporary assignment up north to oversee our participation in the Military's running of our old program."

"And?"

Baier thought back to his time shortly after he arrived to take over his post on the seventh floor as the Special Advisor for Strategic Affairs. He had watched as McNamara, per JFK's orders, had assumed control of the covert action program that was supposed to be infiltrating and promoting a resistance movement while also collecting intelligence during the forays and insertions in the North. 'Do to those creeps what they're doing to the South,' in the words of one Administration official. But JFK and his brother Robert had been sorely disappointed by the meager results won by the Agency between 1961 and 1963, so control of the operations had been turned over to the Pentagon, where McNamara was so sure that a superior commitment of resources would bring the desired outcome.

"Have they achieved anything of note since the Army began running the covert action program?" the Director pressed.

"In the words of the officer who just returned, Sir, 'nothing has changed. Not a damn thing.'"

"You mean all those numbers McNamara and his whiz kids were going to throw at the problem haven't made any difference?" McCone continued.

"He claims the only difference has been that more of the Vietnamese we send into the north get captured or killed almost right away. He referred to them as 'poor suckers.'"

"As I recall, we were supposed to provide several dozen officers to assist the Military in establishing and running the infiltration and influence operations. There was some resistance on our part, which was understandable, and I realize that our people in country wanted to make sure that the Army did not poach any more of our resources for their programs. Has that happened?"

Baier looked over at the Station Chief, who nodded. "Yes, Sir. I believe Colby was right, insertions and fostering an opposition movement are a waste of time in that environment. Look at what we ran into in Eastern Europe and China." Crockett continued to nod, more vigorously as the conversation proceeded. "If I may be so bold, Sir, Frank Wisner's pipe dreams about replicating the efforts of the OSS and British SAS teams in World War II cost us too much. And we got nothing in return. It's the same in North Vietnam."

"Then remind me, just how much do we have up there in the way of resources these days?"

"Well, Sir, not nearly what we promised. We've been able to limit it to nine people so far. And none of them are working on insertions or sabotage or any of that nonsense."

"Why so few, and why exactly does the Military still need our help?"

"It's because they don't have anyone with the necessary experience to build and run a program like that," Baier replied. "The Army brass does not like covert ops, Sir, and nobody's career, and I mean nobody's career, progresses working on that stuff."

"Then what are we doing up there? The Agency, I mean."

"Mostly psychological operations. 'Psyops,' Sir, in Agency parlance. Forgeries, leaflet drops, radio broadcasts. Things like that."

"Has anything been achieved there?"

"Some, Sir, but not much. A few of the forgeries of letters that we sent in have gotten some party bigwigs in trouble. The radio stuff also helps give the people a more realistic view of what's going on down here and in their own country. That is, if they own a radio and have the electricity to use it. Which is probably very, very few. But none of it is going to make much of a difference, if you ask me."

"Why not?"

"Because it's just a pile of pinpricks. There's no overall strategic objective. Nor does it appear to be coordinated as part of a broader US strategy for Vietnam." Baier paused. "I'm sorry to give you such a negative impression, Sir. I hope that doesn't make you the spoiler at the next Principals Committee meeting.

"That's alright, Karl. If that's our view then they'll just have to listen. Whether the actually want to hear that or act on it is something else entirely. That's beyond our purview."

"Yes, Sir."

"But back to the original purpose for my call. It's time to wrap things up, Karl. I want a written report from your visit on my desk by the end of next week. That gives you ten whole days. See that's it done."

"I will certainly aim for that, Mr. McCone."

"And I don't care what else is going on. I gather from the restricted back-channel reporting that you've gotten yourself into some kind of mess with some characters in Saigon. That is not your job. Get back to the real reason you are out there, Karl."

"Yes, Sir. Understood."

Baier let the receiver slip back into its cradle without a sound, with almost no movement on his part.

• • •

It was the tail that he noticed first. It took Baier a while to figure out that they must have been government workers, presumably from the local liaison service. But which branch they represented was anyone's guess at this point. Either that, or they were some very well-disguised Viet Cong–or maybe even some more Binh Xuyen gangsters.

It had been several days since his and Pyle's escape from their ineffective kidnapping, a period in which Baier had been expecting some sort of sign of renewed interest on the part of the KGB thug or whoever else he might have recruited or purchased for his operation. Whatever that was. Maybe the Russian had returned to Hanoi or Moscow for a new set of instructions or a new project, or maybe to spend some time in the cellars of Lubyanka. Then again, maybe he had simply been cooling his proverbial heels and adjusting his operation, or bringing in extra help.

The puzzling thing for Baier was that this crew did not look like anyone he might recruit or use for the same kind of operation. These guys looked like a surveillance team and nothing more. They used scooters, exclusively—from what Baier had been able to pick out anyway. There were some foot soldiers involved, mostly relay men or substitutes when one of the scooter people—basically one, sometimes two guys on a machine—needed to switch off.

All the men wore the business casual uniform of long and lose khaki slacks with short-sleeved sports shirts that hung over the waistbands to the tops of their slacks. Each had a pistol, always a revolver, sitting in a small holster clipped to their belts at the hip. The untucked shirts helped hide those weapons at times. But Baier was almost always able to identify the bulges at the side of their waists.

He had not been able to single out any automobiles. Then again, that would have been a chore, since he would have had to find something distinguishing about any one of the innumerable Citroens or Renaults that roamed the streets, plus all the damn taxis. Besides, with Saigon traffic being what it was—crowded and plodding—surveillance with an automobile would have been a real challenge, and not very effective.

But there had been enough of the guys on the streets and sidewalks that Baier had recognized that established and later confirmed in his mind that he was being followed—and heavily. It was like they wanted him to know that he was not going to get away with anything. Baier was also not going to be able to use the traffic to escape their surveillance, since the traffic police halted all oncoming cars and waved the scooter teams through to make sure they could keep up.

"I can't figure it out," Baier exclaimed to Crockett. "Why the hell all this heavy surveillance? What do they expect to happen? And don't they have better things to do?"

"Apparently not. Have you checked with Melby or anyone on his team?"

Baier nodded. "Yeah, of course. He's as confused as me. Do you recall this sort of thing before? I mean, it has to be the government service. And we're supposed to be their friends."

"I'm not sure I'd go that far. Patrons maybe, or sponsors. But the people here have a long history and long memories. I doubt they see anyone as their 'friends.' And the same goes for those guys on the other side up north, or their minions down here."

"Maybe I should head out to their headquarters to press them on this."

Crockett frowned. "I'm not sure you want to show your hand. Not just yet anyway."

"Hell, Frank, they're probably wondering why I haven't called them on it yet. It's not like they're being subtle about this."

"I don't think subtle is in their vocabulary. At least not when they're dealing with us. If it is the locals, they clearly want something from you. Maybe that's what you should press them on. But Karl..."

Baier turned. "Yeah?"

"Keep the Director's words in mind. He sounded pretty serious and not a little upset."

"Yeah, I know. I know."

• • •

Instead, Baier went to see Pyle first. He was still "resting" at *La Maison des Reves*, sitting upright against a small mountain of pillows in a bed with clean white sheets and a small fan blowing in his direction from the windowsill. Baier was almost envious. He became downright jealous when a young woman brought in a tray with two teas and a plate of American fig newtons. She was not dressed for work, Baier guessed, but she might as well have been. She wore a loose-fitting set of silk pajamas that looked much like the daily wear of the women of Saigon. Baier had quickly determined that the phrase "loose-fitting" was clearly a misnomer for these outfits, since they still displayed a woman's figure as well as any tight-fitting outfit he had ever seen, and this pair was black, which only seemed to heighten the erotic effect of her wardrobe. She smiled at Pyle as she set the tray on a bureau by the door, then turned and left without even appearing to notice Baier's presence.

"Well, it looks like your French friend is taking good care of you," Baier said. "How's the ankle coming along?"

"Oh, pretty well. I guess. About as good as one might expect. Have you been able to find out anything more about who was behind our adventure in Cholon?"

"No, not yet," Baier answered. "But my suspicions about the Russian asshole were right, as it turns out. I just can't nail down at this point what his ultimate objective is. Or was. He hasn't been around lately. Not that I can tell anyway." Baier mentioned the spate of surveillance.

"Now that is strange," Pyle said. "Those guys are usually more subtle when it comes to dealing with us."

"Say what? That's not the way I heard it."

"Oh, come on, man. They've been at this game a lot longer than we have. They definitely want something of you. You might as well ask them directly. I wouldn't try to outsmart them."

Of course not, Baier thought. At least not unless you're sober. "Any ideas as to what they might want. If that is the case."

Pyle turned and beat the pillows at his back to create a more comfortable seating arrangement. "Yeah. They don't want you to act on this thing alone. They'll want to know everything that's going on in their patch."

"How do I know I can trust them?"

"You can't. And don't fool yourself on that score. But they're probably the best friends you can have if you want to operate in this town, and especially in Cholon. They're the only ones who can match up with the Binh Xuyen guys. Even if their power was broken by Diem in the 1950s. The old gangsters might not have much organizational punch these days. But they do still have a network of sorts. Certainly more than you'll have if you go up against those guys alone."

"Speaking of trust," Baier continued, "how's your relationship with de Couget these days?" He glanced around the room. "He obviously likes you, or wants to hold your friendship, judging by the set up you've got here."

"That's right. He hasn't asked for anything in return either."

"You don't wonder why he was nowhere to be found back at the warehouse when we were trapped and beaten?"

"Not really. He says he got away after a gunfight. He may even have shot three of their people. He's not sure."

"Neither am I."

"What else would you expect him to do?"

"That's some pretty fancy gunwork for an older man, and one who's been running a whorehouse of late."

"But remember, he was a Legionnaire. Some things stay with you from a bunch like that."

"So they say."

"Meaning?"

"Meaning we're all human. We all lose a step, and we're all vulnerable at some point."

• • •

The first attack was a drive by. Baier later thought about how at first he felt like he was in some Hollywood set up with the bad guys spraying the café with tommy guns. De Couget had once said they all liked to watch American gangster movies, so maybe that was their inspiration. But it was a single shooter, and he was using an AK-47, held waist high and without much of an aim…and they didn't use an old Model A Ford. Instead, Baier saw the shooter escape on the back of a scooter, disappearing into the vast sea of humanity that parted like the Red Sea to let the bastard through. Those that weren't spread out on the ground already. He also left his automatic lying on the sidewalk as he and his partner sped away.

Baier had just shut the stall door in the toilet when the sound of rapid gunfire erupted out front. He slammed the door open and came out in a crouch to make sure he was alone in the restroom. He moved slowly to the door and peeked out.

The scene before him was one of complete chaos and destruction. From what Baier could see, the gunner emptied his magazine, threw it to the ground once the clip was empty, then turned and ran into the street when a scooter pulled up behind him. He quickly hopped aboard, and the duo raced to freedom. Pedestrians scattered and cars honked and swerved, adding to the panic that spread over the scene like a plague.

People lay all over the floor, many covered in broken glass from the shattered front windows. There were pools of blood and splashes sprayed along the walls. Baier crawled forward to see if he could help with the wounded, several of whom were bleeding profusely, thin streams blood running to a small sea of dark scarlet that seemed to grow and congeal at the same time.

He whipped off his belt to use a tourniquet for one women who had a gash in her thigh, probably from a glass splinter. The man next to her was dead, half his head missing.

There were three more fatalities, each of them with huge holes ripped in the upper torsos from the rounds of the AK-47. Numerous others had cuts from flying glass or bullet wounds, about a half dozen looking pretty serious. Baier ripped a tablecloth into strips and did what he could to halt, or at least slow, the bleeding, cramming fabric into bullet wounds and cuts and instructing the people with sign language to hold the material tight against the wound.

'Keep the pressure on' was his mantra. He doubted many understood.

After about fifteen or twenty minutes, the police arrived. Baier gave them a statement, then left for the Station. He had been lucky, he later admitted to Crockett. "Which is good if you're slowing with age."

"So, you got up and went to the john at just the right time?" Crockett asked. "That is pretty damn lucky."

"Yeah," Baier confessed. "Luck, timing, and advancing old age kept me alive to run away another day."

"Sounds like it was a VC hit, although those guys generally prefer bombs. Gives them an early start on their get-away."

"Well," Baier added, "they were wearing the shorts and loose, well-worn shirt with sandals that one associates with the Viet Cong. The scooter, too."

"I wouldn't be too sure about the scooter. Everyone drives those damn things. I'll have somebody check with the locals to see what they can find out. Either Melby or Hartnett can do it."

"No, that's okay." Baier waved the suggestion away. "I'd rather go out there myself. I have a few more things to follow up on."

"Like what?"

"Like what the hell is going on here. You know, the surveillance..."

"That could have been anybody. The VC, the old gangsters still looking for employment, the local service, some fucking free agent..."

"Or the French. Maybe the Russian showing his hand again. There are a lot of possibilities, and I need to start eliminating some of them."

"Well," Crockett warned, "just make sure you do a damn good job at counter-surveillance. And you know the old rule: vary your routes. Don't make it easy. It looks like you could be a marked man, Karl."

"If I was indeed the target."

Crockett nodded. "True. You could've been in the wrong place at the wrong time. But there's been an awful lot of activity around you lately."

"No shit. I think I'd like to keep a Browning with me from now on." Baier stopped and studied the floor before turning back to the COS. "I haven't forgotten what the Director said. But this is getting kind of personal, Frank. It's getting harder and harder to walk away."

CHAPTER NINETEEN

L e Duc Vien and Nguyen Van Trongh were sitting together on the sofa in Van Trongh's office when Baier entered. He had requested a meeting with Van Trongh and would have preferred to talk to the two men separately. But Van Trongh had outmaneuvered Baier, no doubt aware of why Baier had called. Baier was sure the news of the attack—and Baier's presence at the site—had made its way quickly to these offices.

The two Vietnamese looked as though they had been deep in conversation before Baier arrived, both men leaning forward to exchange whatever they had to say in voices barely above a whisper. Try as he might, Baier could not pick anything up when he stopped for a moment outside the office door. His Vietnamese was non-existent, of course, but he hoped for a sense of the mood in the room.

Nguyen Van Trongh rose from the sofa and walked to his desk. Le Duc Vien rose as well when he saw Baier coming through the door and extended his hand. He also wore a wide and warm smile.

"Mister Baier, thank you for coming all this way," Le said. "I hope it is okay with you if I sit in. I am assuming, of course, that you have come to discuss the recent shooting at the café. If not, I will certainly leave." He paused, staring at Baier for a moment. "Unless, of course, you'd like me to stay."

"And let me add how glad I am to see that you escaped injury," Nguyen Van Trongh added. "My men tell me that others were not so lucky."

"As I have told Frank Crockett and others, I am still here because of luck alone," Baier said. "I wish I could say it is because of my superior fighting skills. But it is difficult to fight back from a toilet." Baier smiled and waved a hand in the air. "I doubt I would have made much a difference in any case. The fire was very rapid and very effective. It was also over very soon."

"But they did not get you," Van Trongh observed.

"No, they did not. That is assuming, of course, that I was the intended target."

Baier took the seat on the end of the sofa opposite Le Duc Vien.

"I can assure you that my men are hot on the trail, as your countrymen like to say, of the Viet Cong gunners who perpetrated this attack. They are a scourge on this country, and we will not give up until we have found the criminals and punished them," Le Duc Vien said.

Those words had all the sincerity of a politician's speech to Baier's ears. "How can you be so sure those two men were from the Viet Cong?" he asked.

"You saw only two?" Van Trongh asked. "The shooter and the man on the motorbike?"

Baier nodded. "Yes. But it does make sense that way. You know, leave a smaller footprint."

"But who else would they be?" Le Duc Vien pressed. His eyes studied Baier as though he were some sort of interloper, just arrived on the planet.

Baier studied the floor at his feet for a moment before looking up at his hosts. "I can understand that that would be your first guess. But I wonder if it isn't little more than an impression. You have no evidence thus far to say with certainty that it was the Viet Cong."

"Well, there is the evidence of repetition and precedent," Le Duc Vien noted. "The past attacks in the capital have all come from the VC."

"But weren't those primarily bombings?"

"There has also been the campaign of assassinations in the countryside of government officials and representatives. There have been thousands of those since the campaign began in the late 1950s," Nguyen Van Trongh added, "when Le Duan pressed the case with Ho and Giap to resume the insurgency in the south. I think it would be a mistake to limit cases attributed to the National Liberation Front, or NLF, solely to one type of weapon."

"And there have been killings in this city as well," Duc Vien stated.

"That is a good point," Baier nodded in agreement. "Do we know if there were any government officials at the café?"

Nguyen Van Trongh shook his head. "We are still trying to determine if that were the case."

Baier held up a finger. "Let me throw out some other possibilities."

"Yes, of course," Le Duc Vien said. "We would be happy to entertainment any suggestions you might have, Mister Baier."

"If you recall from our last meeting," Baier's focus was on Le Duc Vien this point. "I noted the presence of former members of the Binh Xuyen organization at my kidnapping. Can you not see them trying to pull off something like this?"

"Perhaps. But I do have difficulties imagining them operating outside Cholon," Nguyen Van Trongh said. "Even before Prime Minister Diem crushed them in 1955, they focused their energies and operations within Cholon. This would be a real stretch for them now."

"But they would have people available to do so if they were instructed or paid to do that," Baier protested.

"But who would that be? This paymaster you mentioned previously? Your Russian?" Le Duc Vien pressed.

Baier nodded vigorously. "Yes. He would be my prime candidate."

"Have you seen or heard from him lately?"

Baier shook his head. "No, I admit that I have not. I have to say that given how things developed the one and only time we met, there is good news in that. But, no, he appears to have been silent and inactive since then. As far as I can tell. Of course, that could have been because he was preparing something like this." Baier studied his hosts. "Should I assume that your organization had found no trace of the man or any organization he may have set up here?"

"No, we have not. He has become something of a phantom," Le Duc Vien suggested.

"I seriously doubt that."

"I hope you are not planning on hunting for this man or anyone he may have recruited in Cholon," Nguyen Van Trongh said. He had given up his relaxed posture and moved from the back cushion of his chair and was now leaning forward over his desk. "If you are, then please let me have some of our people accompany you. I still believe the assault was a Viet Cong act, but it is always better to be safe than sorry. I believe that is a popular saying in your country. At least it was during the two years I spent in Washington and Los Angeles."

"Yes, it still is," Baier concurred. "But I believe I've already had a good deal of company as it is."

"Excuse me?" Van Trongh looked puzzled. His body had gone rigid, and his forehead wrinkled in frowns, as though he was trying to interpret Baier's words.

"I've had a regular tail for several days now. Probably longer. They're very clever and very capable. But their presence has been pretty heavy and hard to miss."

"I see," Nguyen Van Trongh said. "Then it does look as though you are a target for someone. I do wonder then if you are not already on the Viet Cong radar, as it were. I hope it wasn't because of your trip to the countryside, or any other activity your organization may have you involved in."

"Or it could also be that someone simply wants to keep tabs on you, Mister Baier," Le Duc Vien added. "For whatever reason."

"Such as?"

Le Duc Vien shrugged and looked aside. As he spoke his attention returned to Baier. "Oh, there could be any number of those. Some, perhaps someone like this Russian you've encountered here, may see you as a threat. Others may find you a person of interest and see the need to keep track of your movements and interests. Others may be following you because you are a new American in town, and therefore someone of interest."

"Either way, it is not very encouraging," Baier responded. "The last thing I want to do is draw attention to myself."

"It looks as though it may be too late for that," Le Duc Vien replied. "But either way, we will continue to hunt for perpetrators of this brutal attack on the café, and…" he paused to smile at the American "…we will keep our options open as to the who the criminal might be."

• • •

On his way out, Baier skipped down the front steps, his mind rewinding the conversation with the two Vietnamese liaison officers. When he looked up from the ground, Baier was stunned to see Jacques Schroeder, the French Surete officer, heading in the opposite direction and into the building. Baier started to raise his hand in greeting, but the Frenchman swept past as though Baier wasn't even there. Baier halted and turned to make sure he hadn't been mistaken. Although he was watching the back of the man's head, the build and gait of the Frenchman ensured Baier he had not.

Upstairs, Le Duc Vien and Nguyen Van Trongh stared at each other for several seconds after Baier had gone. Their conversation was brief, if elliptical.

"Yours?" Van Trongh finally asked.

Duc Vien smiled and shrugged.

"Do you think it wise?" Van Trongh continued. "Particularly in such heavy numbers?"

"We shall see," was all Duc Vien had to say.

"And the shooting at the café?"

"No," Duc Vien stated, "that was not us. Of that I am quite sure."

"Let's hope so," Van Trongh replied. "Anything else would be very unfortunate. For all of us."

Le Duc Vien stood. "I am afraid I must go. I have another appointment."

"Oh?" Van Trongh rose from his seat. "With whom?"

"Another foreigner. Duc Vien laughed. "Another nuisance."

•••

Pyle's foot was not nestled in his pillow mountain this time when Baier entered his room. In fact, the entire bed was empty. Baier searched the room for a clue as to the man's whereabouts, and he was still moving the paper notes and pens on the dressing table when Pyle emerged from the bathroom. He was helped by the same woman who had served them tea on Baier's last visit. She was wearing a long, black silk shirt that stopped several inches above her knees and looked like the top piece of a set of pajamas. The effect from this sighting was the same as the last one: a woman of enduring erotic appeal. The image and suggestions that flowed from her immaculately shaped legs were almost impossible to dismiss. Apparently, she had been assigned to Pyle as his nursemaid. Baier wondered what else her duties were.

Pyle limped to the bed, while his nurse held his forearm to steady his balance. Then he collapsed on the bed and raised his foot to its nest in the pillows. Baier was astonished to see that the cast was gone, replaced by an elastic bandage wrapped around his ankle in a professional looking manner. He grimaced as the foot settled into the conclave it had created over the past few weeks.

"Where the hell did you get that?" Baier asked, pointing at the damaged ankle. "And what happened to your cast?"

Pyle angled his head to one side to get a better look at the wrapping. "Not bad, eh?" He looked up and nodded towards his assistant. "Kim here did that."

"But who removed the cast?"

"Oh, that. Henri brought in a doctor who took it off. I just couldn't stand the itching any longer. It was driving me crazy."

Baier looked over at the woman. "So, Kim is a trained as a nurse as well? Or is she just very good with her hands?"

"I don't know about her training," Pyle answered. "But you've got it right about her hands. I mean, look at that bandage. It sure feels a helluva lot better than that damn cast."

"What else have you been doing since the escape? Have you even left this room?"

"Heck, yes. I've been downstairs almost every day. My host has been quite gracious and has invited me to dinner several times. I think he likes to show off his hospitality when he has important visitors."

"Important? Like who?" Baier asked.

"Like guests from the local security service or the French Embassy."

"That's interesting. Do you have any names?"

"Well, as you might have guessed, the Vietnamese have been by to inquire about the kidnapping and escape. A couple times, actually. People from their counter-intelligence or counter-espionage and also the counter-terrorism departments. Twice each, I believe."

"Names?" Baier pressed.

"Different people each time. But both heads of their CI bunch and CT group."

"Le Duc Vien?"

Pyle nodded while he shifted the weight of his foot in the pillows. "Yeah, that name sounds familiar."

"What about Nguyen Van Trongh?"

Pyle shook his head as it settled back into another, smaller mountain of pillows behind his head. "Nope, sorry. That name doesn't ring any bells."

"What did they want to know?"

"Oh, the usual. Who was there, how many, their weapons, the location. Also my guess as to who was responsible."

"What did you tell them?"

"I said there was a European who appeared to be running the show, and that he was using either some VC or former gangsters." Pyle paused to consider his foot, then Kim. "It looks to me like the Russkies or some of their friends are throwing their hand into the fight down here."

"What did they say to that?"

"Nothing. I think they've made up their minds already."

"And?"

"The Viet Cong with the help of some Commie allies. It's the story that gives them what they need and want."

"What sort of a reaction did you get when you introduced the European, or Russian, angle?"

Pyle studied his foot again before looking up at Baier. "Mostly blank stares. But, you know, it's sad if that's the case. About a Soviet or Warsaw Pact service getting directly involved down here. I would have thought Ho would keep his distance from those guys."

"Why? If he needs the help he'll take it from whoever's willing to give it."

"I guess so. They were also curious about de Couget and his role. I guess they found it suspicious that he escaped and disappeared so easily."

"They're not the only ones," Baier said. "Doesn't it make you wonder?"

"Not really," Pyle replied. "I know the guy too well. I just can't see him betraying us, me especially. I mean, look at this arrangement." Pyle sat halfway up and swept his arm around the room.

"That doesn't prove anything. Maybe he has a guilty conscience. Which reminds me," Baier added. "There's one other thing I've been meaning to ask. "How long was it before de Couget set himself up in this business after he came to Saigon?"

"Why? What does it matter?"

"Humor me."

"I'm not really sure. It wasn't right away. He came down from the mountains in Laos after Dien Bien Phu and the Geneva Accords, back in early 1956, I believe, or maybe earlier, in '55. I think he had to stay about a year up there to recover from his wounds. He got pretty sick as well. Or so he says. I'm not sure what he caught."

"Yeah, he probably drank the water. So, what did he do once he arrived?"

Pyle shrugged as his weight sank back onto the bed. "I don't know. But I believe he opened this place about a year later. 1957 probably. I doubt it was much later than that. Why? I'm sure he has all the proper certifications. This place sees a doctor about once a week."

"I'm not worried about his business practices, Pyle. Did he have any connections to the French before they pulled out?"

Pyle gave Baier an incredulous look. "Of course, he did. I mean he served in the Foreign Legion with some of those guys. I thought he would have had to keep his distance, but I occasionally saw him with some of the officers. I guess they didn't hold any grudges, seeing how it all turned out. He supposedly had a pretty stellar record, too." Pyle rolled to his side away from the door and held out his hand to his nurse. "They probably all had a lot of memories to share. Just like we did. And still do." He smiled. "Maybe he gave them some discounts here."

"Do you recall any names from the French visitors? And how often have they been by? Since the kidnapping, I mean. You said some came from the French Embassy."

"No, no names there, except one or two. And there weren't as many of them as the Vietnamese."

"Was someone named Jacques Schroeder here?"

"I don't think so. There was someone once or twice with a name that sounded like Cabernet. You know, like the wine. Some of the red stuff. But I can't be sure. My French is not very good. I've been concentrating on learning Vietnamese since I've been here."

"Me, too," Baier said. He did not mention that a man named Carbonel was actually Jacques Schroeder's boss, the head of the Surete section at the French Embassy.

• • •

On his way out, Baier decided to swing by de Couget's office to see if he was in. Unfortunately, he was out running errands, according his wife. Baier was surprised to learn that she spoke passable English. Probably learning to accommodate the growing American presence. Her short dark hair was combed back into a bun at the base of her neck, and she wore a modest, loose flowered dress that reached to her ankles. It was truly a loose-fitting garment that hid her body well, unlike the dress code Baier usually encountered in *La Maison*.

She leaned against de Couget's desk, her arms crossed in front of her chest. Baier found himself staring and shook his head to free his thoughts. He was struck less by her beauty—she was very attractive-

-then by her presence. Baier recognized for the first time that if she wished, she could easily dominate a room. He found it interesting that she was apparently willing to allow her husband to take center stage whenever Baier was present. She could have easily been a more active player, which made him wonder what sort of role she played behind the scenes, or at least when he was not present.

"I am not sure where he is at the moment," she said. "I am sorry."

"Would he be meeting with any Vietnamese or French officials?" Baier asked.

"You will have to ask him about his schedule. But it would not surprise me if he is meeting with some of our hosts. We have been having trouble lately with our electricity supplies."

"I see. Please tell him that I stopped by. I need to speak with him."

"Of course."

• • •

After Baier left, she walked to the office entrance and shut the door. Then she turned toward another passage, one that led to the kitchen. There she looked at her husband and shook her head.

"It is no use. You must speak to him. He needs to know."

"Not just yet. In good time, though. In good time."

De Couget turned towards another individual, a European looking out the window. That visitor was dressed in a white, light-weight suit that looked as though it had just come from the dry cleaner. The man turned and stared at de Couget.

"You have put me in a difficult position," de Couget said. He spoke in French, and his voice sounded angry, frustrated.

"I have not put you there. The Americans have put all of us in a difficult position."

De Couget sighed. "There are too many masters here in this country now. It is difficult to please them all."

"You must do what is necessary to survive. You have done well so far. I admire that."

"Spare me your false praise, Monsieur Carbonel. I can do without that much."

CHAPTER TWENTY

The second attempt on Baier's life began with a bombing.

He was strolling down Rue de Gaulle on a beautiful afternoon in late February, hoping to enjoy what would probably be the last few days of his assignment in Saigon. He was happy that he would, in all likelihood, miss the monsoon rains, still months away. The stories about the torrents of water that poured down on this part of the earth were frightening enough to give him a quickness to his step, as though he was looking for shelter already.

He had been cautious about varying his routes, certain he was avoiding the kind of predictability that made surveillance easy and allowed something like a terrorist attack to happen. He also avoided narrow alleys and pathways that would have aided another kidnapping attempt by limiting his options for escape, should he need one. The Rue de Gaulle was one of those broad boulevards the French had erected in Saigon to give the town the look and feel of an almost-European city. That also gave Baier the chance to check on any surveillance and to use the many restaurants and stores to check on a tail, which he decided to do right there.

That may have been what saved him. It may have thrown off the timing of the explosion, so that Baier did not feel the full force of the blast.

It still shattered the small world around him. A typhoon of air and pressure knocked Baier off his feet and threw him up against a brick wall that separated two storefronts. His body recoiled from the thudding impact it had to absorb as he slammed into the wall.

He glanced to either side and realized that somehow his luck had not deserted him yet. Broken shards of glass framed storefront windows on either side. He would have been cut to into small pieces had the blast tossed him through those.

Baier lay momentarily stunned on the sidewalk. The only sound he could hear was a ringing in his ears. Everything else around him seemed to move in silence and slow motion.

He looked down at his body to make sure all his limbs were in place. They were. His hands were blackened by some kind of soot, and his trousers were ripped. His right shoe was also missing. He ran his hands through his hair to check the condition of his scalp and felt strands of dried dirty hair poking out in all directions like a used and battered mop.

He forced himself to stand but needed the wall that had nearly broken his back to balance himself. His legs were wobbly. He gasped for breath to get more oxygen into his lungs and looked out on a scene of utter devastation.

Wounded and dying or dead covered the sidewalk and street, also spotted with human limbs. Several cars and a number of rickshaws had been destroyed by the blast; the mangled bodies of their drivers and passengers littered the street and sidewalk. There was blood everywhere. People were crying and screaming from the pain and shock. Sirens shrieked in the distance.

Baier fell back down on the hard ground. His head was beginning to clear, and he sat with his back to the wall. He prayed there would not be a second bomb, one intended to wreak more havoc and misery as the local authorities responded to the strike.

Baier looked up through the drifting smoke. At first he could not be sure. His vision was impaired, and he wasn't sure what the effect of the shock from the blast was on his sight and perception. But he was pretty certain that a larger than usual figure approached from the street.

Baier was amazed to see that someone had emerged from the apocalypse around him untouched. It was as though this man had just arrived from another planet. Maybe he had—or from another country, at least. Because Baier was pretty damn certain that it was Vladimir. The Russian stopped in front of Baier and smiled, his hands on his hips, and his head nodding approvingly.

"You see," Vladimir said in that heavily accented English Baier had come to hate over the years for what it so often portended. "I have not been away. In fact, I never left."

CHAPTER TWENTY-ONE

"**Y**ou look like the devil," Baier said. The Russian had appeared from a haze of smoke and thin air, sirens blaring and screams echoing through the air. His clothes had miraculously escaped the rubble and the dirt and smoke that still filled the sky and lay like a carpet on the ground. "But I know you're only an asshole. What the hell do you want now?"

Vladimir took a few steps towards Baier. "I want to take you out of chaos and death here. We finish our business from other day."

"Fuck you. I'm not moving. I'll wait for the police."

Vladimir glanced behind himself and motioned with his head towards Baier. "Take him. And hurry."

Two Vietnamese thugs—neither of whom Baier recognized, not that it mattered—hauled Baier to his feet by each arm, then dragged him into the street. A battered Renault sedan was waiting, also free of any of the dents and dust or broken glass that marked everything else on the street. They tossed him onto the back seat next to Vladimir. Both men then jumped into the front, one in the passenger seat and one at the steering wheel. The car sped off away from the chaos that reigned behind them. Baier wondered where the hell the police had gotten to, since none had showed up yet at the scene of the attack. Shit, timing really was everything.

After about twenty minutes the car was weaving its way through the back alleys of Cholon. Not this again, Baier said to himself. I'm really getting to hate this place.

The car pulled up in front of a different building, this one more of a shop front. Baier was dragged once more through an alley to a door at the back of the shop, where two more Vietnamese gunmen were waiting. One held the door open for the party; the other one rested himself on the edge of a desk that had a telephone and little else. The two men from the car left Baier standing on his shaky legs. After several seconds he collapsed on the floor.

"I can't stand anymore. So, fuck you, Vlad." He looked up at his erstwhile captor. "I need a doctor. No more talking until I see a doctor."

Vladimir ambled to the desk, where he pushed the Vietnamese gunman off the corner and took his place.

"You get doctor when I say so. Now, tell me why you are here. You do not look like another Lansdale. He fit in much better. Had better contacts."

Baier looked up again and shook his head. "Lansdale? So many people have that guy on their minds. No, he is not a part of the game here anymore."

"That is good."

"For whom?"

"For everyone. Well, maybe not for you. Which means it is good for us. Your people, your country will spend much more time here. And money. And men."

"Perhaps. But that does not mean we won't win."

"Hah. You will go where French went."

"Is that your government's position? I thought Mister Khrushchev supported a negotiated truce, or even a peace."

"What you people say, pipe dream? That is what that is." The Russian studied Baier for a minute. "So, what you do here? How you fit in?"

"You will have to figure that out for yourself. I might be willing to talk more if you get a doctor in here."

Vladimir shrugged and waved his arm at the door leading out into the alley. "Go," was all he said. The Russian scowled at one of the guards, who slipped out the door. Baier hoped it was for a doctor. He noticed that his leg was bleeding again and his head was pounding now that he was still.

"You know, North Vietnamese are aware of you here. South, too. I told them all about you and our little misadventure."

"Our what?" Baier was silent. "And who did you tell?"

The Russian shrugged. "No matter. They already knew. How you think I stay here so long."

"Who knew, goddammit? The government? Here?"

The Russian nodded. "*Da*, parts of it. The important parts."

"You mean the security service?"

The Russian smiled. "*Da*, some. Not all. But I do not need all."

"Then what is your game? What is in it for them? And for you?"

"We do not care about government in South. Those guys not very good or capable anyways. They will not last long. You cannot win with them."

"What do you care about?"

"We care about the day after. And our real competition here. Like I say, you will lose and go home."

"Then who is your real competition?"

"Hah, can you not tell?"

Baier sat in silence. He shook his head and waited for the punch line.

"It is Chinese. They want to make themselves leaders of our world, our side. We will not let that happen."

"I thought you two were friends and partners. What happened?"

"Mao happened. Mao and his gang. They too greedy. You see it up north. So much weapons. So much men."

"But the North needs all that. I thought your people would be more active."

Vladimir shook his head. "Not really. Kremlin wants to practice peaceful competition. America too strong right now. We need time to catch up." The Russian stood and approached Baier. His right index finger jutted out and came within inches of Baier's nose. "And we will. Your time is doomed. History shows it."

"Yeah, right. Good luck with that Hegelian crap. We will be able to kick your ass for years to come. Decades." Baier pushed the finger away. "So, what have you been up to? Spying on the Chinese here? Wouldn't that be done better up in Hanoi?"

"Maybe we already do that up there. Checking on things. We need to be busy down here, too."

"Doing what?"

"Working with others to block Chinese. Plenty of allies, too, among Vietnamese."

Oh, shit, Baier thought. "Like who? Who and in which service have you been working with?"

"Hah, none of your business. And too bad you will not be able to find out for yourself."

"Why not?"

"Because today is your last day. Here in Vietnam or anywhere."

The Russian stared at Baier, as though working to make up his mind. When he spoke, Vladimir was no longer smiling. "I am sorry, but I cannot let you leave here. You already know too much about me. Just knowing I am here is too dangerous for me."

"I wondered why you were so talkative. You're pretty damn sure of yourself, Vlad."

The Russian drew a pistol that had been stuck inside his belt at the front. "Bye, bye, Mister Baier. This is present from Chernov and those he betrayed."

The shot sent an echo through the small room that rung inside Baier's skull and pounded on his ears. Baier asked himself why he would take the chance of firing his gun in such a packed neighborhood. But then he realized the few who would hear the shot would probably dismiss it as just another gangland shooting, or a Viet Cong attack.

He also wondered why he didn't feel anything.

Then he saw Vladimir standing upright, his arm at his side. The pistol dropped to his feet. A red stain was spreading across the Russian's chest. He did not seem to notice, however. His eyes were focused on some distant spot on the wall opposite, as though that would explain the sudden turn of events, one that took things out of his control. Something he never thought he would lose. It was a spot with a small hole, rough cut and uneven, where the bullet that had just left his chest had broken against the brick.

Then his knees buckled, and he collapsed in a heap on the floor at Baier's feet.

One of the Vietnamese gunmen stood behind the dead Russian, his right hand holding a Makarov pistol. A thin trail of smoke drifted towards the ceiling. He looked at Baier and nodded. Baier didn't know what to say, or what to do. He could only think of the irony of it all. Vladimir shot with a Russian gun.

The other gunmen stood impassively at the side of the room against the back wall, apparently unconcerned over what had just happened.

Baier didn't know what to say. He was too stunned to think coherently. Finally, he asked a question, one that would later come back to him as perhaps the stupidest thing he could have said.

"Where the hell did you get that thing?" Baier nodded at the pistol.

The gunman looked at the gun, then shrugged. "We have lots."

The shooter turned then and walked to the desk, where he picked up the phone and dialed. He said something in Vietnamese, nodded, spoke another word, then hung up. Next, he dialed again, but this time he spoke in French. Again, Baier understood nothing...well, almost nothing. He did pick out the word 'Charbonel' from the string of conversation.

Still holding the receiver in his hand, the shooter looked right into Baier's eyes and smiled. He also nodded in recognition. Baier was too tired and in too much pain to acknowledge the salute.

After he hung up, the shooter and two of the others picked Baier up off the floor and half carried, half dragged him out to the Renault. They placed him more carefully in the back, then the shooter joined him. The other two, the same driver and guide who had driven them to Cholon, took off in the midst of a crowd that did not seem to care in the least about what may have just transpired. Nobody appeared to even notice the group, or the condition of the American in their midst.

It was either the pain or the end of the excitement, or possibly both, that caused Baier to pass out in the car. After what seemed like days but was actually another twenty or thirty minutes, rough hands shook him awake, then pushed him out of the car and onto the sidewalk. Baier struggled onto an elbow for some leverage so he could attempt to stand. When he looked up, Baier saw the familiar curved façade of the American Embassy.

Finally, he thought, I can get to an infirmary.

• • •

"Jesus, how the hell did you walk into that truck?" Crockett asked.

It was actually more of an exclamation. Crockett had run down to the Embassy's infirmary as soon as he got the call about Baier lying on the sidewalk out front from the Marine Guards. Without saying a word, he had pushed the Marines aside and pulled Baier up from the cement, threw his colleague's arm over his shoulder and duck-walked him inside. The two of them drew a series of curious—almost unbelieving—stares from others in the hallway. Baier noticed that he was leaving a small trail of blood on the linoleum floor, which picked up the glare from the overhead light fixtures to send a pink reflection in their wake.

As soon as they burst through the swinging doors, Crockett shoved Baier onto a gurney and wheeled him towards the reception desk. A doctor rushed forward after about thirty seconds of Crockett demanding, in a very loud voice, that someone attend to this officer.

"Easy, Frank, I'm not dying. And it wasn't a truck. It was a bomb."

"Yeah, no shit. We've been hearing about it all morning. I'd say you were one of the lucky ones."

"Well, I don't feel so lucky right now."

"Hell, Karl, you've got to be running out of your extra cat lives by now. How many do you think you have left? Three or four?"

"Very funny. Any word yet on who was responsible?"

Crockett shook his head. "Naw, not yet. Everyone's assuming it was the VC, of course. That's where the precedent lies. Motive, too, I would guess."

Baier leaned up on his elbow, as though he wanted to make sure his words reached the Chief of Station. "Fuck, the precedent and that particular motive, Frank. The Russian was there."

"That Vladimir prick? At the bombing? Where is he now?"

Baier tried to shake his head, then gave it up. "He's dead. But not from the bombing."

Crockett's jaw dropped and his eyes went way wide. "You think he was behind this thing?"

Baier let his head fall back against the pillow. "It's possible. I mean, it was like he came out of nowhere. Untouched. But he must have been there already. Somewhere. And he had a car waiting to carry me away. It was like he had everything prepared."

"That sounds pretty damn suspicious. In fact, it sounds pretty damn certain."

Baier waved his hand in the air. "Yeah, he had a car, some thugs as gunmen. Everything had been prepared. He must have known."

"Man, I wish I could get my hands on that son of a bitch."

"You're too late. Like I said, he's dead. He was just about to shoot me, when one of the Vietnamese thugs there dropped him. And the other guys just stood there and watched. It was like he was the one who had been set up."

"But by whom? Surely not the Viet Cong?"

"That's where this gets really interesting. Once the shooter killed good old Vlad, he walks over and uses the phone."

"Where were you guys? Back in Cholon again?"

"Yeah. And he makes two calls. One in Vietnamese and one in French. And guess who's name he uses?' Crockett stared and pulled his hand in close to his ear, as though pressing Baier to continue. "Charbolet. The head of French intelligence here."

"You think the French were behind this? They have not been our best friends here, for sure. But that is one helluva step forward. Really fucking forward, I might add."

"Well, my French is just about non-existent…"

"Yeah, other than ordering a meal or buying some wine."

"Right. So, I can't be sure what he said. But the French must have been aware of some part of this affair."

"And the Vietnamese? If you guys were in Cholon, that means it could have been anyone, but probably the old Binh Xuyen gang."

"Sure. But they wouldn't have been acting on their own here. More like guns for hire, if you ask me."

"Okay, where do you want to go from here? That is when you get released."

"Oh, I'm getting out of here as soon as they patch me up," Baier said.

"I wouldn't be too sure of that." Those last words came from a young medical officer, who had finally shown up, his white cotton medical jacket wrinkled and spotted with blood. Baier guessed that he couldn't have been older than his mid-to-late twenties, probably on a medical assignment in a military hospital paying off the ROTC loan that had allowed him to afford medical school. "I'll let you know when you're well enough to leave."

"Oh, come on, Doc, you probably need the beds, what with all the wounded trickling in here after the bombing." Baier actually found himself smiling at this point. Only then did he notice that he must have bled on Crocket's nice white shirt and slacks during the trip in from the sidewalk. "Oh, Jesus, frank, I am sorry about that." Baier pointed towards the Station Chief's shirt.

Crockett looked down and shrugged. When he looked up at Baier, he was smiling, too. "If that's all it takes to get you fixed up, then I guess it was worth it. You will get a bill, though, for the dry-cleaning."

"Hell, you're not going to get that stuff out. I'll buy you a new shirt. You're on your own for the pants, though. I do have another favor to ask."

"Yeah? You're not planning on dodging another bomb, I hope."

"No, not for now. But could you have someone pick up a set of clothes for me? I'll need something clean and un-shredded to wear when I make some calls later today."

"Sure, thing. I'll send Melby or Hartnett over to your room." Crockett pointed at Baier's feet. "You'll probably need a new pair of shoes while they're at it. Socks should be okay, though."

"You might want to wait until tomorrow on that," the young doctor said. "You've lost a lot of blood."

"Look, Doctor Kildare…"

"I prefer Ben Casey, actually."

"Whoever. I've got important things to take care of. And they won't wait."

"They might have to."

A nurse strolled in at that point with a set of medical tools and vials on a tray. The medical officer selected a hypodermic needle and approached Baier.

"Wow, there, Madame Curie. What the hell is that?"

"It's an antibiotic," the doctor explained. "I want to make sure you don't suffer from an infection. It looks like you could have picked up any range of bacteria out there, and with all your bleeding, I think this is the safest course. I'm assuming you've had a tetanus shot recently."

Strange, thought Baier, I never realized I was bleeding that much. He nodded, surprised at how difficult it had become. "Yeah, before I…."

A minute later he was sound asleep. The last thing he remembered hearing was something about shock.

CHAPTER TWENTY-TWO

Pyle's appearance at the infirmary the following morning was another surprise for Baier. The American walked with a steady step that showed barely a hint of his previous injury. He also looked washed and manicured, as though he had been to a spa that included not only hygiene and health but a good dose of dry-cleaning as well. His pants and shirt, white and beige, respectively, were not only spotless but pressed, too...and his hair had been trimmed and combed.

"Geez, you look like a new man, Pyle. What's up?"

Baier's guest looked a bit sheepish as he swept the floor with his foot and held his hands behind his back. "I think I'm in love."

This brought Baier up with a shot to a sitting position on the edge of his bed. "What did you say? With whom?"

"Kim. You know the woman who's been looking after me. Man, she is amazing."

Baier squinted with suspicion. "But isn't she...pre-occupied? You know, kind of spoken for?"

Pyle shook his head. "Not anymore. I've spoken to de Couget, and he's taken her off the rotation, so to speak."

"Is Kim aware of your feelings and the conversation with de Couget about...her career?"

Pyle's head bobbed up and down vigorously. "Oh, yeah. She's fine with it. Man, she never really liked doing that. I guess that's no surprise, although the money was always pretty good." Pyle glanced around the room as though it encompassed the whole world. "Plus, it provided some security in this place. Vietnam, I mean."

"So, what are you going to do for income? A place to live? All that sort of stuff?"

"Well," Pyle answered, "I've got my trust fund. It's not a lot, but you don't need much to get by here. And Kim can find other work. De Couget even said he'd help. Hell, I might even find something to do."

Baier smiled and slid off the bed. "Well, okay then. I guess you've got it all worked out." He extended his hand. "And congratulations. Now, help me get into my clothes. I want to get the hell out of here." Baier put a hand on the bed to steady himself, a mild case of dizziness having hit him as his feet found the floor.

Pyle held up a hand. "Sure. But first let me tell you why I came. It wasn't to make a proclamation of my new love."

"Okay, what is it then?"

"It's Kim. She's the one who pushed me on this. She thinks you should know that she might have heard something about the bombing. Who was behind it."

Baier stood up straight, as he suddenly found his balance. "Say, what? She knows who did it?"

Pyle grimaced and shook his head. "Not exactly. But she overheard a couple of the guards the other day, and they mentioned something about the Vietnamese security services being involved in something. The French, too. It wasn't clear just what, though."

Baier had to steady himself once more on the edge of the bed. "Goddammit. What did they say? Can she remember the exact words?"

"I don't think so. It was just something about the old gang members having some cover from people in the government. And they could always turn to the French, if necessary."

"Those motherfuckers." Baier felt his cheeks going red. His lips closed tight, and he ran his hand through the ruffled mop of hair piled on top of his head. "Motherfuckers," he repeated. "Anything on who might be responsible?" Baier pressed. "Individuals, I mean. Or even offices. And what sort of link is there between these Vietnamese and the French?"

Pyle's head swayed back and forth slowly, as though it were carrying a great weight. "No, nothing like that. I'm sorry." He chewed his lower lip. "We can't even be sure it had to do with the bombing."

"It's still a lead. Of sorts." Baier studied Pyle, whose focus remained on the linoleum floor at Baier's feet. "And it took Kim to get you here to talk to me?"

Pyle raised his head. "I was going to come anyways. But I wanted to be sure what I told you was accurate."

"Accurate? How so?"

"I didn't want you to read too much into it. The information is pretty spotty. You have to admit that."

"You mean you didn't want to do anything that might implicate de Couget."

Pyle's head started to shake again but with extra weight this time. Baier could see now that Pyle carried a burden that was mixed with recognition and denial. Pyle had built up a friendship with the Frenchman over the years that had tied their fates in this changing country and culture together in a bond of friendship that included a mutual desire for how they should coexist and how things would eventually—hopefully—turn out. Theirs was a comfortable and beneficial world that deep inside both men knew would come to an end at some point. Until then they would make the best possible present and future they could in the middle of that. And now Pyle was beginning to recognize that that sort of denial and self-deception carried other consequences as well.

In the back of his mind Baier had suspected as much of this expatriate American. And in spite of himself, Baier had come to like this guy, who had been lost since his time and experiences in the OSS. He realized how much of an indelible print this country had planted on his mind and his character during that period of uncertainty and wandering. Baier also suspected that neither man was alone in this dilemma. He truly hoped it did not come to a tragedy for either one. Because he also found the Frenchman a congenial enigma that made him an occasional adversary and friend. Kind of like the whole damn country.

"You know I'm going to have to follow up on this, don't you?" Baier said.

Pyle nodded. He had tears pooling under his eyes. "Yes, I know. But I really can't see de Couget being a part of this."

"Come on, Pyle. The man's hand has been visible in so much of this. Just think back to our run in at the warehouse."

"I know, I know. But that can be explained."

"He's already tried. And I was not convinced. I don't know how much blame he carries, but he's going to have to come up with a much better explanation." Baier pointed his finger at his American colleague. "And don't you dare warn him."

Even as he spoke those words, Baier knew they were fruitless. Pyle would follow his heart and try to press the Frenchman on his own.

● ● ●

This time Baier made sure he could meet with Nguyen Van Trongh alone. His desire was based largely on a guess. As the deputy chief of the counterterrorism unit, Nguyen was less likely to be directly involved than someone like Le Duc Vien, the head of the counterintelligence branch. Working CT, the man would certainly have an interest and probably knowledge of what had transpired. But that, hopefully, came after the fact, not before. If Baier's suspicions about the people and the motives behind the attack were correct.

He had developed a certain impression of Nguyen Van Trongh, the man and his interests, one that was more favorable than he had of the others he had met. He just hoped he hadn't misled himself. It can happen. In any case, Baier did not want to have to confront the two men together.

He drove straight there. Fuck the countersurveillance. He was in too much of a hurry.

Baier, however, found Nguyen's office empty. His secretary said that the deputy chief was in a meeting, but that he should be back within the hour, perhaps even sooner. Baier told her he'd be happy to wait. The secretary brought Baier another Orange Crush, which helped the time slip away.

Van Trongh reappeared after little over half an hour. He was surprised to see Baier waiting for him in the outer office but immediately invited him into his inner sanctum, as it were.

"I am so sorry to have heard about your injuries from the recent bomb attack. I hope they are not serious," Nguyen Van Trongh said, his hand on Baier's left shoulder. "You appear to be recovering quite nicely, however."

Baier thanked his host, then moved towards the sofa. "I hope you don't mind if I sit. There is still some pain in the leg if I stand for too long."

"No, no. Of course not." Van Trongh took the seat in the opposite corner of the couch. "This visit is unexpected, a real surprise. If that is your only pain, then I believe we...you have been very fortunate. What can I do for you?"

Baier hesitated. He needed to press someone in the service, even if it was only to find out where else someone in the South Vietnamese government might sit, someone who could have been involved in the bomb attack, and possibly an assault on his own life. But he did not want to reveal the source of his information, or his suspicions.

"It has come to my attention that those involved in the bombing may have had some kind of connection to people in your government."

Nguyen Van Trongh's face registered genuine surprise, shock even. At least as best Baier could tell.

"How did you come by this information? And how certain are you?"

Baier paused. "I'd rather not reveal that. But the sourcing, at least, is genuine."

It was Nguyen Van Trongh's turn to hesitate. His eyes studied the spot of fabric on the sofa between the two men. "I am aware that your organization will often spend a good deal of time to verify its sources. Have you done the same in this case?"

This time, Baier did not hesitate. "Yes. I am reasonably certain that the information is valid, if inconclusive. But I believe it warrants further investigation."

"And who do you believe is responsible for the bombing itself. The Viet Cong are a usual suspect, a suspicion that generally proves to be correct."

"Not in this case. I cannot say for certain, of course, but I believe a stronger suspect would be members of the old Binh Xuyen gang. If the VC were involved, it would only be as an agent of action. Not as the organizer, or even in the selection of the target."

"Yes, but the Viet Cong often works to disrupt the stability of this country and does not care about the innocent victims they harm. Besides, killing you would be a nice bonus. That is why we suspect them in this case. At the least, they would be happy to hit someone from the country that is becoming their principal enemy, even if they were only acting for others."

Baier shook his head. "I understand all that. But it is just as credible that Binh Xuyen thugs carried this one out. That is the information I have been hearing. And there was the presence of the Russian, who so magically appeared at the scene of the crime, and who did not have a single mark from the bombing. He also had a car waiting to take me away."

"It is not inconceivable that that someone from the KGB would be working with the Viet Cong," Nguyen Van Trongh protested.

"But that has not been the man's M.O."

"M.O.?" Van Trongh queried. For the first time that morning, the Vietnamese interlocutor looked confused to Baier.

"It means the 'method of operation.' He has been involved from the start—at least the start of my confrontation with him—with members of the old criminal organization, one that your government worked so hard to suppress almost a decade ago. I believe he was behind this attack."

"And his motive," Nguyen Van Trongh pressed. "Simply to kill you? If that was the case why something so spectacular? He could simply have shot you."

"He may have had several motives. I may have been one of opportunity. And it is not necessarily easier to shoot someone, not if he is aware and prepared." Baier paused. "Besides, that may have been tried once already."

"You mean the shooting at the café?"

Baier nodded. "And a bombing makes it look like a VC operation. After all, you immediately suspected they were behind it."

"I see." Nguyen Van Trongh was silent, as though he was considering a new range of possibilities.

Baier continued. "Have you considered a Chinese angle?"

Nguyen Van Trongh looked up suddenly, as though his thoughts had been interrupted. "How do you mean? What would the Chinese have to do with this?" He smiled for the first time. "Mind you, I would not put such a thing past them."

"Not necessarily as instigator," Baier suggested. "But as a player, nonetheless. At times the Russian seemed to be more concerned about a Chinese presence in this battle, especially down here, than in our growing presence."

"Why is that? I would have thought those two nations would work together in this fight. Do not the both of them want a Communist takeover here?"

"Perhaps," was Baier's single worded response. This appeared to confuse Nguyen further.

"Moscow and Beijing do not always see eye-to-eye on a number of issues," Baier continued. "The Chinese were not happy, for example, with Khrushchev's compromise on Cuba two years ago."

"But this is different."

"Not necessarily," Baier continued. "What is going on here is still part of a larger strategic game. And the Russians are much more careful and open to negotiations. The Kremlin has made that much clear."

"But are they serious? You know well, Mister Baier, how the Soviets can be rather disingenuous in these matters. Look at your own experience in eastern Europe and Germany."

Baier nodded. "I suppose you have a point. But I think we may be seeing a growing divergence between the two capitals of the communist revolution."

"Well, that would certainly make things in the world much more interesting," Nguyen Van Trongh conceded. "You are also aware of how much we distrust and dislike the Chinese based on our own history..."

"Yes, I am," Baier interrupted. "Which could make for some strange bedfellows here in Vietnam."

Nguyen Van Trongh stood. "You have given me much to think about, Mister Baier. And I thank you for that. I suggest we stay in touch to discuss this matter further, as we accumulate more information."

"I would appreciate that very much," Baier said. He leaned forward and held out his hand, hoping he had found an ally among his country's partners in the growing war. On the way out, Baier glanced at his half full bottle of Orange Crush. He decided to leave it behind.

● ● ●

As soon as he saw Baier descend the stairs and get into his jeep, Nguyen Van Trongh asked his secretary to summon Le Duc Vien, or to arrange a meeting later in the day if necessary. Le Duc Vien was available later that afternoon. So, shortly after lunch, Nguyen Van Trongh walked slowly down to his colleague's office, assembling his thoughts as he went.

"I am sorry to make you wait, Nguyen," Duc Vien said as he invited his colleague into his office. "What is so urgent?"

"Your special operation. Is there any chance it was connected to the recent bombing on Rue de Gaulle?" Nguyen Van Trongh asked. He took a seat in one of the armchairs facing the desk and the window behind it.

Le Duc Vien was taken aback and stumbled around to the other side of his desk, where he took a seat in the tall straight-backed leather chair across from where Nguyen was seated. "Why do you ask?"

"I had a visit earlier today from the American you have been tailing. You know he was wounded in the blast and barely escaped more serious, life-threatening injuries."

"Yes, I was very sorry to hear that. But what does that have to do with my operation?"

"It is strange, is it not, that your men were unable to prevent either the bombing, or his involvement? As a target, I mean."

"Oh, come now, Nguyen, we cannot prevent every Viet Cong atrocity in this country, or even this city. You know that."

"Of course not. But how are you so certain that it was the Viet Cong?"

"Who else would it be?"

"What of the Russian you claimed to have no knowledge of? He apparently was well connected to some of the remaining members of the Binh Xuyen gang. Don't you use them on occasion?"

"Very rarely."

"But still." Nguyen Van Trongh studied his colleague. "You know what I believe?"

"What is that?" Le Duc Vien asked.

Nguyen Van Trongh noticed that the man was beginning to perspire, as beads of sweat ran across his forehead. Duc Vien rolled his chair closer to the desk and leaned forward, as though to be sure he did not miss a word of what was about to be said.

"I believe that you were aware of the Russian's presence all along," Nguyen Van Trongh continued. "And that you were using him to check on Chinese activities in Saigon. And together you found the old Binh Xuyen gang to be convenient soldiers for this. They remain present, to a point, in Cholon, where the Chinese would be most likely to try to work."

"That is speculation, Nguyen."

"And I have learned about the possibility of a rift between Moscow and Beijing here in Vietnam." Nguyen Van Trongh paused. "You know, I have no problem with you running an anti-Chinese operation. We all hate those bastards. Even our countrymen in the north."

"Then why are they so eager to accept Chinese help?"

"Because they need it. But you let your operation here get out of hand. You almost caused the death of an American, not to mention the deaths of all the innocent Vietnamese."

Le Duc Vien stood. "That bombing was not part of the plan. The Russian must have acted on his own. He was obsessed with the American. It was not our fault. We were not informed and would not have approved. The operation as we planned it, however, was necessary, and he was a useful idiot, if I may use Trotsky's own words."

"It was your responsibility. You should have been aware of what that man is capable of. The Russians are thugs, especially those from the KGB." Nguyen Van Trongh paused as though considering a new thought. "And the murder of Kim? I suppose that was a part of all this as well. I never could understand the change in the Viet Cong's approach on that one. Have you anything to add?"

Le Duc Vien simply stared straight ahead, his gaze passing right through his colleague. When he spoke the words seemed to be directed at the air in the room, rather than his colleague.

"I will look into it."

The two Vietnamese squared off for several moments. Neither one could have said how long it lasted, if only because their pounding heartbeats distorted the time. Eventually, Nguyen Van Trongh turned to leave.

"You will need to sort this out," he said.

"How," Le Duc Vien asked.

"Who else is involved?" Duc Vien was silent. "Whoever they are, you will need to take care of them and be sure they stop whatever it is they are doing. And I will need to know who else was involved at your level. Or above."

Le Duc Vien stood then stumbled backwards into his chair again. He gripped his knees for a few seconds, then stood once more. He turned and walked to the office door. He gripped the handle and held it open for his colleague. Then, he turned, his mouth open, as though he was preparing to say something else.

But Nguyen Van Trongh cut him off. "This was, after all, an act of terrorism. And that falls to my responsibilities."

CHAPTER TWENTY-THREE

They met at the same café on the edge of the park down the street from the French Embassy...the same table even. It was as though this one spot in all of Saigon was reserved for the Surete's use alone. A small awning had been erected to provide cover from the harsh Indochinese sun for the guests. Schroder was dressed more casually this time: no coat or tie—just a short-sleeve, white cotton shirt. Even that felt as though it must be too warm and confining as the heat and humidity never seemed to let up. Baier was dressed similarly: slacks and a light, linen shirt. But he at least was wearing shoes. Jacques Schroeder had on a pair of sandals.

"It keeps the weather from destroying your shoes. The superiors in my embassy look the other way, especially after the rains break."

"Lucky you," Baier said. He studied the Frenchman, asking himself how much the man knew regarding the bombing and the Vietnamese role in the affair. And just where did the French stand? Were they also aware of the Russian and his part in all this? Baier sipped his café au lait before proceeding.

"Do they do that often? Look the other way."

Schroeder sipped his espresso in return. "What do you mean? In terms of office dress?"

Baier smiled, although no joke had been intended. He was sure of that. "No, not that. I mean on operational matters. Or liaison work with the local service. I know you are involved in the latter."

"How do you know that?"

"Well, it's fairly obvious. I mean, that would be a major part of your office's mission here. Is it not?"

"Yes, of course. But how do you know what it is I do?"

Baier paused to see if Schroeder was serious. "I saw you there the other day. At the security service headquarters. We passed on the front steps. I was sure you had seen me, even though you breezed past without a word or nod of acknowledgement."

"I am sorry about that. My mind must have been somewhere else. Are you sure it was me?"

"Yes, quite. Can you tell me whom you were visiting?"

Schroeder fingered his coffee cup. "I suppose there is no harm in that. I would probably have been visiting Le Duc Vien. He is my principal contact there."

Baier leaned forward and pushed his coffee to the side. "Now that is interesting. Have you seen him lately?"

Schroder swallowed the rest of his espresso, shaking his head. "No, I have not. He seems to be missing. His office could not—or would not—tell me where he had gone."

Baier sat back. Goddammit, he thought. "You know of the Russian and his death, I presume."

"Yes. Is there something more you want to tell me?"

"Let me give you an inside story from his passing."

Schroder's eyebrows arched. "An inside story? From whom?"

"From me," Baier said. "I was there. And that fucking creep almost killed me. In fact, he tried to. But one of his Vietnamese thugs shot him first. And the others never lifted a finger to stop the gunman. I thought that when he grabbed me at the site of the bombing, that it had been a setup, in part, to spirit me away once more. But instead, it was a set up to get rid of him." Baier paused and shrugged. "Perhaps not at first, but then others must have decided that he had gone too far and needed to be removed."

"That is an interesting scenario," the Frenchman said. "But why would you tell me this?"

"Because after he killed poor old Vlad, the shooter made two calls. I could not follow the conversation in either one, however.

But I know he called a Vietnamese first because that was the language they spoke."

"And the second?"

"Ah, that conversation was in French. And the name of your boss, Monsieur Charbonel, came up. That wouldn't have been you on the other end of the line, would it?"

It was Schroeder's turn to sit back. He studied the residue in his coffee cup for several seconds, perhaps longer. When he sat forward and put his cup back on its saucer, it was as though he had made up his mind.

"I will tell you something, but only in the strictest confidence. Because of your role in all this, that of being a victim, of sorts…"

"Of sorts?"

Schroeder shrugged. "Yes, of sorts. You know the risks that our profession carries. But that does not matter here. I believe it is important for you to know more about this matter. Our countries are, after all, allies. And we both desire the same end for this country, even if we do want to go about it in different ways."

"Okay. Go on."

"We were aware of the Russian's presence here. You see, he was working with the Vietnamese. And we thought it important to monitor his presence and his work."

"Just monitor?"

Schroeder nodded vigorously. "Yes, yes. Monitor. We wanted to know more before we interceded. We would have informed you immediately, of course, once we were sure."

"Well, that's a relief. What do you mean by working with the Vietnamese?"

"They were quite open with us, although they made us promise not to inform you. They did not trust you, or what you might do. You see, they and the Russians had a common enemy in this regard."

"Who? Us?"

"No, no. It was the Chinese. You are aware, I am sure, that the Vietnamese do not like the Chinese, or trust them. In fact, they hate them."

"Yes, I've learned that much in my time here."

Yes, well," Schroeder continued, "they wanted someone's help to limit or constrain how involved the Chinese became here. The Chinese will always be a presence here, but the Vietnamese wanted someone closer to Beijing to help balance their role."

"But isn't that why we're here? In fact, that's a big reason we're here in the first place. It is a major part of the rationale in Washington for our presence in Vietnam." Baier paused. "And beyond. In Indochina, I mean. To prevent the expansion of Chinese communism."

Schroeder smiled and shook his head. This time it looked more like an act of disbelief. "Don't you see how you have replaced us as the colonial masters here. Your presence is overwhelming. Many Vietnamese complain that you Americans are not just running the war and telling the government what to do, but you are also undermining traditional Vietnamese culture."

Baier spread his arms wide to encompass the city around them. "You mean like the French did when they built this 'Paris of the Orient,' or whatever it has been labelled?"

"Yes, okay, I will concede that point. But it does not change how the Vietnamese see you. And even fear you. So, they were looking for some balance. At least some were." Schroeder picked up his cup to drink more coffee but replaced it on the saucer when he saw that it was empty. "These people have been playing at this game for a long time."

"But all you were doing was 'monitoring' things, as you said? What was that phone call I mentioned all about?"

"I cannot be sure. I was not on that call. But surely you can guess that we had assets of our own within the old Binh Xuyen gang. And we told them in no uncertain terms that no Americans were to be hurt. That may have been why one of them killed the Russian. But I believe that Vietnamese probably had given them the same instructions." Schroder shrugged as he played with his coffee cup again, then waved to the waiter. "The Russian obviously had gone off on his own tangent. In any case, I am glad no further harm came to you. I hope we helped that much. We never thought it would go so far."

"Thank you for your good wishes. But you are professionals. You should have known that it could get out of hand."

"The Russian must have frightened the Vietnamese in the room with you and brought about his own death by overplaying his hand. I am not sure why he got so carried away."

"I know why," Baier said.

• • •

Baier sped to *La Maison des Reves*. He wanted to get there before Jacques Schroeder had an opportunity to warn de Couget. Although Baier could not be sure just what role this Frenchman had played, he was certain that de Couget was involved. Somehow.

He left the jeep parked at an angle in front of the entrance, right in the middle of the walkway leading up to the porch. Baier rushed up the steps and trotted down the hallway, not bothering to look in either direction at all the eye candy on display. He burst through the door and into de Couget's office without knocking. Fortunately, the door was unlocked. The thought brushed through his mind that the door was never locked—not that he had encountered in any case. It was as though this particular Frenchman had nothing to hide. Well, we'll see, Baier thought.

"Mister Baier, what a surprise," de Couget announced. His smile was wide, reaching almost as far as his arms spread before him. "To what do I owe the pleasure?"

"I think you know," Baier answered. "And if you don't, you will soon."

The smile evaporated, and the arms fell. "Hmmm, that sounds ominous. What is wrong?"

"What is wrong, *Monsieur*, is the recent bombing in the city center, my second kidnapping, the death of the Russian whom I suspected was active in Saigon all along, and the people who have been behind this activity." Baier paused, but only for a moment to add some emphasis to the words that followed. "And your part in all this."

De Couget looked to his right, then left, as though he might find the answers to Baier's riddle hiding behind a door or underneath the furniture. "Mister, Baier, I assure you, you are mistaken. I concede to you that I was wrong about the Russian, who did visit my establishment on numerous occasions. But I told you that already. In fact, I admitted that he was quite taken with one of the ladies here, and I even offered to have her attempt to acquire some information for you."

"Which never brought that much out, and certainly not anything about his real mission here."

De Couget shrugged and glanced at his desk before looking up again. "But as an experienced intelligence officer you are aware that not all sources can deliver golden nuggets of information. So, you keep trying."

"Let's go over your escape from the first kidnapping attempt."

"The first? There have been more?"

Baier nodded and approached the desk. He stood less than a foot from the front.

"You know there was another one. I still don't buy your story about how you shot your way to freedom. You may remember how to handle a gun from your time in the Legion, but there is no way you could outgun those others in the room. At the most, you could have gotten one of them, when surprise was on your side. After that, we would all have been picking lead out of your liver."

Baier paused while de Couget tried to digest this line from *The Maltese Falcon.* Hell, they all supposedly liked gangster films so damn much. "The second kidnapping was even more serious. It nearly got me killed. You hadn't counted on that. I was saved only by the act of one the Russian's Bien Xuyen thugs, who shot him before he could finish me."

"And. How does that involve me? You may not believe my story, but it is as good as any you can suggest."

"He was one of your security guards. Like the others from the first seizure. I thought he looked familiar, but I only placed him at Pyle's opium hamlet afterwards."

"Mister Baier, surely you are aware that I cannot exercise full control over those men. If they choose to work elsewhere as well as here, I can do nothing to stop them."

"There is also the matter of Pyle and his girlfriend Kim. They gave me some very useful information about the people who work here." Baier stopped to look around the room. He took a step back from the desk. "By the way, where is Pyle?"

De Couget sighed and rose from his chair. It sounded and looked like a surrender. Of sorts. "He has disappeared."

"Again? What have you done?"

De Couget shook his head. "No, it is nothing like those previous episodes. I arranged this one."

"Where do you have him? And why? I thought you cared for the man."

De Couget nodded and studied Baier for a moment before answering. "But I do. Very much. That is why I helped him escape."

"Escape? What the hell are you talking about?'

"Unfortunately, Mister Pyle knows too much. As does his new paramour Kim. That knowledge in this case can be very dangerous. It has already killed Le Duc Vien."

Baier was stunned. He stared at the floor, then at the Frenchman. Baier stumbled into a chair beside the desk. "What the hell has happened? I figured that Duc Vien was probably behind the operation with the Russian, but I assumed there were others involved as well. Most likely people higher up in the service."

"Oh, there were. You are right there. That is why he had to be removed. Once things went sour, he had to be removed. He became a threat himself."

"And you feared for Pyle as well? What danger could he pose?"

"It was his friendship with you, Mister Baier. He could provide additional evidence, possibly even proof of your suspicions."

"So, where is he?"

De Couget shook his head and smiled. "I am afraid I cannot tell you. That must remain a secret."

"Goddammit, the man is an American. I want to protect him and bring him home. He deserves that much."

"I seriously doubt he wants to go home. Or to the United States, I should say. He has a new home. And I will do my best to ensure that he can remain here and survive."

Baier studied the Frenchman. He failed to hide his skepticism. "What makes you so sure you can do that?"

De Couget shrugged. "I cannot provide a guarantee. But I can probably do a better job than you."

"Because of your relationship with the Sûreté?"

"Ah, you have ascertained that much. Bravo, Mister Baier. You are more clever than you look."

Baier let the backhanded compliment pass. "We are not done here, de Couget. I know you have been facilitating French operations here, especially the one that nearly killed me and Pyle. I will continue to look for my compatriot to see that he gets through this. I can assure you of that much. And you can tell your countrymen like Charbonel that, too."

"You are obviously going to do what you believe is right, Mister Baier. I know I cannot change that. But have no doubts that I will continue to do whatever I can for my friend Pyle." He paused as another smile returned, almost as wide as the first. "But I think you will find yourself busy with other matters in the days ahead. Your country is heading into a quagmire, much like the one we barely escaped from."

"This time it's different."

Baier spoke those words in anger. Almost as soon as he said them, though, he realized he no longer believed them.

• • •

"I'm not sure how much of this the new Ambassador will take on," Crockett said.

Baier looked out the window of Crockett's office and shook his head. "I know it's hard to digest, much less believe. And I'm not recommending any sort of response. At least not for now. That's beyond my purview. As you know."

"And it would get you…us in all sorts of trouble if you tried." Crockett studied the paper in his hands for a moment, then looked up at his colleague. "You think it's over? The operation, I mean."

Baier nodded. "Yes, I do. At least, it is insofar as we probably never will know who all was behind this thing."

"Just what do you think Le Duc Vien's part was? Was he just a middleman or more like the brains behind this op?"

"Oh, I'm pretty sure he was more than just a middleman or the guy who put things in motion. Someone in his position had to know more about the plans and assemble the cast. I think he also ran the operation himself, approving the daily plans and operations, selecting the targets…"

"Like you?" Crockett interrupted.

Baier paused, then nodded his head again. "Oh, hell yeah. Me especially. At least in terms of keeping tabs on me and trying to limit what I might find out. It must have been his people who were tailing me in order to keep tabs on how far along I was getting. I wonder, though, what else they were supposed to do. I mean, they weren't very effective in preventing a bombing or a shootout. If that ever was a part of their instructions." Baier went silent while he considered the inconsiderable. "I doubt he was worried enough to want me dead, though. That was where the Russian took over. His part in the whole thing, anyway."

"What about the broader relationship with the Russian?"

"That one is actually easier to figure. And it must go higher than just Le Duc Vien. That part gets at some longer-term strategic planning. You know, finding some kind of balance to our growing presence and influence here. Considering who they chose to work with, they must have been pretty desperate," Baier concluded. "Or naive."

"Someone else to help keep the Chinese in check? Or us?"

"Both, but primarily the Chinese. They need us right now. In any case, I think Ambassador Taylor will have his proverbial work cut out for him, given all the competing interests and visions for this place. I mean, just look at the sort of allies he's going to have to work with."

Yeah," Crockett agreed, "that's why I think he needs to know what went on here. Maybe it will help open his eyes a little bit more. He—and others in Washington—need to recognize that we're not just dealing with a military problem. There's a serious political dimension that our policy needs to address. These guys are not just going to roll over and do whatever we tell them." He stopped to catch his breath before continuing. "Even if we do threaten to bomb the hell out of the North."

Baier paused, as though to catch his breath as well. "What's the word on our military effort? Any troops getting ready to come over?'

Crockett shook his head. "Not yet. We're still just sending advisors, but the word is that LBJ is going to increase their number from 16,000 to over 20,000. Maybe go as high as 22,000."

"Well, sadly, once those guys start getting killed in any number, it won't be long before a regular troop presence becomes necessary. I'm sure they're a big help to the ARVN troops—and Lord knows they need it—but they're also targets out there."

"And there are also reports that the Khanh government is reaching out to the VC. I don't know if you've had the chance to read our reporting of late…"

"I have been kind of busy getting shot and bombed."

"Yeah, I've noticed. You'll need to work on that, Karl. Anyway, the reporting points to a widespread war weariness and a popular interest in negotiations to bring the fighting to an end."

"What kind of an end?" Baier asked.

"Any kind of an end."

• • •

He found the waves soothing. Maybe it was their natural rhythm, or the consistency of their arrival and departure—their dependability. The sound was certainly refreshing and reassuring at the same time. There was an unquestioning beauty involved, a natural beauty, the blue sea and white-topped crests that covered the sand and left it a deep brown that almost immediately reverted to its original whiteness. It was a kind of rejuvenating purity, like a phoenix for natural beauty and meaning.

Pyle glanced over at Kim, who leaned against the railing separating their back porch from all this wonder. The flowered sarong was wrapped around her lower body like a sheet of silken skin. Her legs were crossed at the knee, and the bikini top left her lightly browned stomach and shoulders open to the sky and the sea breeze that drifted in from the free air beyond.

He could hardly believe his good fortune: this incredible woman, who was happy to be with him here in paradise. And then there was their miraculous escape from the hell that Saigon and the South were becoming. Yes, de Couget had proven to be a true friend. Baier may still have his doubts, but that was no longer a concern of his.

"Do you think we will be safe here," Kim asked. Her English seemed to be improving day-by-day.

"Thailand is as good as any place," Pyle assured her. "Certainly better than staying behind in Vietnam. Although I am sorry you had to leave your home."

"That is okay," Kim replied. "It is no longer the same country. It probably won't be for quite some time."

"Well, when it is, we can always return."

"That would be nice. But let's concentrate on staying alive here for now."

"Yes. And enjoying this idyll." Pyle looked out over the beach and the ocean again. "We've found our bit of paradise at last."

CHAPTER TWENTY-FOUR

It was now March 1, 1964. Baier sometimes wondered where the time had gone, even though he had been in Vietnam for just two months, two to three weeks longer than the Director had wanted, but still not long enough to really know the place. But he believed he had seen enough…at least enough to fulfill his original mission. He reread the opening lines of his missive to the Director that would go out to Washington in an "Eyes Only" cable for the Director. It would be up to him to determine who else saw the report.

Baier had briefed COS Crockett on the broad outlines of his report, to which the Chief had wholeheartedly agreed. He even offered to send it back as an "Aardwolf" cable, meaning it was a report direct from the Chief of Station. Baier thanked Crockett for the endorsement, but he declined the offer, noting that this was supposed to be his product alone.

"Well, I'll be sure to put in a plug in the accompanying ops cable."

If it ran into serious opposition or challenges back in Washington, Baier would have to stand by his observations and analysis on his own. He had little doubt that it would meet with resistance and even rejection in several quarters, but Baier was confident in his conclusions—even after a mere two months in country.

He was ready to go home. Sabine's presence in Virginia loomed larger than ever for him. He hadn't been able to communicate as often as he would have liked, so he wanted to make sure he hadn't created a new gap in their marriage by his extended absence in this evolving war zone that threatened to swallow up so much more of his and every American's life.

"In my brief period in Saigon and South Vietnam I have come to the unfortunate conclusion that our policy is badly mistaken and our future prospects for achieving our objective of establishing a functioning and popular democratic government in the South while inflicting a military defeat on the Communist forces are exceedingly poor. That conclusion rests on several basic observations and analysis."

Baier studied his opening line for several more seconds. He liked it: bottom line up front, direct, and succinct. The supporting evidence and assumptions would follow, and, hopefully, sway the Director.

"First, our senior policymakers have made a basic mistake in approaching the insurgency in Vietnam as primarily a military problem. To be sure, there exists a serious military challenge. However, it is much more than that. It is, at its heart, a political challenge that we and the South Vietnamese Government are neglecting. Without addressing this first, we and our allies in Saigon will never be able to overcome and supplant the broad base of support that Ho Chi Minh and his acolytes enjoy not only in the North, but also throughout the South as the true patrons of national liberation.

"Ho Chi Minh is clearly a Communist who would establish a dictatorship if victorious in the South. That, however, dissuades few here, especially in the countryside. (Ho's embrace of Lenin's thesis on Imperialism and Communism as the best venue for liberation from colonial rule is due in no small part, I am convinced, to our and our Allies' neglect of him and his mission after the two world wars. But what is done is done.) In the minds of a majority of Vietnamese, Ho Chi Minh may be a Communist, but he is their Communist, and one who represents the best chance of freeing them of foreign oppression—something which is now identified with the U.S. presence.

The entire notion or concept of communism means little for the majority of Vietnamese, especially in the countryside. The prospect of a dictatorship also carries little meaning to a people who have never enjoyed the fruits of a civil society or self-rule in the past. Moreover, their government in the South appears to be no better. It is also oppressive and corrupt. That is what the people in the countryside see and perceive. They also see in the Viet Cong a presence that can enforce its will, often in the absence of a government that is ineffective in protecting them. Unless the rulers in Saigon can offer more, the broad swath of Vietnamese outside Saigon will remain aligned with the Communist insurgency—even those that disagree with its goals and dislike its practitioners. As a result, they care nothing for the broader strategic implications that drive our policy.

"Second, our policy of promoting the country's democratic development and stability is correct, but its implementation is deeply flawed. It is hard to imagine how it could be otherwise, given the material with which we have to work. The coup that overthrew the Diem regime was, I am convinced, a terrible mistake. Granted, the man and his family were corrupt and unpopular. Nonetheless, governance in South Vietnam—never a strong point even at its best--has been on a downward slide ever since the overthrow and execution of President Diem and his brother. Our primary objective of finding a government in the mess we helped create with the coup against Diem that will prosecute the war while making a stab at building popular support remains a valid but exceedingly difficult objective.

"We have tried in the past to promote a more open approach to the opposition and dissidents in the South, efforts that were unsuccessful. For now, our policy towards the opposition and a broader government is governed by our concerns over the impact on the military effort. Moreover, the Vietnamese in the government here are more concerned with fattening their own profits and illicit income from the war and their positions of power than in establishing the kind of government that can win the support of the people and win the war. Diem had been making some progress in that regard, but those approaches floundered and stopped near the end of his regime. What has replaced his reign is one of organized confusion and self-service.

"Third, our military leadership appears to be misreading the nature of the insurgency and how best to defeat it. Like many generals in years past, ours appear to be intent on refighting the last wars. They are developing and promoting a strategy that seeks to build a South Vietnamese army capable of resisting an invasion of conventional forces from the North, as opposed to a guerilla insurgency in the South. They also appear to believe that creating and sustaining an overwhelming superiority in firepower will allow our ally to prosecute a war of attrition and is the path to victory.

I am not a military officer, nor do I consider myself an expert in military tactics and strategy. But I do believe that the insurgency will not be defeated through an attempt to attrit its manpower and resources. For one thing, there is no way to quantify the enemy's losses when you cannot find him. Indeed, many of the casualties reported are undoubtedly innocent civilians. There is also no shortage of men and resources the enemy is prepared to put into this contest, and the foreign sources of support—albeit limited as they are at present—will continue to provide important assistance.

Moreover, that support can increase at any time the North chooses. And the leadership there is almost certainly determined to do so whenever necessary. There are already reports of Northern involvement with the Viet Cong as front-line leaders of VC units in the south and, in some cases, of entire North Vietnamese units, although this role remains small at this point. Even so, they will be difficult to defeat in battle, because the Viet Cong and the North Vietnamese are unlikely to adopt such a convenient strategy that would enable us to confront them directly.

I also believe our analysts are spot on with their assessments that the bombing campaign the Administration is considering will not have a measurable impact on the insurgency or the North's role in it. The unyielding belief in the impact of our air superiority is yet another illusion in Washington and at MACV Headquarters.

"Finally, our Washington strategists are misreading the regional dynamics at play here, as well as those behind Ho's strategy and objectives. The dynamo theory about the spread of Communism and the Chinese pursuit of hegemony is misguided and almost certainly wrong. For one thing, it neglects the internal dynamics and political cultures of other countries in the region. Landsdale demonstrated that through an effort that combined an active pursuit of political and social reform along with a military campaign that Communism can be defeated, as it was in the Philippines.

"We are also underestimating the degree of opposition to and distrust of the Chinese, especially in Vietnam. It exists elsewhere as well. The Chinese may well have imperial ambitions in the region. They have displayed those throughout their history. But that has also generated a great deal of opposition to the Chinese and their presence. True, Ho Chi Minh needs them now. But once the insurgency is over, he will no longer need—and probably not welcome—their presence. The Vietnamese people will undoubtedly support any government of a similar mind."

As Baier reread his message, he thought it fair, but also hard-hitting. McCone might not want to share it, but Baier hoped it would at least help inform the Director and give him additional perspectives in the policy discussions downtown. He had not included his own adventures with the KGB, the expatriates, or the Vietnamese themselves in this report. Those were available in the restricted cable traffic in any case. But those had clearly helped inform his message and develop his own perspective. He also realized that as long as OPLAN-34 remained the basis of the U.S. approach to its role in Vietnam, then this cable and the follow-up conversations with the Director would probably be filed away for posterity.

But he could still hope. Baier felt he could be satisfied with one thing at least: he had remained true to the Agency's mission to provide objective reporting and analysis to the policymakers and elected officials in Washington, regardless of their preferences or beliefs. What they did with the information was their responsibility.

EPILOGUE

It was August 4th. The humidity hung in the air of Northern Virginia like a blanket. It was almost as bad as Vietnam...at least as bad as he remembered it. He had gotten used to the heat in both places, back home, as well as in Southeast Asia. But the humidity was something else. He would never be able to adapt to that, regardless of where he lived or served.

Baier shifted his weight in the chair behind his desk on the seventh floor in Langley, and gazed out over the lush green foliage that surrounded the CIA headquarters like an extra layer of security. He thought back to his last day in Saigon, standing before the bed to retrieve his suitcase and the several carry-on bags with gifts for Sabine and a few mementos of his time in Vietnam. He had purchased a nice, albeit small, haul because he did not plan to return. Then again, you never knew about those kinds of things in this business. But he felt relatively secure now that his future assignment would be limited to Headquarters, where he could actually help direct Agency policy and operations in his current position as the Special Advisor for Strategic Affairs. He reached over and dialed the number of the Chief of Station in Saigon. Frank Crockett answered after just two rings.

"Is it true?" Baier asked.

"Is what true? That your alma mater hired an Armenian Presbyterian to be its next football coach?"

Baier smiled and shook his head while he fiddled with a pen on his desk. The cardboard sheet on his blotter was covered with doodles of palm trees and Vietnamese hamlets.

"No. I mean this incident in the Gulf of Tonkin. Did the North Vietnamese really attack the USS Maddox?" If so, you know damn well it was not unprovoked. Not with all the support we're providing for those half-assed covert operations the Pentagon is running up there. You know damn well that destroyer was running people and arms into the North."

"Of course, they were. And there are reports filtering in about a second attack today. Although this one is a lot murkier."

"How's that?" Baier asked. "I suppose we were running more stuff up there. The U.S., I mean. Not our own guys."

Crockett shrugged. "I can't say for sure. Hartnett might know. You remember him, don't you?"

"Yes, of course."

"Well, he keeps in touch with our people still involved in the psyops work. But yeah, you're probably right."

Baier's fingers gripped the pen in a stranglehold that actually left an imprint on his palm. He cursed. "Goddammit, Frank."

"What? Are you saying your shocked?"

Baier shook his head, although Crockett was thousands of miles away. "I was afraid of that. The Director said something about the Administration taking this to the Hill."

"Well, no shit, Sherlock. Of course, they will. If they haven't already. The Ambo said something about a resolution. One that will give LBJ and his boys a virtual blank check." Crockett laughed. "Hell, he probably helped write it."

Baier shook his head again and sat silently for a moment. "In that case, I guess my report won't make it much further around town. And it will have even less of an impact."

"Have you gotten much a reaction so far?"

"Not really. The Director took it to a Cabinet meeting and included it in the President's Daily Brief shortly after I got back."

"And?"

"He said the President just snorted and turned the page. Nobody else ever said much after they heard that."

Crockett sighed through the wires. "You did what you were asked to do, Karl. You made an honest effort to provide

Washington with an objective assessment of the situation and prospects here." Crockett laughed again, lighter this time. "And you did some other good stuff, too. Regular spy shit, you know. And against some real-live bad guys."

Baier leaned forward and wound the telephone wire around his wrist. "I guess there was some good in my time there after all."

"So, what's next *Kamerad*?"

Baier turned and shrugged. "Who knows. Something in Europe, I hope. The battle lines are lot clearer over there."

"Yeah," Crockett agreed, "But for how long?"

Baier did not respond for several seconds. "Whatever happens, Frank, I think we'll both remain gainfully employed for the near and distant future."

ABOUT THE AUTHOR

Bill Rapp began his professional life as an academic historian of Modern Europe. He received his B.A. from the University of Notre Dame, his M.A. from the University of Toronto, and his Ph.D. from Vanderbilt University. After a short stint teaching at Iowa State University, Bill left for a less sedentary career at the Central Intelligence Agency. He spent the next thirty-five years as an analyst, diplomat, and senior executive at the CIA; after his retirement Bill continued his service as a consultant and trainer with the Agency. His Cold War spy series draws on his experiences in both those careers. He has also written a stand-alone thriller—*Berlin Breakdown*—set during the fall of the Wall, which he experienced first-hand during his assignment there-- and a three-book private detective series set outside Chicago, where he lives with wife, their older daughter, and their two dogs.